Secrets Maple Keeps

by Emersyn Park

Laurie —
So nice to meet
you! LBelle's is my favorite!
Hope you enjoy the
drama & mystery
EP ♡

Secrets Maple Keeps, 1st Edition

All rights reserved. Copyright ©2023 by Julie Frank

Cover design and image by Sandy Fritz (www.sandyfritz.com)

Editor: Caramie Malcolm

ISBN: 979-8-9-87-9022-9-5 (print) 979-8-9-87-9022-8-8 (ebook)

Library of Congress Control Number has been applied for.

Website: www.EmersynPark.com

Instagram: EmersynJulesPark

Facebook: EmersynPark

"The journey may be fraught with challenges,

yet it continues,

for even the smallest leaf must embrace destiny...

Persistence is the key."

-Virginia Alison

Prologue

Tiny, sharp, bright sparks of blinking lights invade my vision, like fireflies flickering in the darkest part of night. I blink several times, trying to refocus my vision. I command my mind to slow down and concentrate on the twinkles, but they disappear as suddenly as they appeared. Because my eyesight narrows and widens too quickly – unable to adjust – my sense of gravity is hindered as I teeter back and forth, making me feel dizzy. My brain is embodied by a dark gray fog of confusion. I can feel a pounding headache building behind my eyes. As I inhale and exhale a few deep breaths, my nostrils flare open wide, ingesting the cold, nighttime air. My nose hairs are encrusted in layers of frost. I feel inebriated, but I don't remember taking any magic pill that would warrant this out-of-body experience. There are no empty vodka bottles near my feet. No syringes scattered about. I struggle to recall the recent events that would place me in my current situation. The only emotion besides confusion that I recognize is anger. It boils in my bloodstream making it impossible for me to see clearly.

Where am I?

Besides the flickers of light in my blurred vision, everything is black. A sick, heavy pit forms a massive boulder in the bottom of my weak stomach, and before I can react accordingly, I swallow a bit of bile that forces its way into my throat. I don't feel in control of myself. Knowledge from my wild, drunken twenties rudely reminds me that I lack complete control over what comes out of my mouth or what morals I might lower while being intoxicated or high. But I'm neither. The next emotion that registers is regret.

What do I regret? And why? What happened?

My intense anger blinds me and has resulted in violence, of what I'm not sure.

What have I done? How long have I been out here? How did I get here? What am I capable of?

The only sound that echoes in my ears is my own deep, out-of-shape breathing. Night has driven every living thing asleep or indoors. As the fog in my head struggles to clear, I recognize that I'm standing at the end of my neighbor's driveway, breathing heavily. I can't recall how I arrived here. An odd prickling feeling overwhelms my toes. I can't feel them.

What am I doing? How did I get here? Why am I not wearing my coat and shoes?

My twenty-twenty vision is blurry as I struggle to focus on the images right in front of my face. As I look down, I notice that I'm barefoot. When I lift my arms that were resting at my sides, I realize that my hands are covered in blue disposable latex gloves. I'm wearing plastic clothes but no shoes.

Where did I get these medical gloves from? What was I trying to avoid getting on my skin? Or was it the opposite and I didn't want my fingerprints left behind?

My breath is deep and heavy from my heart beating with adrenaline. Even though I feel like everything is in slow motion, my heart rate is at least one hundred and seventy-five, a perfect rate after a quick mile run. Except I hadn't run a mile, and I wasn't sure what I did. In order to answer the questions bouncing around in my brain, I examine the evidence in front of me. My gloved hands and out-of-body experience would both lead me to believe that I should see bright red blood, instead of a brown, muddy-like substance staining my gloves. I lift them to my nose. The smell is ripe and putrid.

Suddenly, I do see red, but it is not blood. My hands – that, thank goodness, were protected– are covered in warm, fresh dog feces. In the middle of the night, I'd been smearing my dog's excrement all over the neighbor's freshly waxed, *red* Corvette.

Chapter 1

now

"The bail is set for one million dollars because the defendant poses a flight risk – "

Frank rockets straight into a standing position. "Excuse me, Your Honor. How does she pose a flight risk? My client is a law-abiding citizen without a prior record, not even a speeding ticket. She has a stable family and a part-time job. How is she a flight risk?" Frank has been a lawyer for over twenty years. When he accepted the job to represent me, he confessed that he'd only argued in court a handful of times, because most of his cases were usually settled out of court or didn't require a trial by jury.

"Evie, I have to be honest with you. If your case makes it to court, arguing in front of a judge isn't my strong suit. I'm a better behind-the-desk-and-file-a-thousand-motions type of lawyer. Mainly, because I have no filter. Whatever I'm thinking explodes straight out of my mouth. Judges tend to not appreciate my candor. Most of them view my frankness as a sign of disrespect."

"*Frankness*...good one, Frank. But that's exactly why I need you."

I've known Frank longer than I've known my husband. Frank Baker and I attended undergraduate college together where we met at a popular bar. Calling a bar in a college town 'popular' isn't necessarily a compliment. It simply referred to the enormous amount of alcohol spilled by its overserved patrons to make everyone's feet stick to the floor. Because the bartenders mixed stiff, inexpensive drinks, word spread that Charley's was the place to be. From the time the doors opened at noon until closing time fourteen hours later, the bar stools welcomed butts from the overnight mining shift to the nine-to-fivers and later in the evening to the college students who needed to release some tension earned from long hours of concentration. In the back of the bar, a long U-shaped counter was built to guard the auburn-colored liquor bottles that lined the glass shelves. Six kegs of different brews were always tapped and ready for distribution. A long corridor extended as an appendage, paving the way to the three beer-stained pool tables, the sticky, worn-out dance floor, and the overused, unsanitary bathrooms. Even a poet couldn't romanticize this run-of-the-mill tavern, but day after day customers returned to the bar for cheap entertainment, tasty liquids and familiar fellowship.

For me, Charley's was where I practiced my billiard skills. Since I looked like the girl-next-door with my thick-framed glasses, my opponents often doubted my abilities, and I used this miscalculation to my advantage. To my worthy opponents, my unmanageable, wavy brown hair implied that I was neglectful and undisciplined. My slim physique suggested I was malnourished and desperate. My old school style of clothing gave the impression that I was clueless and innocent.

While I kept my blouse buttoned to the top, I pocketed hundreds of dollars from the intoxicated, eager young fools who underestimated me and challenged me to a game. Every weekend, I grabbed my pool cue, coated it with blue chalk, and knocked in a few balls while I leaned over the pool table, hoping to entice a few overconfident men into playing a game or two. I lured unsuspecting victims with my sex appeal and innocent appearance. I teased them with my sharp wit while claiming each shot was pure luck. My puppy dog eyes and round behind were foolproof. Until Frank.

Sitting in the shadows of the low bar lights, he sipped his bourbon on the rocks as he studied and analyzed my shots. Night after night, he watched me flirt and tease men. He noticed that I arrived alone and always left alone. I was reclusive, but instead of being weak and vulnerable like I tried to appear, my solitude was a choice. After a few weeks of watching me collect money for my living expenses, he approached me and asked me to join him for a drink.

"Don't you want to see if you can beat me?" I nodded my head toward the pool table. I wasn't interested in dating anyone, and I didn't need a man to buy me a drink. I wanted another hundred bucks to pay for my utility bill. "One hundred dollars says I can beat you in three shots."

"Nope. I already know you'll beat me. I'm more interested in seeing if you can hold your liquor. Name's Frank by the way." He raised one eyebrow in a competitive manner. I looked the attractive stranger up and down. He was dressed similar to me – a pair of khaki pants and a button-down, starched white oxford – and stuck out like a sore thumb. Style wasn't something either of us had in common. While his natural wavy hair was shaggy and in need of a trim, his face was freshly shaved and revealed his unwrinkled baby face. He seemed harmless, so with a shrug of my shoulders, I accepted his offer. I'd already earned enough money for my garbage bill, so why not enjoy one free drink?

Over the course of several drinks, Frank admitted that he had been watching me pound my opponents for a while. He referred to my talent as an art, a mathematical puzzle. At first when he started spying on me, he was simply entertained, but then he started to watch for patterns in my shots. He saw through my act and understood that every move wasn't luck, but methodical.

"You're a thief, stealing their hard-earned money like that." He gestured to the loud, stumbling twenty-somethings behind us making a fool of themselves on the dance floor. With each hip thrust, beer spilled onto the already soiled floor.

I shook my head. "Are we talking about the same drunk fools who are wasting their trust fund money on alcohol and blow?"

"Not all of them. Some of them, yeah. A few of them work hard for their money."

"Well, then those pretty, rich boys better learn fast. There are scarier, more skilled thieves than me out in the real world." I gulped down the rest of my drink and excused myself. "Thanks for the drink, Frank. Maybe I'll see you around."

And I did. I saw him a lot in the weeks after our first conversation. Every Friday and Saturday night, he quietly watched me from a far corner. After I would earn enough money to pay for whatever bill I had pending, I would stroll over to him and encourage him to buy me a drink. Each encounter was entertaining, and I started to look forward to our conversations. Our banter was comfortable and easy, plus we had a similar sense of humor. He was good looking, polite, honest, well-educated and in his second year of law school. He was a catch.

"A good looking, single law student. I bet all the girls are banging down your door." I'd never seen him talking to anyone else but me; therefore, I assumed he was interested in me. Otherwise, why would he only direct his attention toward me?

"Evie, I'm gay. Completely still in the closet, but nonetheless, I'm one hundred percent gay."

"I'm sorry – "

"Sorry? What are you sorry about? Nothing to be sorry about."

"I'm sorry that I read the situation wrong. I thought you were attracted to me and were waiting for me to make the first move." I grabbed his free hand that was resting next to mine on the bar, and I lifted it up to my face. "Plus, your hands are huge, and I'm sorry that I'll never be able to prove if the old wives' tale is true."

"Which wives' tale are you referring to?" His smile grew to meet his eyes as he realized that I was about to tease him.

"The one that says you can tell the size of a man's penis by the size of his hands. You have the hands of a giant."

I was torn between being relieved and disappointed regarding Frank's sexual preference. This man had broken down some walls, and even though I told myself I wasn't interested in any type of relationship, I hadn't envisioned this outcome.

He bellowed out a deep, hearty laugh. "Evie, you're witty and adorable, but unfortunately, I prefer a bratwurst over a taco. And yes, I guess you'll have to take my word for it that my manhood is relatively large because my fingers are meaty and long." He wiggled his long, thick fingers at me, toying with my imagination.

I raised my glass to him. "Well, cheers to hoping that your polish sausage never yearns to attend a fiesta, because that party is invitation only."

Our glasses clinked to our mutual admiration for each other.

***

The judge clears her throat to bring the attention back onto her. "Well, Mr. Baker, if you hadn't interrupted me, I could've gotten to that point – "

"I'm sorry, Your Honor."

"Yet, you did it again, Mr. Baker." Judge Crawford's lips were pinched in a fine line as if the bun on the top of her head was slowly getting tighter and tighter as her patience for Frank was getting smaller and smaller. Everyone in the courthouse can hear the edge in her voice. I tug on Frank's suit jacket and shake my head. I can't handle him losing his cool. He'd been so level-headed and calm while he supported me in the last few days. "Mrs. Stanton's bail is set for one million dollars. Case adjourned."

The crack of the judge's gavel hitting the sound block bounces off the thin walls. Her decision has been made.

Classic small-town courtrooms are nothing like the movies. Obviously, I know this isn't a movie set, but I was expecting it to look more official, full of doom. Instead of tall, intimidating ceilings being held in place by white granite pillars, the courtroom where I made my first appearance as a defendant is surrounded by thin, cheap-looking office walls that block off a square room. Because the walls are so paper-thin, I can hear the phone ringing in the next office.

In the back of the courtroom, many pairs of eyes return my curious stare. The people sitting in the hard, wooden pews aren't reporters dressed in fancy suits ready to write down every detail of the juicy charges. There are no camera flashes as I enter through the side door that leads to the jail. No one is shouting vile names at me. The group gathered aren't overly concerned citizens making sure the town's laws are being upheld. No one is demanding the judge to punish me harshly. The men and women returning my blank stare are the next innocent or guilty parties waiting their turn to face the judge. All of them look scared and worried about what fate the cards will deal them today. Most of the time, they sit alone or with their attorney. Their families have long ago abandoned them.

But what is just like the movies is the gut-wrenching feeling in the pit of the defendant's stomach. I wait on the edge of my seat to hear my fate.

Except this isn't the movie set for the iconic scene where Jack Nicholson delivers that famous line, "You can't handle the truth!"

I knew the battle was over as soon as I looked at Judge Crawford's tired, gray eyes. She lost her patience with Frank. Sure, she is sworn to uphold the law and never judge someone before their trial, but she was also human. When her eyes met mine, I recognized strong contempt. She masked her personal feelings very quickly, but it was there. She senses something and holds me accountable even before we can argue against it. Her years behind the bench tell her that a higher percentage of people that she comes into contact with are guilty of something, and that guilt got them arrested.

Frank and I need to save our strength. I'm safe behind bars. And if I want to approach my situation as half-full, I'll remember that I have less things to focus on behind bars. I have time to think and plan. Of course, I would've preferred to be home with my family, snuggling on the couch or cooking a homemade meal, but I'd have this murder charge hanging over my head. Would I even be able to relax and enjoy the mundane things of everyday life? I doubt it. I'd be overthinking everything and making mountains out of molehills.

As the bailiff, who stands over six feet tall and weighs about three hundred pounds, escorts me from the defendant's table to the door of the long, narrow hallway leading to the jail, I quickly steal a glance for familiar faces. I see my husband of twenty years, William, sitting next to my only daughter, Hazel. While one arm is draped over her shoulders, he uses his free hand to pet her head as a continuous flow of tears fall down her face. She can't look at her own mother. She is ashamed. She thinks her mother is a murderer.

Chapter 2

then

Babies are born with a clean slate. A squeaky new sponge yearning to learn. A soul begging to be filled. Each experience, each encounter will shape who they will become. Researchers refer to it as the formative age when everything is a possibility. Before they learn to grasp an object, their chubby little arms flail about. As soon as they learn to control their arms, they clench the toy tightly in their little fists. If it happens to be your hair, good luck. Before a parent realizes it, their little one sprints past that stage and is crawling or walking and getting into everything. Curiosity is what drives them. And of course, some babies learn quicker than others.

I remember hearing a comedian discuss how childhood safety has changed over the years. "When I was a kid, my parents had a nine-hundred-pound television on top of a TV tray. My dad's theory was, 'Let him pull it on his head a few times, he'll learn. You wanna put a penny in a light socket? Try that out. Oh! Hurt like hell, didn't it? Won't do that no more.'"

Children have natural curiosity and little understanding of what consequences are. Curiosity makes them interested, and if the consequences are rewarding enough – negative or positive – the child will learn from the adventure. Some children are slower learners than others.

Remember that stage when your toddler dropped food on the floor from their highchair just to earn a reaction from you? He holds the chunk of cheese over the side of his plastic tray, looks you in the eye, and opens the palm of his hand. The cheese lands on your kitchen floor. The first couple of times that it happened, you may have giggled and picked it up. After five days – possibly five hours, depending on your patience level – of this entertaining, new game of bending over and retrieving spaghetti noodles, carrots, and cheese from your soiled, crusty floor, you start leaving the food on the floor. Or if you are completely honest, there were a couple of times that you chucked the mushy food back on his tray. *A little gravel or hair won't kill him. It'll make his immune system stronger. Right?*

"I can't wait until she can walk."

"I can't wait until she can vocalize what she wants rather than throwing a fit."

"I can't wait until he can drive himself to his practices."

As parents of young ones, we are constantly wishing away time. I remember waiting for the day my children would become more independent, stop hollering, 'Mom' from all ends of the house, stop throwing a public tantrum at the grocery store every time they heard the word, 'no,' stop complaining about eating their vegetables, stop requiring to be tucked in each night so I could just remain rooted to my cozy spot on the couch, and stop needing me every second of every day for simple, mundane tasks. My kids are older now, and all of these prayers were answered; however, they were replaced by new ones. Prayers deep in meaning and heavy with worry become the new norm for a parent with teenagers.

I wish I could go back in time to when my kids would wrap their chubby little arms around my legs, when their sticky little fingers would cling to my finger as we walked on the street, and when their infectious giggles filled the walls of our home. Wishing away their youth and childhood also takes with it those heartfelt, raw moments that you can never duplicate.

We wish for time away from our never-ending responsibilities because we are exhausted and think that the next stage in life will bring the benefits that we so desperately crave. Our children learn independence and grow as sensitive human beings. However, in some cases, we wish we could turn back time and find out where it went wrong – where we could've changed the course of the future. What we wouldn't do to turn back the clock and change the present that we are currently suffering through.

Our firstborn, Hudson, was a sensitive, tentative old soul. When he met a stranger, his right hand jutted out for a formal handshake. I remember Hudson's third grade teacher telling me that he was the most thoughtful, considerate student that she'd ever met. When a new student joined the class, he was the first one to introduce himself and the first one to invite the child to play. She also told me that he was polite and even helped her. He would hold the door open when he would see her coming down the hall. In her arms, she carried a stack of books and tried to balance her lunch and coffee cup. He was the only student who recognized her struggle and took the time to help.

People always complimented my husband and me on how well-behaved and gentle he was. "Please" and "Thank you" were phrases he used on a regular basis. He was quiet, sweet, and easy to have around. We felt blessed and believed our amazing parenting skills were the reason Hudson was such an angelic child. Never in a million years did we imagine being in the reverse situation where we felt that our parenting skills influenced Hudson down a dark path of addiction and self-destruction.

I remember when a classmate bullied him. Hudson returned home from school one day with a black eye and a tear-soaked face claiming that Brit House - a name that will be eternally engraved in my brain - had pushed him down during first grade recess and kicked dirt on his face.

"He called me a toothpick." In between sobs, he tried to explain what had happened on the playground. "Said my fuzzy, white hair reminds him of one that he uses to clean wax from his ear."

Q-tip. Even though it was vaguely true - a thick mop of white blonde hair rested on the top of his head and he was underweight - steam rolled out of my ears as my temper ignited. My Mother Bear qualities erupted. I googled his family, I even Facebook stalked them. I wouldn't let someone hurt my kid. *What kind of child are these people raising?*

Then, two days later, Hudson bounced through the front door and asked if Brit could come over for a playdate. *What? No, we hate him. We want him to be expelled from school even though he's only in the first grade. He called you a mean name and hurt your feelings.* I was so confused and still angry. But he forgave him in a heartbeat and wanted to be friends again.

Hudson and his big heart.

Then there was Hudson's first crush, his first teenage girlfriend. I was so excited for that experience. This was something I knew about. Feelings, love, girls – I could talk for countless hours about relationship stuff. Basketball, football, baseball... I didn't understand the significance of the outfits or the reasons for the different numbers in scoring in the same sporting event. *Only two points if you shoot from the straight, black line but three points if you make it from the red curved one?* Made no sense to me. But girls, now girls I could talk about. And feelings, yep, I could talk about them too. I was ready for this adventure.

Until she broke his heart. Ripped it completely out of his chest and stomped on it on the sidewalk just outside our front door. I remember her name too, but I choose not to say it out loud. Kind of like saying, "Beetle Juice" three times. If I said her name three times, it might summon her. I didn't want that. The night that they broke up, I was there. Laying next to him in his big bed, rubbing his head, telling him that he would be okay.

I couldn't actually mend his heart for him, but of course, I would try. I would do anything for my child. Anything.

Chapter 3

then

Mama Bear. The two words sound endearing together. A fluffy, cuddly teddy bear with a little pink bow in her hair. Long, dark eyelashes surrounding her big brown circular eyes as she blinks rapidly to portray a flirtatious, friendly nature. She cocks her head to the side to appear timid and shy.

A Mama Bear's mothering instincts are simply to protect her son. Unconditional love. She adores her cub. She licks him clean while he looks up adoringly at her. She feeds him fresh fish from the nearby stream that she caught with her bare hands. She is hungry as well, but her cubs' needs come first. She eats the leftovers – the crumbs. As he becomes sleepy after his meal, she tucks him into her side, and he falls asleep next to her with a full, satisfied tummy. By keeping him close to her side, she can protect him from harm and make sure he doesn't wander off. Her sole purpose is to keep him alive. Her eyes droop as sleep takes over.

Very picturesque scene. A perfect image to paint onto a canvas. That is the Hallmark version.

In the wilderness, as soon as the female bear realizes she is pregnant, she goes into hiding. To protect her unborn cub and herself, she hides in the safety of her dark, damp cave for months. She trusts no one. After a seven-month-long pregnancy in isolation, Mama Bear climbs out of hibernation with her newborn safely by her side.

A female bear has every right to be overly protective of her innocent baby. Male bears – the same ones who fought each other to impregnate her – want to tear the baby bear cub to pieces simply because of their powerful desire to procreate. Sex and murder. A male bear instinctively knows that if he can kill the cub, Mama Bear will go into heat again. Hence, more sex. Without her baby, she'll be interested in mating again. But if her bear cub is alive, she is solely focused on him and uninterested in a male companion.

Mama Bears have earned a bad reputation. Out in the wild, when a human meets a Mama Bear, the odds of surviving the encounter are slim. Can you blame her? She can't even depend on the baby's father to help protect her and her baby. Even he will turn on her. Her baby's survival and happiness is her sole priority. She had no one else to count on. It's the Mama Bear and her cub against the world.

***

William received a substantial bonus when Hudson was five and I was waddling around pregnant with Hazel. We decided to take our little family of three on one last vacation before the busyness of a new baby interrupted our lives. As soon as the money hit our bank account, I booked a trip to a warm, sandy beach. While winter in the Black Hills was remarkably beautiful, Vitamin D was lacking, and we wanted to introduce Hudson to the wonders of the ocean. I reserved a little cottage in Outer Banks, North Carolina on the Atlantic Ocean. We didn't plan any excursions. We were only interested in relaxing and enjoying the calm before 'the storm,' a nickname we awarded the baby even before she was born. It was an accurate description. During the first trimester, I was completely miserable. I couldn't keep any solids or liquids down. Nothing agreed with me. In the second trimester, I suffered from insomnia, which was worse than feeling sick all the time. I paced the house all hours of the night wishing for a measly hour of slumber.

When the third trimester came, I was completely afraid to see what the next three months would bring. Each morning I'd wake up and I'd check myself to see what felt different. *Did I have a headache?* Nope. *Was my tummy turning?* Nope. I felt great. Besides the basketball that I was carrying around under the front of my shirt, I felt wonderful. So, William and I nicknamed Hazel 'the storm' and the period before her arrival 'the calm.' We enjoyed every minute of it. I was a new woman. The six months before seemed like a nightmare – something of the past. The worst that our young lives had ever been.

Our little beach cottage was everything we had hoped for, and we fell in love with it, the surrounding area, and the life we could imagine living here. A small front porch overlooked the Atlantic Ocean with two rocking chairs that pointed east and beckoned us each morning as we sipped our coffee and Hudson constructed sandcastles thirty feet away. Mornings were colder so we wore sweats, but by noon we stripped off the baggy clothes and opted for tank tops to allow the Vitamin D to penetrate our skin. It was a slice of heaven. Our slice of heaven for seven whole days.

Until it wasn't.

One afternoon, after lunch, Hudson was itching for some splash time. He'd already adjusted to our daily routine of morning coffee and sandcastles, followed by a light lunch, and then he knew it was time to play with the waves. As I cleaned up the aftermath of lunch, William accompanied Hudson for a swim in the warm water. While I washed the dishes, I'd watch them through the little picture window. As he jumped over the waves,

Hudson giggled every time a wave would splash him or nudge his little body back to the shore. Each wave was a loyal playmate.

My heart felt full of love and contentment, but I wondered if I'd have enough love to share with the new baby. Hudson was my boy, my first born. When I looked out the window, I saw my whole world.

A smile emerged on my lips as the baby kicked, almost like she was saying, "Of course, you will love me." I rubbed the spot where the baby's foot had pressed on my abdomen. It fluttered a bit more. Even before she was born, our little storm had a feisty personality.

That fifth day of our routine, I decided to lay down on the couch for a quick cat nap, and then maybe I'd be able to stay up with William after Hudson went to bed. Our marriage could use some quiet time alone without any distractions.

Sleep came easy while on vacation. Maybe I was more relaxed, or maybe it was the ocean air. As I closed my eyes, I could hear the repetitive crash of the ocean waves hitting the shoreline. Sea gulls chirped at one another, announcing the discovery of an afternoon snack in the water. Faintly, I could hear the mumble of William's voice. I imagined the two of them splashing each other in the warm water. My eyelids were heavy, and my breathing became even and steady. A little breeze from the ocean filled the air with a wonderful salty scent. I could stay here forever.

Suddenly, William was shaking me awake. "Eve! Couldn't you hear me yelling for you?"

It took a moment for me to wake up and realize I wasn't dreaming. As my eyes adjusted their focus, I noticed William was hysterical. His brow was tense and wrinkled.

"What...?" I heard his voice outside, but I thought he was playing and laughing with Hudson. I bolted upright from my reclining position on the couch. "Where's Hudson?"

Possibly the scariest two words ever asked until I heard William's four-word reply. "I can't find him."

That afternoon, when I dozed on the couch, letting the hypnotic waves lull me to sleep, William answered a work phone call and became distracted. Simultaneously, Hudson noticed a hermit crab and followed him along the beach. However, we didn't know this at the time, and the sheer panic we felt was the most heartbreaking, desperate feeling that I had ever experienced. The unknown. The possibilities. The fear.

In a matter of a few seconds, I experienced every emotion humanly possible, from anger – *how could you lose our child?* – to fear – *did the ocean snatch him without a sound?* – to complete heartache – *my baby! I can't live in a world without you.* I pushed William away, knocking him over as I darted out of the door and onto the porch while I screamed his name.

"HUDSON!" As his name erupted from my lips, I could hear the desperation in my voice. This Mama Bear had been separated from her cub. No one was safe.

Obviously, we physically found Hudson, or I wouldn't be disclosing the horrors that led up to emotionally losing him, but nothing compares to the feeling of being hopelessly desperate and completely afraid that I felt that afternoon. While running around frantically on the shore, I made pacts with God and the Devil. I didn't care who found my son or how, but I'd do anything to erase this nightmare.

I'm not sure which one is worse: physically losing a child or emotionally losing a connection with a loved one. I've felt both.

Chapter 4

now

"If a grizzly bear and a buffalo are fighting, do you want to know who would win?" I honestly don't care, but I raise my eyebrows in the form of curiosity anyway. Silently, I vote for the bear because I can sympathize with her.

"The buffalo. A grown-ass buffalo weighs about a thousand pounds while a mature grizzly bear weighs about three hundred pounds. The buffalo ain't gonna win just because it weighs more, but because the buffalo has sharp-ass horns and can run faster than any dumb-ass bear. Even though they can't see worth shit, the buffalo listens. Their hearing is crystal-ass clear. That big-ass, fluffy, solid mass of muscle can hear a pin drop in a dusty, ole field. A dumb-ass bear wouldn't stand a chance." Caramie Rae, one of the first 'friends' that I made while incarcerated, is from Wyoming, where she grew up on a farm that raised bison, and one of her many talents is that she can randomly insert the word buffalo in almost any conversation. Another one of her talents that I found amusing was that she included the word 'ass' at the end of almost every adjective. She had been arrested for the attempted murder of her abusive boyfriend. Unfortunately for him, depending on how you look at it, he survived but, at the moment, is confined to a hospital bed in a coma.

I asked her once – before I knew that you weren't supposed to ask other inmates about their crimes – why she was in a South Dakota jail and not Wyoming. She must not have heard that inmate rule about keeping the facts of your crime to yourself, because she completely word-vomited her story. Another one of her talents is telling a long-ass story.

"You can tell when you pissed off a buffalo because its tail shoots straight up. Points right to the sky. There is no sneaky-ass, don't-know-where-you-stand bullshit from a buffalo. And do you know what buffaloes like to stomp on? Snakes. My old man was devious like a cobra, the worst-ass snake. Cobras can't hear shit, but they stare at you like they're listening to every word. But instead of hearing, they are dreaming of ways to project their evil on the innocent. Cobra Craig was sneaky and silent, masking every emotion until he would lash out and strike. Mean SOB thought I was his own personal punching bag. Crazy-ass mother-fucker. That's why I decided to finally be a buffalo and stomp on that mean-ass snake.

"Anywho, after he drank himself into a stupor, I decided it was now or never. As soon as he was good and comatose, I yanked his ugly ass out of the house, down the front steps, and threw him into the back of my truck. Then I drove across the state line to bury him alive in the Badlands because I figured that no one would find him there. I planned to bind his arms and legs and bury him in the hard, unforgiving dirt of the Badlands with only his eyes visible. He would be able to see but not able to move. Scavengers would pluck at his beady-ass eyes while he was still alive, and he'd not be able to defend himself. Craig deserved to suffer a long-ass, painful death."

She never answered my question about how she ended up in jail because she became sidetracked with another story about a precious buffalo who climbed up her front porch. I decided not to ask again for fear that she'd tell me another long-ass story.

Some inmates concentrate on healthy hobbies, like getting physically fit. Caramie claims that she could bench a thousand-pound buffalo, but I have my doubts. While she is extremely fit, her blonde hair and blue eyes cause me to underestimate her, and she has no way to prove it since we don't have any buffaloes in jail to toss around.

Other inmates better themselves by getting educated. Knowledge is power. Jilli Jones, my cellmate and the only other friend I've made, is taking online courses to earn her Bachelor of Science degree in Business. Even though her previous business was a huge success, it was completely illegal. She's a natural entrepreneur.

"My momma didn't think too highly of educated white folk," she informed me one night as we lay on our thin mattresses. "She said since I wasn't White, I shouldn't be wastin' my time workin' on my brain when I could use my God-given charm and killer good looks that I've already been blessed with. She was right! The woman was dumber than a box of rocks and uglier than a two-headed warthog, but she nailed genius on that. I made ten g's in one month while I was in Vegas. For fuck's sake, I was livin' the good life."

Jilli's story is simply that she knifed her pimp. "I sliced him on the side of his neck so I could see the fear in his eyes and watch the life drain from his body. He bled like a stuffed pig. His blood completely ruined my favorite pair of Gucci horsebit white leather sandals, but he deserved it. He was bad. Real bad." She slyly avoids answering all questions about how she ended up in a South Dakota jail. Honestly, I'm surprised she shared as much as she did about her arrest.

I'm the only one who continues to proclaim my innocence, but of course, my new friends think my claim is hilarious and laughable. I believe in the philosophy, 'make your dreams become your reality.' I think; therefore, I believe.

"Evelyn, Evelyn, girl, you don't have to pretend with us. In cell block E, we got your back. You ain't gotta lie to your ladies." Jilli didn't believe that anyone was innocent of anything. She said she'd seen too much crap in her life to not question what she was told.

"But I'm not lying. I didn't touch him." My proclamation is met with a loud cackle.

"Okay, Evelyn, whatever you wanna believe. I think we'll call you Snow White because you think you're livin' in a fairytale."

Jilli compared our female inmates to princesses from childhood fairy tales. She'd nicknamed everyone in our cell block a princess name. She called the blonde whose weekly chore was scrubbing shit stains from the community room toilets 'Cinderella,' and Ariel was the red-haired woman who was missing the majority of her teeth. "I named her Ariel because she is missin' so many teeth that when she talks she sounds like she is underwater." Jasmine, Mulan and Esmeralda were the three musketeers who no one wanted to mess with. They were lifers who solidified a firm pact to have each other's back until they died.

While my new jailhouse friends earn an education or become physically fit, I think. I over-think.

Chapter 5

then

William and I met at the same bar, Charley's, where I'd had my first conversation with Frank a year before. After I'd successfully smoked a couple of over-served frat boys in a game of pool, Frank and I planned on celebrating my effortless victory with a cocktail. Winning never got old.

As soon as we were belly up to the bar and our drinks of choice – a vodka club soda for me and a Knob Creek neat for Frank – were deposited in front of us, I pulled out my winnings and offered to pay for the first round. We always drank water until the first game was over. Kind of felt like a ritual, and we didn't want to jinx it.

"The devilishly handsome guy at the other end of the bar bought this round. And that's the *exact* adjective he paid me to use to describe him." The bartender gave me a little wink and pointed at the above-average, overconfident guy dressed in jeans and a white T-shirt at the opposite end of the bar. When we made eye contact, a huge grin spread across his face, and he raised his hand in a polite, eager wave.

"Oh, he's dreamy." Frank sipped his drink after a long sigh. "But the Mister looks like he only has eyes for you, Evie. He's making his way over here, so I think I'll excuse myself and head to the restroom while this poor lad makes a complete and utter fool of himself." He picked up his free drink and gave a polite nod in gratitude to the guy who was now taking over my attention.

Frank had witnessed many attempts of men hitting on me over the past year. *Some* of them were the naive ones who I took money from. *Most* of them were hoping to win back some of their pride by bedding the female pool shark that robbed them. And *all* of them didn't have a chance in hell. I usually let them buy me a stiff drink while I batted my eyes at them for a few painful minutes before I looked for an escape route.

Frank didn't return the first few times while the potential suitor was attempting to woo me because he wasn't aware that I wasn't enjoying the unwanted attention until I texted him an SOS message asking where he was and why he wasn't assisting me in getting rid of the guy. His response was, "What am I supposed to do about it?"

Me: *"You're my best friend. Do something."*

Frank: *"I'm your best friend? You've never said that before. I have tears pooling up in my old, dried-up eyes."*

Me: *"Can we discuss this later? I need this Mister gone."*

Frank: *"As 'the' best friend, please be aware that I don't want your filthy, second-hand rejects, and I have a vote in the one we keep."*

Me: *"Deal. Hurry up."*

However, before he would agree to anything, Frank had a few more ground rules that he established from the start since he felt he was receiving the raw end of the deal.

"What's in it for me? I have to benefit in this scenario somehow since my evening with you is cut short by some jerk who fancies and desires Eve's unmentionables." With Frank at my side, I was sure I'd always be entertained. If I chose to escape before Frank returned, I'd excuse myself to the bathroom, claiming that I needed to powder my nose. I would sneak out of the door undetected. If I couldn't wait for Frank to return,

I promised to leave more than a drop at the bottom of my free drink. After the young men finally realized I wasn't coming back, Frank would finish my free drink and make random excuses for me.

If Frank returned to claim his bar stool while the young man was still trying to woo me, I promised to go with the flow while he practiced his improv skills. His performances were wildly entertaining. I was never sure what scenario he'd create for our evening amusement. Honestly, I looked forward to this adventure as much as the lucrative pool games.

After I beat the hunky accountant named Zack in an aggressive game of pool, Frank pumped up his chest and played the role of my knight in shining armor. He cleared his throat to earn our attention, "Excuse me, Eve, but is this *the* Mister that gave you that awful case of herpes?" Zack's dark chocolate skin turned an almond color in a matter of seconds. He jumped off his stool before he gave me a second glance. Zack set a record for the quickest exit.

After a quick game where my sharply dressed opponent didn't hit more than three balls into a pocket, a new Mister named Jeremiah turned on the charm very quickly by placing a firm hand on my bare knee even before my drink had arrived. Frank returned from the restroom as I started to squirm.

"Hey, cheap ass, I paid her for the *whole* night. Go find your own hooker." Jeremiah looked me up and down and apologized for misinterpreting the situation. He laid down a hundred dollar bill and hailed a cab before I was even able to discover what he did for a living. Frank felt validated since he had told me before we went out that my skirt was too short and my shirt too sheer. "Guess I was right."

A few other lines that Frank was famous for were: "Dude, this one is all dried up. I banged her hard all the way to Cleveland earlier." and "Don't bother with this one. She has a permanent case of lockjaw."

Sometimes Frank, the jealous boyfriend, would return to discover that his seat was taken by an eager, young buck talking to his girl. "Hey there, fella. This one is taken unless you wanna meet the exit door." On his right bicep, he had written in permanent marker, 'exit' and the left one read, 'door.' "I suggest you beat it." And then he made a gesture with his hand that earned him and the Mister a trip to the alley.

Most of the time that scene played out smoothly, but twice Frank had been challenged to a fist match in the back parking lot, where he *tried* to defend my honor. Physical aggression isn't Frank's strong suit; he is more of a lover. But Frank, always the good ole boy, would laugh off the black eye and bloody nose, saying he couldn't wait to brag about his fist fight to his law friends. His famous line to every one of his stories was always, "You should see the other guy."

No matter what scenario or line he would deliver, I always cracked up. "Frank, I think you should've chosen a career in theater, not the law."

"It's the same damn thing, Evie." He pretended to tip his hat and bow.

But the night that William cozied up to me at the bar something changed. Something I can't explain. As he strolled over and quickly obtained Frank's deserted seat, I turned to him getting ready to lay on my pretend charm. I lifted my glass in the form of a salute and thanked him for the drink. Then I forced out a flirtatious smile and batted my eyelashes a couple of times so he wouldn't feel immediately rejected. I wasn't completely rude. I was capable of using a few manners.

As our glasses clinked in a hi-there-stranger cheer, the self-proclaimed devilishly handsome man said, "You're welcome. Where did your boyfriend rush off to? If you were mine, I'd never leave you alone."

I took a deep breath. I've heard that lame pickup line a million times, and Frank and I had played out all the possible scenarios for our own amusement.

In Frank's momentary absence, I usually responded, "He's not my boyfriend. We're just friends." But this time, when William's eager smile appeared on his chiseled face, I didn't sputter out my usual response. Instead, I looked at William and stopped breathing for a moment. He smelled so good – Irish Springs soap and Tide laundry detergent. Behind his glasses, his hazel eyes sparkled as his grin reached them. They were grayish green with golden speckles all over them. While his attire suggested he was relaxed and casual, his thick, dark hair was trimmed and perfectly styled. Not a hair out of place.

The difference that I noticed in William was the twinkle in his eye. Frank had taught me to analyze people based on first impressions. "There are two types of people, Evie. The ones who are worried if they look like they have it all or the ones who don't care that they have it all. If you are more worried about appearances, you stop enjoying the game of life. If you are always wishing for tomorrow, you miss the importance of the present adventure. Don't be worried about the next win, instead think about what you can learn from a loss. Take me for example, I look like I have it all, but I could care less; therefore, I'm a wonderful person." Then Frank flashed me his smile with that twinkle of fun in his eye, the same one I recognized in William. Like Frank, he enjoyed the chase. The game wasn't completely about winning but more about the journey.

Instead of creating a fictitious response, and then sneaking out within the next ten to fifteen minutes, I decided to treat him like a human who had real feelings and an actual, beating heart. Flirt back a little, and see what happens. After all, his boy-next-door hadn't left a group of buddies from the other side of the bar. There were no goons snickering and making catcalls egging him on. He was alone and seemed harmless. The last person I let my guard down around was Frank, and look how good that turned out – we were best friends.

I returned his smile with one of my own. A genuine smile, only reserved for when I was truly happy. "Actually, he's not my boyfriend. He's a serial killer. He kidnapped me earlier by flashing a big, shiny knife at my body-guard. Any chance your name is Clark Kent, and under those glasses and tight tee, you are Superman here to rescue me?"

He pushed up his black-rimmed glasses and chuckled. He looked down at his chest and then back up at me with that damn twinkle. "This T-shirt reveals too much, huh? I was going for rugged and carefree, but I guess I should have gotten a large." He laughed again. "You're right, and I deserve that. Bad pickup line. I know he's not your boyfriend because he hit on me a few months back. I found him in the back alley nursing a bloody nose, and he told me that I should see the other guy."

As I laughed, I choked on a big gulp of alcohol that I'd thrown back as he started talking. The wet contents landed in a big splash on the bar in front of me. *Nice.*

My spitting out my drink all over the place made Clark Kent laugh again, yet he still managed to be a gentleman and handed me a napkin to clean up the drips on my chin. "I decided to help the poor guy and buy him a drink because he looked like his best friend had abandoned him." Frank's last roll in the alley that I knew about was over six months ago. He didn't mention a recent one. "Now, I can see that you must be that best friend."

"Yeah, and that totally sounds like Frank. He hasn't won a fight yet, but he'll die trying."

"I'm William, by the way." He extended his right hand in my direction. Not Clark Kent, but he was still polite and nice looking, and I was a sucker for dimples, of which he had one on each cheek.

"Evelyn." I shook his hand. He had a firm, confident handshake.

For over a half hour, we discussed what brought us to Miner City and what kept us from leaving. In William's case, he had accepted a job transfer with his company, Waldner Investments. "They flew me here a few months ago to help start up a new branch. I fell in love with the place. So much to do and see. I've always loved nature, and this truly is God's Country."

The Black Hills had a way of seducing visitors with its gorgeous scenery, untamed wildlife, and laid-back lifestyle. It was South Dakota's secret, and hopefully, it would never catch the eye of a big corporation that sought to melt it down and ruin its true beauty.

"When I returned home to Iowa after a couple of months, I decided this is where I wanted roots. I loved Des Moines, don't get me wrong, but the Hills..." He had a dreamy, romantic look in his eyes. "There is nothing like it."

Even though the feeling was genuine and pure, the notion wasn't. I felt the same way as many others have. The Hills had been our family's only vacation destination for all of my childhood years. We teased my dad by informing him that the interstate led drivers to the east as well as the west. Whether he believed us or not, our car always headed west.

The bartender had made her way back to us as we drained the round. "Would you two like another one?"

That's when I noticed Frank hadn't returned from the men's room to save me. He snuck out. For the first time ever, I enjoyed a second and then a third drink with this new Mister.

Chapter 6

then

Frank reluctantly accepted William into our exclusive group, even though he only once voiced that William wasn't good enough for me. But I shrugged off Frank's overprotective concerns because he was like a big brother to me, and I didn't think anyone would ever measure up to Frank's expectations. Our friendship didn't feel complete unless all three of us were in attendance, which helped maintain my ability to stay a virgin while my hunger for William grew. I fell for William quickly. Once I let my guard down there seemed to be no turning back. Luckily, those intense feelings were mutual.

One evening when Frank declined my invitation to join William and me for dinner and drinks, I begged him to reconsider. "You can study afterward. I'll even help. I can quiz you on whatever you need. You know I'm invaluable to you."

"Not tonight, darlin'. I'm staying in. I'm tired of being the monkey in the middle. Why are you scared to be alone with William? We've known him for months now. He won't bite – Oh!" He recognized the nervousness and the wide-eyed expression on my face. He pointed his index finger at me. "That's why you don't want to be alone with him. You're afraid you won't be able to deny your lady urges anymore. You'll finally surrender your jewel to the handsome treasure hunter." Frank giggled. He couldn't believe that in this fast-paced, instant-gratification generation, I wanted to wait until I was married to have sex.

"Frank, my virginity isn't a joke. It's important to me. Just because my jewel doesn't turn you on doesn't make it any less important." We were curled up on the couch of our little apartment above our favorite bar, Charley's. During one of our nights bellied up to the bar, the owner had approached us and offered the little place to us.

"You two are harmless, and I need harmless to live above my bar. I'll cut you a deal if you promise not to kill *all* my pool business. I know you gamble on my tables to pay for your bills, Evelyn, so I will cover the utilities. In return, you don't need to steal from *all* my pool customers." Mr. Avery was like a sweet teddy bear. When he chuckled, his beer belly would jiggle like good ole St. Nick. When he directed his attention to Frank, he said, "And you, I'd like to ask you for random legal advice, if and when needed."

Frank and I looked at each other. We hadn't even discussed living together, but honestly, it was a perfect idea. We were together whenever we were free, we enjoyed each other's company, and my lease was up at the end of the month. Frank lived at home, so he just needed to break the news to his mom, who would prefer to never let him leave her sight. Suddenly, a grin spread across his face, which of course ignited one to grow on mine. We shook Mr. Avery's hand and the details of our upcoming move began.

After we'd settled into our new place, we didn't venture out as often. We enjoyed the solitude and each other's company more than we liked a crowded bar with sticky floors.

"You can't expect to use me as your crotch-clutch forever, Evie. You need to tell him your hoo-ha is locked tight and see if he sticks around, or you could give it up like a normal hormone-raging human. Bend a rule, for heaven's sake." Frank, who wanted to bed any man that had a pair, didn't understand my desire to remain a virgin after twenty-five years.

"Frank, you're the biggest hormone I know. And since you can't seem to keep it in your pants, I figured I'd help the universe by not providing it with one more slut." He hit on anyone with a pulse. It was a standing joke between us.

When Frank strutted straight out of his imaginary closet, he admitted his sexual preference to everyone that he met except his mother, who openly prayed that Frank and I would finally see the light and start dating. Vera Baker wasn't known for her subtle opinions. "Children should be seen not heard," or "People who claim that they came from old money are just relatives of a long line of tightasses," or "Men and women can't be just friends. There is always sexual tension." And our friendship was one opinion that was even included in the dinnertime prayers.

Vera was a tidy housekeeper who never let a dirty dish rest at the bottom of her sink. No dust bunnies or things out of place. Even though she had a great fondness for being neat and organized, her house did not feel stuffy like a museum. The complete opposite actually. When we walked through the front door, the distinct smell of fresh garlic and bread dough filled our nostrils, and colorful wildflowers were exploding in vases on the entryway table, the living room coffee table, and the centerpiece for our intimate dinner reservation. Booming music cascaded down the hallway, indicating that she was working in the kitchen.

While she made the finishing touches on dinner, she floated from the edge of the counter to the stove with a dance-like grace. *Chop, chop, slide* into the steam pot. *Kerplunk* then slid back to the cutting board to *chop, chop* again. Even though I wondered, I never asked why she didn't move closer to the pot while she cut up the vegetables for the meal. It seemed like if she had been closer, she wouldn't have to keep dancing over to drop in the vegetables. No matter what her reason, she was entertaining to watch. As soon as I popped a squat on a counter stool, Frank would glissade toward

Vera, kiss the top of her head, and glide to the refrigerator where he would pull out two beers. The conversation was reserved for the dinner table because while Vera was cooking, the Beatles bellowed out their hits at the highest volume. Vera believed that cooking preparations were foreplay for the main event, which was stuffing our faces, and she enjoyed each stage for completely different reasons.

After the dance recital was finished, we gathered around her table to savor her hard work and shared some lively banter. Holding hands as we bowed our heads in prayer, Vera led the prayer. "Dear Lord, help my Frankie and his Evelyn find their fondness for one another. Help them to get over themselves or their preconceived notions about marriage. Oh, but no premarital sex. I don't wanna be a granny before they get married. Hear my prayer, heavenly Father. Amen."

It was obvious where Frank inherited his bluntness and creativity for using the English language.

However, Frank, like many of the current generation, did not inherit his mother's strict beliefs on abstinence. "Darling, the universe is over your lock and key, Rapunzel in a tower philosophy. In fact, you should ask this Mister to check for mold." I tossed a throw pillow from our hand-me-down couch at him.

He was right, but I'd never tell him that. I was a bit apprehensive about being alone with William. The more I got to know him, the more I fell for him. I was scared, and honestly, didn't quite trust myself. William had been the perfect gentleman, never trying to push me past the fondling that I was comfortable with. He was amazing with his big, strong magic hands. I melted under his touch. I understood why Vera enjoyed the foreplay.

***

The first time I had sex was the same day that I knew I was in love with William. Besides never pushing me into doing something I didn't feel sexually ready for, he opened every door for me and politely pulled out my chair before I sat down. In conversation, he listened and advised when appropriate. His manners were impeccable and old-fashioned. Dating William was a dream, and I never wanted the dream to end. But it wasn't his manners that I wanted to join me under the sheets.

My sexual knowledge was limited to books, movies, and jokes told at the bar. Because my all-time favorite movie was 'Grease,' I assumed that I'd fall for the bad boy, the greaser with the muscles and sly smile. I couldn't sing or dance a lick, but I figured if I fell in love with the perfect guy, he would inspire my body to move rhythmically to the beat of the music. I was a romantic, a dreamer. Instead, I fell for the business nerd who worked hard to earn a living, and he couldn't dance or sing like John Travolta, but he did have irresistible dimples and oozed a manly confidence. I decided I could just buy him a black leather jacket. William was everything that I needed.

Following a wonderful dinner at a local steakhouse, we tipped back a few cold ones at Charley's and played a lively game of darts. I had chosen my lucky, brown leather skirt that barely covered my bottom half. It was deemed lucky because whenever I wore it to Charley's looking for a pool game, I won more money than I needed for the pending bills I was hoping to pay. Lucky wasn't the word Frank adjective to describe the skirt.

"That small piece of cowhide that you call a skirt is snatch-revealing. It's so minuscule that only the cow's ear was required to make it." Even though Frank pretended to be appalled by it, he often suggested I wear it when we headed to Charley's, especially when we were short on our phone bill. Along with my short skirt, I strapped on a pair of high heels. The top half of my body was covered by a pink, faux cashmere sweater.

As William pulled the darts out of the dartboard and walked toward me, I noticed his eyes looking me over. He handed me three darts. "I've seen you play pool. I don't have a chance at that game so let's try something we are both virgins at." Luckily for William's male ego, darts wasn't my game. My bullseyes were few and far between. Therefore, I didn't purposely *let* him win, and it earned me adoration from my attractive opponent.

By the time we left the bar, we couldn't keep our hands off each other. I knew Frank was at the law library studying for an exam, so William and I would have the apartment to ourselves. Before I could overthink it, I invited William up. He accepted my offer within seconds of the proposition leaving my mouth. We practically sprinted up the stairs.

His mouth was hungry and wet as his tongue explored mine. I fumbled to get the key into the lock. We giggled at our reckless desire.

"I was hoping I'd be smoother, but I've been thinking about getting you naked since the first time I noticed you lean over the pool table." William's cheeks were slightly pink and he seemed out of breath.

"Really?" As I grabbed his head with my free hand and pulled his lips toward me, I kissed him hard to reward him for his patience.

"Ummm...hello, yes! The fact that you have no idea that you're incredibly beautiful is an extremely attractive quality." With his hip, he thrusted the front door to our apartment closed and started to kick off his shoes while still managing to keep his hands cupping my face. "With one hundred percent concentration, you would stare at the colorful maze on the pool table, looking for your next shot. You had no idea what was happening around you. You were lost on that green felt pool table. There could've been a fire, and you wouldn't have noticed. It was so hot."

I kissed him back as I tried to kick off my high heels before I remembered that they were strapped to my ankles. *Damn it.* I leaned down to unbuckle the straps. As my face was near his waist, I noticed the large bulge in the pleat of his pants. *Oh my*. But for the first time in my life, I wasn't scared of it or losing my virginity. I was amazed that my body - little ole me - caused such excitement and desire.

Once my high heels were removed, a big sly smile played on my lips as my hands I reached for his face to pull him for some more tonsil hockey. "That's one massive bulge, Mr. Stanton." My eyes darted down to the magical area below his belt buckle.

"Well, thank you for noticing, Miss Eve. That bulge is about six months old and about to burst."

William didn't know I was a virgin, and I didn't want to tell him for fear that he would deny my advances and suggest that we wait. I was convinced that I was ready to take the next step. I would tell him afterward, or maybe he'd figure it out for himself if I didn't appear too experienced once we dove under the bed sheets.

"I might know how to help you with that."

"I'm all ears. I mean, I'm interested." William seemed nervous as well, which of course made him even more charming. "You know what I mean..."

"I'm no doctor, but I think I have something in my bedroom." I'd read enough books and watched enough movies to know how to flirt, but I had no idea how powerful and sexy I'd feel at that moment. The fact that he was excited about me was thrilling. I couldn't believe I had that power. Literally, he was eating out of the palm of my hand. Too bad I didn't have any real sexual experience because I could've asked for something wild and adventurous, and he would have agreed without hesitation.

As I turned to playfully jog down the hallway to my room, a sexy growl that I'd been practicing escaped from my lipstick-stained lips. I was full of surprises.

William tossed his coat onto the back side of the couch and eagerly chased me down the narrow hallway. The scurry of our chase and hungry giggles echoed throughout the apartment. Since his legs were longer, he caught up to me in no time, and when he tackled me, we landed on the top of my bed. We were out of breath and aroused.

William pushed off me and stood next to the edge of my bed. He started to unbutton his pressed, light blue oxford shirt exposing a perfectly sculpted six pack. This boy next door was insanely ripped, and his bare chest made me warm in places that had never been warmed before.

Breaking my own rules, I seductively invited him into my bed as well as my heart.

Chapter 7

now

For obvious reasons, most of my days are not filled with rainbows and sunshine. In jail, there isn't a plethora of color or warmth. Everything is different shades of gray with sprinkles of inmate orange. If I ever get out of here, I will never paint the walls of my home gray or wear orange again. I will never drive a silver car with a gray interior, or let my hair become aged and gray. Gray is the color that represents surrender, defeat. It is a combination of dark, scary black and crisp, pure white. It is the in-between color, the hue that you settle for. *I can't be bold black or angelic white, so I give up and lie somewhere in the middle.*

Inmate orange has a similar story. Blending blood red and vibrant yellow, orange resolves to be the color that screams 'caution' and alerts everyone to proceed with a warning that indicates trouble is ahead. Orange is avoided at all costs.

Since I feel forgotten and partially dead inside, my heart doesn't pump enough blood to warm my body. The tips of my fingers and toes are the furthest from my frozen heart, and they are left suffering from a lack of blood flow. Most often, I'm chilled to the bone as I try to mask my true feelings or concerns. If my heart remains a frozen shell, I will survive the heartache in silence. Gone are the nights of cozy sweats under a plush blanket listening to the crackle of the fireplace. Gone are the days of lazy

Sunday afternoon football doused with the smell of freshly made pizza and the taste of cold beer. Gone are the moments of pure pleasure of being surrounded by the ones you love. Gone are the simple things that I took for granted.

Most of my days fuse together. At six in the morning, mushy oatmeal breakfast is served with a half-slice of a flavorless apple or a bruised banana and lukewarm coffee that tastes as if it has been warmed up one too many times. Then I usually crawl back onto the hard, cold steel slab that the jail defines as a bed, hoping sleep will overtake me so I can shut off my brain for any amount of time. Lunch in the overcrowded cafeteria is served at eleven, followed by fifteen minutes of yard time where we all steal deep breaths of the fresh air.

Today, my heart feels heavier than usual because, during Frank's quick visit yesterday, he confessed that his mother had recently been diagnosed with stage four lung cancer. She didn't have long, and even though she accepted the news quite well, Frank was having a hard time imagining a life without her.

"And she is so stubborn that she won't even consider chemotherapy or radiation to slow it down. She is too ornery to die, right?" Frank's eyes searched mine hoping to find comfort that would reassure him that his mother could avoid her death sentence. I had nothing to give him, not even words of compassion. "I'm praying the devil will refuse to take her and spit her out. I need to hold onto that hope."

Vera and Frank are two peas in a pod. Since their personalities are very similar, they tend to butt heads because of their strong opinions and ability to vocalize them, but they both appreciate each other and value their relationship, so their healthy disagreements never diminished their love. Being around both of them was not only entertaining but also heartwarming. I could only hope that someday Hudson and I could enjoy that deep of a bond, and all this pain will be worth it. "I know she drives me crazy when she gets up in my business, but without her, I'll be lost. " I didn't doubt it, and I felt the same admiration for his mother. When some people leave this world, they leave a gigantic void. Vera will be one of them.

The ringing of the phone echoes in my ear until I hear her husky voice. "Hello?"

The automated robotic voice announces, "This is a collect call from an inmate at the South Dakota Correctional Facility. If you accept the charges, press one – "

Beep.

"Hello? Evelyn, is that you?" The scratchiness of her voice reminds me that she was a heavy smoker during her youth, back when smoking cigarettes in restaurants and businesses was acceptable and slightly promoted. She likes to remind us 'youngsters' that when she was a receptionist, she had her own built-in ashtray at her workstation. When the FDA confirmed that smoking tobacco led to lung cancer, Vera stopped cold turkey. "Now, what the hell am I gonna do with my hands?"

"Hi, Vera. Yes, it's me. How are you?" I wanted to respond with a smart comment like, *of course, it's me, Vera. How many other friends do you have rotting in jail?* But I couldn't.

"Dying." She giggles at her own bluntness. Obviously, her sharp wit hasn't been affected by the growing cancer. "But isn't everyone? It isn't like I can get out of this world alive. I just earned a warning flag so I can say goodbye. Kinda reminds me of a grenade. The sinister sizzling of the wick gets louder and louder before it finally reaches the tip and blows itself up into a thousand little pieces. I can hear the sizzling, Evelyn."

"Oh, Vera. I miss your spunk. It's so good to hear your voice." I promised myself that I could cry *after* the phone call, not during. I lasted about three seconds.

"Well, it's the same shit, different day out here. Frank's been working round the clock to free his girl. You stay strong until he does. You hear me?"

"Yes, ma'am. I'm trying to be strong." I swallow down the huge lump that formed in my throat. Because I didn't have a healthy relationship with my own mother, I always tried to earn Vera's approval. It hurt to think how much I must've disappointed her. "I'm so sorry, Vera. Is there anything I can do? I know my ability to help is quite restricted from here, but I wanted you to know I'd do anything for you if I'm able."

"Anything? You know I have only one dying wish." I hear a little, feisty spark in her weak, cancer-ridden voice. She's still Vera, always with a witty comment and a hidden agenda. I must've paused long enough to indicate that I wasn't sure what her dying wish was because she responded before I had the chance. "Make Frank an honest man."

"Oh, Vera..." Stubborn, one-track mind, Vera. She was never gonna let that idea of hers die. Even though we are discussing her pending death and her dying wish, Vera has managed to make me smile and shake my head. This woman is one-of-a-kind, and the world needs more like her. Life isn't fair.

"Don't patronize me. I'm aware my boy is light in those shiny, little penny loafers and skin-tight pants, but it doesn't change what a mother wants. Since you two were young'uns, you shared something special. So, what if it's a deep friendship and not a bang-me-sideways sexual attraction. I've always said best friends make the best partners." Yes, she's been saying that since I met her. Frank and I joked that we believed that she thought if she repeated herself enough times it would make it true. I guess Vera and I had that in common.

"Vera, I love you and you know I'd do anything for you, but I'm already married."

"Everyone makes mistakes – "

"Vera..."

"Yeah, William gave me the only grandbabies I'll ever have, but he wasn't and still isn't good enough for you. Plus, I've heard there's some trouble there. Time to cut your losses, Evelyn. Know when to call it a game. Retire the pitcher and sub in a fresh buck. You still have time." Vera loves her analogies.

"Vera, I know your heart is in the right place, but right now, I just need to focus on my case, proving my innocence and getting out of here. I'll deal with whatever is left of my marriage after that."

"Maybe that's your problem in the first place – you only focus on one thing at a time. In the meantime, you allow the rest of your life to suffer. How are you ever going to reach the top of the hill, Evelyn, if you keep circling around it?" I love this woman and her ability to always tell it like she sees it, but sometimes her honesty stings a bit because it isn't far from the truth.

"You're probably right." I knew there was no point in arguing with her, and furthermore, I did have a one-track mind, but in most cases, it proved to be an asset.

"I know I'm right. Now, promise a dying woman that you'll grant me my last wish. I want to hear you say it, Evelyn."

She knew I'd have a hard time promising something that I didn't intend to fulfill. I may have a hard time focusing my attention on more than one major life event at a time, but I always followed through on my promises. It was a curse and a blessing. If I said I was going to do something, I did it. But at the moment, I had no idea how I could make her wish come true.

I take a deep breath and quietly respond, "I promise."

"Thank you. That's all I need to hear."

A dying woman's wish is like not any other plan because she has nothing to lose.

Chapter 8

now

C igarettes are gold in jail. Rather than paying a friend for a favor with a five-dollar bill, you promise a 'five point of chicken,' which is the code word for cigarette. I've never been a smoker and never wanted to be one. In fact, my allergy tests indicated that I was highly allergic to smoke. But to survive in jail and pay my dues, I need to deal in cigarettes. It is the one vice everyone is allowed in here. 'Allowed' is a term used lightly. Our jail is smoke-free like the rest of the institutions in the state, but the underpaid, greedy guards need to earn extra money somehow. So, a five point of chicken it is.

During one of my first days behind bars, I received my first jailhouse economic lesson. Jilli informed me that, "cigarettes as prison currency dates back to Hitler's POW camps. Those damn Nazi prison guards were not just hoodlums, but savvy businessmen. Behind desperate people are desperate actions, I guess. Because the prisoners were starvin' and dehydrated, I read that they would trade a cigarette for a glass of water. Can you imagine being denied water? Thank the Lord, that we have some laws to protect us. We got it pretty good in here, Snow White."

Jilli had no idea how good I had it before stepping foot into this place, and it made me wonder what her life was like before she became incarcerated.

The fact that cigarettes have become an important currency in my life reminds me how ironic that is in comparison to my life before jail.

Before living behind bars, I held the belief that I should enjoy everything in moderation. If Jilli or Caramie would've known me before this fortress of depression, they would've called me a prude. Everything was in moderation, especially if it was a vice, and they would've laughed hysterically at my definition of a vice.

Coffee – two cups filled to the rim was all that I allowed myself. Wine – I could personally only handle three glasses, but like my coffee cup, the glass was always filled to the top. Dessert – only once a week and it had to be worth every calorie. Sex – three times a week and always on Sundays, and only with my husband. Smoking – No thanks. Not only was I allergic to smoke, but I couldn't stand the lingering, tobacco smell. Drugs – I wasn't interested in screwing up my life. Not being in total control of myself and my actions scared the hell out of me.

I liked rules, and I taught my kids my fundamental guidelines for life. William and I didn't just say no to our kids, we explained why, hoping that our reasoning would resonate deeper than the resentment of not getting their way. Every guideline was followed by an explanation.

At five years old, Hudson was very observant and pointed out things that he learned through our progressive parenting. Always a rule follower like his mother, Hudson often called out wrongdoings. For example, on the car ride to the courthouse to pay our property taxes, I had removed a hard, crusty booger from my nose. From the backseat securely strapped into his fireman-approved car seat, Hudson was beyond mortified.

"You just picked your nose, Mommy."

"Sorry, yes, I did, Hudson. It must not have gotten out when I blew my nose earlier."

"You flicked it out the window."

"Yes, I did."

"Why?"

"I didn't want it to be hanging in my nose when I talk to someone today."

"You tell me not to pick my nose, Mommy, but you did."

"I realize that, but sometimes you have to bend rules in certain situations."

I had lost him. He turned to stare out the window, lost in trying to understand the adaptation of a new rule in his black and white world. Just because he was a rule follower did not mean Hudson wouldn't question authority or vocalize his questions. We encouraged him to seek understanding and were always intrigued by learning how his brain worked. The curiosity and the sponge of his young, moldable brain was amazing.

When we arrived at the courthouse, Hudson reminded me to lock the car and that I needed to hold his hand as we made our way across the parking lot. "Drivers can't see me, Mommy, because I'm not big like you yet. But someday, I will be."

Suddenly, he yanked down on my arm to request my attention. Unfortunately, he did not know better than to point, and to a five-year-old, sometimes that instinct was hard to resist. Maybe it's like picking a crusty for an adult.

"Mommy, look. That man is bad." Hudson's chubby little finger pointed toward a man around twenty yards away. Dressed in stained, oversized clothing, a bearded man who was leaning against the courthouse as we walked into the building was the focus of Hudson's attention. His lips were pressed into a puckered face as he inhaled the tobacco from his lit cigarette. I gently bent Hudson's finger back down into his hand and shook my head. As we walked past the 'bad man,' Hudson crowded closer to my hip. I tipped my head to politely acknowledge the man as we made our way past him. Thankfully, Hudson was too intimidated to utter another word.

While we were standing in line to make our payment, I decided to use the downtime for a teachable moment.

In a hushed, motherly voice, I leaned down toward my son. "Hudson, that man isn't a bad man. He is an adult, and he is choosing to smoke the cigarette even though he knows it may harm his body. We don't judge strangers for their choices. In our family, we don't allow smoking because we believe it is damaging, and we want to be healthy." Again, I could see that Hudson was trying to make logical, five-year-old sense out of what I was telling him. Sorting it out in his young brain. As the old soul that he was, he needed to process the information internally.

When it was our turn at the counter, the helpful registrar commented on Hudson's good behavior. "What a polite young man you are. Waiting so nicely with Mom." She leaned over the counter to aim her big, toothy grin at Hudson, but he was still comprehending the new lesson and sorting the amendments to rules. I silently prayed that my son would not notice and comment on the bright red lipstick stain on her teeth.

"Hudson, please acknowledge – " I glanced at the registrar's name tag. " – Kathy."

He looked up at the stranger, and without even flashing a smile, my serious wide-eyed child said, "My mommy picked her nose and flicked the crusty out the window. And the bad man outside the building isn't bad, he just isn't very smart."

Chapter 9

now

I've been locked up for six days, eleven hours, and about thirty-three minutes – but who was counting? Of course, I am. There isn't much else to do.

And finally, it's visiting day. I can't wait to see my family. Even though I'm sure William hasn't been able to stay faithful to me during this stressful week, I miss his coffee breath. Every Saturday morning after a good night's sleep, he leaned over for a good morning kiss, and I turned my nose away and let his kiss land on my cheek. I miss Hudson's not-a-fan-of-morning personality, as he grumbled his greeting before stuffing his face. He loves breakfast food but hates rolling out of bed to ingest it. Hazel – I miss everything about her. Hazel is just easy to be around. She is laid back, pleasant and kind. While her brutal honesty sometimes puts people off, William and I get a kick out of the comments that roll off her tongue. Her comeback is often, "but you told me to always tell the truth."

"Little white lies are more socially acceptable than brutal honesty." I explained to Hazel as we both cleaned up the kitchen after breakfast – part of our Saturday morning routine. We were a good team; while I washed, she dried and put away the dishes. That morning, we'd made biscuits and gravy, which was Hudson's favorite. He had blessed us with his presence before quickly disappearing back into his basement hole where I was sure he'd buried himself back under the covers.

"Aren't all lies dishonesty in disguise? No matter what color they are?" Hazel adored debating any topic, even the most elementary issues. William and I imagined Hazel becoming a lawyer someday, and Frank was thrilled with the prospect of mentoring and molding his godchild.

"Hazel, sometimes we have to decide if the truth is worth hurting someone else's feelings."

"Well, you've always taught me not to care about what other people think of me. Now, as I embark on the dawn of adulthood, you are renouncing the childhood lessons that you so firmly planted in my ear and replacing them with white lies and peer pressure." Hazel was thirteen years old but wise beyond her years. "I'm disappointed, Mother."

I giggled. My Hazel is always one to question everything. I never worried about her falling into the wrong crowd or succumbing to peer pressure. As a natural leader, my daughter paved her own way. She *was* the 'in crowd.' Her self-confidence radiated, and it drew people to her. As her mother, I'd never describe her as being cocky; instead, I'd refer to her as being confident. Since she wasn't scared of rejection or what people thought of her, honesty was simply a part of who she was. It was a breath of fresh air.

"Hazel, I know you're smarter than that. I'd never tell you to be anything true to yourself and others. I'm merely explaining that even though you aren't worried about how other people perceive you, you should be concerned about how you make them feel."

As she took the freshly washed coffee cup from me and started to dry it with the dish rag, our eyes met, and I detected a sparkle in her eyes. "Okay, Mother. Please resume my daily lesson on social acceptance with a small side of guilt."

"Thank you." I grinned. "White lies are statements that aren't intended to be life-altering declarations, but more of a quick regard for the moment. For example, when a friend asks you, 'Do these mom jeans make my butt look huge?' If you choose to respond with a harmless white lie, you can simply respond with no and move on. Spare some unnecessary heartache. But if you choose to tell the harsh truth - "

"Like if I said, 'Yes, Peggy, in fact, they do. Rip them off your body before your caboose morphs into that unflattering shape forever.'"

"Precisely, my point. That is why Peggy won't return your messages."

"Peggy is an over-sensitive adolescent who needed to hear the reality of the situation. She shouldn't have inquired if she didn't want the truth. She'll thank me later."

"Hazel, that's not nice. She won't thank you. Instead, your honesty hurt her feelings so much that she'll never forget how your words made her feel. You cut down her confidence." I stopped washing the last dish and turned my attention to my youngest. "When a comment does more harm than good, it isn't worth it."

Hazel understood where this conversation was headed. Peggy had been Hazel's best friend for years. They were joined at the hip during their elementary school years, followed by surviving the tornado of teenage hormones during their seventh grade year, and recently stopped talking after Hazel rudely explained to Peggy that yes, in fact, her new jeans made her look overweight and chubby.

"I get it. I get it." Even though Hazel was confident, independent, and headstrong, I knew she missed her best friend. She could see reason, even though it meant admitting she was wrong. Peggy was the only one with whom Hazel relaxed her guard and showed vulnerability, similar to my friendship with Frank. With Peggy, Hazel allowed herself to be natural.

"Last lesson for today." After I towel-dried my dishwater-pruned hands, I grabbed Hazel's two hands in mine. "A truly wonderful human can admit when she's said something wrong and apologize for it."

"And that human is me." A small thin tear fell out of her eye as she responded softly.

"Yes, Hazel, I think it's time to say you're sorry."

"But...Mom...what if I still think her butt did look mammoth?"

"That is your *opinion*. It may be true, but that is also my point. A little white lie would've saved you two from the fight that you are currently in. And so what if she wasted her own, hard-earned babysitting money on a pair of jeans that you don't like? It's no skin off your back like the old saying goes. If you told her you were sorry, what would you be sorry for?" My lessons always concluded with a summary of my point, but I wanted Hazel to vocalize what she was apologizing for, and that would prove she learned a lesson.

"For hurting her feelings..."

"Lesson learned." I pulled her into a tight hug.

"Mom, can I tell you something?"

"Is it a little white lie? Like, that I look stunning in this ratty, old shirt of Dad's?"

"Ummm no." She giggled. "I mean, as a little white lie, you look amazing! You should wear that baggy, pit-stained shirt every day." I winked at my vulnerable, maturing Hazel and nodded for her to continue. "You're an amazing Mom, and that isn't any color of a lie."

That conversation was only a few months ago, but after the last couple of weeks that my family has suffered through, it feels more like years.

During my quick, supervised shower, I lather, rinse and pat dry all my crevices. I wish I could shave my legs – I hate hairy legs – but razors are obviously not allowed in the prison showers. The clean soap smell reminds me of William. He likes the smell of soap and cleaning supplies. When we were first married, he loved coming home from work to smell a freshly polished kitchen floor and bleached bathrooms. I used to take great pride in my clean house and my hairless legs.

Right now, though, I don't feel worthy of being clean on the outside when I feel so broken on the inside. My heart is black and rotten, so it feels odd to smell like freshly cut flowers and soap. I dress in my least stained prison uniform with my inmate number printed on the back, 9343162-506. It's the only time in my life that I'm thankful that I can't overthink my outfit.

As I zip up my bright orange jumpsuit, I remember completing a gossip magazine poll with Hazel last year that claimed I should never wear the color orange with my cool colored skin tone. The results of the survey indicated that I should wear emerald green or dark lavender. Well, I guess I didn't have much choice today. Maybe no one will notice how pale my skin is.

But still, I'm nervous about the visit today with the people whom I love the most. I haven't talked to them since I was arrested. I'd only seen William and Hazel sitting hunched together in the courtroom on the day of my bail hearing. That seems like so long ago.

I received a letter from William informing me that he planned on attending visitors' day. His note was very brief, so there weren't many lines to read between, but I managed to catch one hint of mystery. On the top of the stationery, a big letter 'S' was monogrammed. It was my personal stationery that I used for handwritten notes that accompanied a care package. *"Get well soon, Mrs. Anderson,"* to the neighbor who had fallen and broken her hip while getting the mail one icy winter morning. *"Coach Sundem, thanks for helping Hazel reach her full potential this season!"* to her volunteer volleyball coach.

To most people, the fact that my husband wrote me a note on a fancy piece of paper wouldn't cause them any alarm. In fact, most inmates would be thrilled by the arrival of a hand-written letter from a loved one. However, that beautiful, heavy paper had been a wedding gift from my grandmother who valued personalized notes and passed on her love of reading to me. It was a gift that I cherished and used only sparingly and on special occasions. William also knew these facts, yet he used this stationary and not a plain piece of notebook paper.

That specific stationery was kept in the top drawer of my little secretary's desk, which I had inherited from my grandmother. I paid our bills, organized the family calendar, and locked up some personal belongings in that desk. Seeing William's handwriting on my personal paper caused butterflies to flutter around in my stomach. And not the butterflies of excitement. It meant he was looking for something... questioning me... doubting me. Normally, I was the one in our marriage who carried the doubt, and I didn't like being on this side of the coin. I questioned William and his loyalty, but he never had any reason to question mine...until now. *What else did he discover? What if he found the random key? Would he figure out what it was for?*

Although, the logical section of my brain pointed out that he needed to look for our monthly bills, possibly some stamps, or maybe Hazel's fundraising packet for school. Logical reasoning. All these things were stored in my desk. There were many reasonable explanations for why William would need to sit at my desk.

However, the paranoid part of my brain said he purposefully used *this* stationery because he knew I'd recognize it and realize where he found the paper. He was going through my personal effects. He was proving a point and wanted to make me sweat.

And because I had a lot of extra time to overthink everything, I did sweat. I did worry. I wondered what he found and what he thought he knew. *Did William doubt my innocence?*

I'm stiffly sitting at a small, round, ivory-colored cafeteria table when he enters the room. The room is a grayish-white color with no pictures or artwork displayed. Near the top of the walls are six windows with bars across them lining the west side of the room, which allow for a gorgeous view of the sun in the late afternoons if you were allowed to stand on the top of a chair. The limited sun that peaks through the glass glistens on William's head making his gray hair glitter. William looks older, if that is possible, in only a week's time. His hair is cut a little too short – meaning it was recently trimmed, possibly for today's meeting. He is dressed in a stark white button-down oxford. It is freshly pressed – and I instantly wonder who is ironing his shirts for him. Clenching his jaw, he acknowledges the guard who is talking to him with a slight nod. Even though I can tell he is nervous, he is trying to appear calm and passive. But to his partner of two decades, I notice the subtle clues that give away that he is uncomfortable in his own skin. He is biting his bottom lip, his nostrils flare open and close in a steady rhythm, and his blood-shot eyes blink rapidly.

As soon as my eyes scan William, I crane my neck around to glance behind him for the heads of our children. My eyes search for Hazel's brown bouncing curls and Hudson's dyed blonde spiky haircut. He is a head taller than William and several heads taller than Hazel, so I expect to see his unique spiked hair first. But no one is trailing behind him. I don't see my children; it is only William. Before I can completely mask my disappointment, my smile fades as William and my eyes meet. He recognizes my letdown. When he sits down, the first thing out of his mouth is heartbreaking. "They aren't coming. Sorry to disappoint you. It's just me."

Even though I'm bummed that I didn't get to see my kids, one familiar family face is better than none. Plus, there are many things I need to discuss with William, and it would probably be best if the kids weren't here. "It's okay. Thank you for coming, William."

"I was strictly informed that we can't hug until the end of our hour." He blurts out as if he needs a reason not to touch me.

I smile at him from my side of the table. Yes, I knew that we aren't allowed to hug. The guards stationed throughout the room often strolled near the tables to eavesdrop on conversations to make sure everything was docile and harmless. I haven't had any visitors besides my lawyer, so this is my first time in the visitor's area, but I was made aware of the rules.

"I've missed you all so much. Time moves very slowly here."

"You aren't on vacation, Eve. It's jail. It isn't supposed to be a walk in the park." In a matter of a few short seconds, I have already managed to irritate him. The speed at which I can annoy William has improved, even when I'm not trying and am not currently living with him. If I wasn't in jail and it was a normal Sunday afternoon in our Miner City home, William's snarky attitude would signal that it had been too long in between our quick rolls in the hay. On a normal Sunday afternoon, I would've suggested a 'nap', which he would've readily accepted and chased me into our bedroom. But this isn't a typical Sunday afternoon.

Furthermore, he is more than simply horny. He is mad, angry, and disappointed at how his current Sunday is being spent. He is probably missing his favorite team's football game, which is the cherry on top of this situation. Or perhaps, he canceled plans with a new mystery woman so that he could visit his wife behind bars.

"Sorry, William. Yes, I wanted to see the kids, but I'm glad to see you. How are you?"

His eyes are as dull as his expression. He isn't going to make this visit easy for either of us.

"Obviously, not good, Eve. Ever since your arrest, our lives have spiraled out of control. We've been going full speed down a San Francisco hill without working brakes."

"I'm sorry, William, I really am." Normally, I would use the nonverbal signs that suggest my regret and heartbreak – look to the ceiling, dab the corner of my eyes, maybe even let out an exhausted sigh – but I know those things wouldn't work on William. He hates weakness. "Have you spoken to Frank lately?"

"I've been too busy worrying about our mounting debt, dodging reporters, maintaining our house, and parenting our two emotionally destroyed kids to shoot the shit with your ole buddy Frank."

"I was only asking to see if you have spoken with him regarding the case. My case. That's all." As I glance across the table at this man who's shared my bed – and a few other women's – I try to remember the man I fell in love with long ago. I don't recognize this man. He is the outer shell of the man who bought me flowers on Labor Day because it was cheaper than Valentine's Day, the man who rubbed my feet when we relaxed on the couch, the man who told me that I was nothing like my mother and didn't need to worry about losing my mind. His appearance suggested that he was William Scott Stanton, but inside the physical frame was someone I didn't know. He was distant, cold, and angry – nothing like the guy who swept me off my feet years ago in Charley's bar.

When he looks at me, I don't see the foundation that our marriage should've built during our twenty years together. I don't see the trust and loyalty that years of stability should've earned us. All I recognize is annoyance, pity, and some resentment. It amazes me how quickly our infrastructure was poisoned. My arrest was only six days ago. Even though my half of the marriage has been dissolving for years, I assumed that William's half was holding steady, and he was comfortable with my constant ability to overlook his numerous flings. Every night after work, he always returned home, even if he briefly visited another female for some extra attention. Our marriage wasn't perfect, but whose was? I'd looked the other way for years, confronted him when it had gotten out of control, and demanded counseling to repair the trust. William would beg me to forgive him, proclaim he'd never do it again, and treat me like a queen for a while. This messed-up pattern seemed to work for us.

"Eve, I don't have time to check in with Frank regarding your mess. Things have been insane. I've been busy not drowning in the mess that you left behind. Neighbors are treating us like we have the plague. My partners at work are probing me with questions. Even your wicked sister read about your arrest and reached out. Bills are piling up, and reporters call the house at all hours. Your case is at the bottom of my priorities right now." His eyebrows shot up as he remembered something. "Frank's strange, nosy mother stopped by the other day – "

"Vera?"

"Yes, her. She pounded on the front door until I finally disconnected from my conference call and answered the door. And you know what she was doing when I pulled the door open?" His eyes are wide open as he continues without waiting for a response from me. I didn't realize the question was rhetorical. "She'd lifted the doormat and was looking under it for a hidden key. To. Our. House. When I asked her what the hell she thought she was doing, she got all flustered, said she was confused and thought she was at Frank's house. Then she forced her way in, and she bee-lined it for the bathroom. She proceeded to lock herself in there. After thirty minutes, I knocked on the door to inform her that I needed to leave for work. All kinds of strange noises erupted from the other side of the door before she told me to leave her and that she would call a cab as soon as her bowel movement subsided. She is completely nuts." William is shaking his head. He never was fond of Vera and her brashness.

"I'm sorry, William. I wish there was something I could do to help. I feel helpless."

Vera...loyal, too smart for her own good, Vera. William's recollection of her recent visit does make me smile, but I stuff down my happiness until later when I have time to overthink.

"I'm sure you do." I catch a bit of sarcasm in his voice.

"William, is there something you would like to say, something you would like to get off your chest? You're obviously pissed at me, and I don't want to spend the limited time that we have together fighting." I've already apologized, but he doesn't seem to hear me, so I suggest a truce.

He crosses his arms over his chest and responds, "What would you like to talk about then?" His question is laced with sarcasm. He is going through the motions of the visit, but he plans on making every moment painful and uncomfortable for me.

As I contemplate his question, I realize that I'm not sure if there is a safe topic that we *can* discuss. If I ask him how work is, I'm sure his response will include how my arrest makes it more stressful. If I inquire about Hazel, I'm sure I'll be to blame for her depression and mood – not saying I'm *not* to blame, but I don't think I could handle more guilt. If I seek information about Hudson, I'm sure I'll be to blame for his possible relapse. *Oh crap...*

"How's Hudson?" My heart skips a beat waiting for an answer that I hope I can stomach.

William's lips pinch together as if they plan on squeezing in the truth; however, his vocal cords are stronger, and he yearns to devolve more heartache onto my pain. Through his clenched jaw, he responds, "He didn't come home from Tallgrass."

Tallgrass is the addiction care center that Hudson had been admitted to after he overdosed on prescription pain medication – pills that had not been prescribed to him. Before my arrest, he had served three and a half weeks of the mandatory four weeks that he'd been sentenced to. He'd been scheduled to be released the day after my arrest. I'd been so consumed with my own doom and drama that I'd just assumed he'd been released and was now at home adjusting to life and sobriety.

Before I can even censor what comes out of my mouth, I ask, "Oh, no. What happened?"

William's response is a motion that magicians use after they complete their performance. He raises his hand and waves it with his palm facing up, as if he is suggesting I'm the next circus act. *Ta-da.*

Oh, no. What have I done?

"William, I completely understand why you're upset, but please tell me what happened." I try to reach across the table to grasp his bare hands when the guard standing near the visitor's door loudly clears his throat to indicate his disapproval. William quickly removes his hands from the top of the table and puts them under the table onto his lap. I regrettably do the same.

"There isn't much to tell. After he learned that his own mother had been arrested for murdering his best friend, he requested to extend his stay and signed himself in for another month. I guess your arrest put him over the edge."

"Oh..." The last time I talked to Hudson, he'd turned a corner in his rehabilitation. He'd finally accepted that *he* had made the choice to use drugs and that *he* needed to be the one to choose to stop. He'd taken ownership of his mistakes, which is a huge step. He recognized that he'd been in a tailspin and needed to take control of his life. He contacted his high school to get caught up on what he was missing. With a clear head, he yearned to graduate with his class and take charge of his future. I'd been so proud of him after his phone call. For years, I prayed that he'd become more concerned with how he treated the people around him and how his choices affected the course of his life. After all the drama and heartbreak, he was finally becoming the young man that I knew he could be. Unfortunately for Hudson, he was also learning too quickly about disappointment and not being able to control the actions of those around him. As soon as he was strong enough to stand on his own two feet after a month-long, painful rehabilitation, his childhood best friend had died, and then his mother had been arrested for the murder. Life punched him square in the jaw, sending stars into his vision that only helped produce a pounding headache and flipping stomach. The poor kid couldn't catch a break.

I feel terrible for him. As his mother, I have always tried to shield him from unnecessary pain, holding little concern about becoming a helicopter parent, or even worse, a bulldozer parent. But when all of your own human rights are stripped from your everyday life, it makes it almost impossible to shield your child from any tragedies of life. No need to worry about the helicopter or bulldozer because my current motorized vehicle is without wheels.

But an even worse feeling than not being able to protect him was knowing that I caused it. I caused his continued weakness and inability to face life. I added one more stress to his already stress-filled anxiety. How could I ever make it up to him or help him heal from the heartbreak that my arrest had caused him?

A lone tear rolls out of my left eye. I promised myself that I'd be strong for my family during our first meeting while I wore a god-awful orange jumpsuit, but I lost the battle. Betrayed by my own weakness.

Before I can wallow in too much self-pity, William sneers at the question that I'd been waiting for him to ask the entire visit. The real reason that he was here. "Where's the money, Eve?"

Chapter 10

now

*D*earest Hudson,

    Dad told me that you signed up for an additional month of treatment at Tallgrass. I'm proud of you for making that tough decision and for taking responsibility to get your life back on track. You're an amazing, young man. I'm so sorry for the heartache you're experiencing.

    As your mom, I've always felt that God blessed me with you so that I could teach and love you as He would want. But lately, I think God is using you to teach me. *I'm learning so much from your example– how strong and patient you are through this tough road to sobriety. Six months ago, I didn't think you had the strength or courage to face the overwhelming battle of addiction. I was wrong, and I've never been so glad to be wrong.*

    Frank has advised me to not discuss the charges against me. He says nothing is safe. I guess I understand that, but it's hard not to defend myself or try to explain what is going on. Just know that I love you and Hazel with all my heart, and I'm still the same mom who raised you and has loved you for your whole life. We'll figure this all out and rise above it when the time comes. I have faith, and I hope you do too.

    I'd love to hear from you sometime, but I understand that it might be difficult for you right now. Losing a friend so tragically is never easy, and under the current circumstances, it's even harder.

xxoo – Mom

***

I'm so tired, and sleep won't come. My whole body is filled with exhaustion from head to toe. I thought maybe if I released my feelings into a letter to Hudson, my heart wouldn't feel so heavy, and then I'd be able to sleep. No such luck.

In the corner of our tiny cell, my imagination creates two teenage girls standing and staring at me. I imagine one of them is named Sleep and the other is Karma. The two catty girlfriends are always plotting and scheming with their foreheads touching in the intimate way that only close friends do. They talk in a secret code and giggle at their private jokes. Sleep throws her head back as a sinister laugh escapes her throat, and Karma teasingly slugs Sleep in the arm. Like the mean school girls loitering in the hallways, they whisper in hushed tones while sneering and judging anyone who crosses their path. Life is a game to these two comrades, and everyone in it is a chess piece, willing or unwilling. Without formal instructions, Karma and Sleep invent games that the players aren't aware they are participating in. The two girls are the only ones who know the rules, and the odds of winning against them are impossible. Another deep, throaty laugh bursts from Sleep as she overhears a familiar prayer being whispered: "Now, I lay me down to sleep, I pray the Lord my soul to keep. Angels watch me through the night and wake me with the morning light. Amen."

"Good one! Like that is gonna work." Sleep gives Karma a high five.

In order to join their exclusive club, I need to surrender my conscience and moral compass. I haven't laid down my cards yet. The game is not over.

I close my eyes, begging my imagination to quit. I roll over and face the cement wall, ignoring their childish taunts.

The fact that I can't sleep is contributing to my mounting depression, something for which I was not prepared. I never knew I could feel so sad. So helpless. Previously, I thought that if I planned out every scenario, I could handle being in jail and away from my family, but even my major over-thinking and preparation had not foreseen this turn of events.

I'm relieved that Hudson is seeking professional help, but I worry about the lasting impact of this crisis and how it will scar him. My heart breaks thinking about him being alone and struggling. On the bright side, I tell myself that he's in the best possible place for what he's experiencing. For a month, Hudson had been undergoing therapy to help him create healthy options to deal with stressors that life would forever throw at him. And unfortunately, a major stressor had occurred one day before he was sched-uled to be released. Hudson had decided on his own that he wasn't ready. As his mother, I know his core is solid and his heart is wholesome, but in the last couple of years, drugs and alcohol have clouded his judgment. He lost sight of right and wrong.

His phone usage is limited similar to mine. We are both locked up and stripped of our everyday distractions. Furthermore, I'm sure his therapist frowns upon him making phone calls to his mother at the local jail, so my snail mail letter will have to suffice for now.

During the last year of Hudson's addiction, I remember feeling the same helplessness that I do right now. I had no control. There was nothing I could say or do to make him stop. Every word that came out of my mouth caused him irritation. He was repulsed by my suggestions and allergic to my advice. As emotions poured out of my mouth, begging him to stop, I noticed that his body reacted with a shiver– a full body shiver – which reminded me of the icky feeling that involuntarily happens to me when my car tires roll over roadkill. That is what Hudson felt the need to do when I spoke. Full body shiver.

I sensed his hatred towards me. I was human. When I entered the room, he immediately exited it. At first, I shrugged it off as a normal teenage reaction; however, he didn't run away when William spoke, even if it was to reprimand him. Hudson listened. Somewhere between the teenage rebellious years and when he asked me to drop him off at school a block away, even in the dead of a Midwest winter, which in South Dakota was below zero, I lost him. I had completely and utterly lost my sensitive, firstborn's love and respect.

If I could pinpoint when and why it occurred, I'd publish a parenting book and become famous for the wealth of information that it provided. I'd be a guest on every talk show, answering questions from famous mothers like Kelly Ripa who wanted to know my secret. If Ann Landers was still alive, she'd seek my advice. Mothers from all over the world would crown me royalty - Princess Evelyn - and thank me for saving their relationships with their hard-to-love teenagers. The headlines would read, "Evelyn Stanton is a Teenage Whisperer." I'd be rolling in money.

I would not be sitting here in a jail cell, begging for sleep to take over my body.

But unfortunately, I can't label the exact action or timeframe. It just gradually happened.

Because it was so gradual, I didn't fight to save it. I didn't recognize the warning signs. Because I wasn't prepared for battle, I didn't pressure him into sharing his feelings. I let him be. Was that the mistake I made? Probably not the only one.

I know it wasn't *all* my fault. Logically, my head knows that, but my heart feels differently.

I blame the space in our relationship for letting his addiction grow. Without the distance between us, I would've seen the warning signs. If we were still communicating, I would've noticed his dilated eyes and withdrawal from his normal routine. I would've smelled that earthy, sweet distinct stench oozing from his pores. His baggy clothes would've been a sure sign that his taste buds had changed and his weight had diminished. These flashing neon lights would have alerted me to pay attention. I let him down by not paying close enough attention. His failure was mine.

Chapter 11

now

While Sleep avoids me and plays her unstructured game of hide and seek, I surrender to my nightly ritual of rehashing the last few years of my life. Trying to pinpoint where everything went wrong. Examine every memory for a conversation that forecasted my family's doom. If I can narrow down where the weakness began, I will find my answer.

I imagine our lives as a game of dominoes, white tiles made from a synthetic material to give the appearance of ivory with grooved black dots. It takes years of love, patience, and perseverance to stack each rectangle into a perfectly spaced pattern, a lifeline. Every brick stands tall and on solid ground, proud and upright. A combination of lies, disloyalty, and secrets weakened the pattern and made the ground quake. A domino can stumble backward and have no repercussions, or it can fall forward, causing an avalanche of consequences. A small quake might only knock over a few tiles, but a vibrating quake can cause a nosedive of destruction. Suddenly, one domino becomes shaky and pushes the others down until nothing is left standing. An unorganized pile of bricks is all that is left from the years of love and dedication that it took to build the stable pattern.

I recall an evening a few months before, when William had cracked open a bottle of my favorite wine and asked me to join him in our four-season room. We had a peaceful dinner, just the two of us, and I was loading the last plate into the dishwasher.

William was in good spirits, so I assumed he was horny. When William and I got engaged, Vera, who always delivered the best – yet politically incorrect – advice explained to me that "Men are capable of only three emotions: happy, hungry, or horny." And since William had just eaten supper, I figured hungry wouldn't describe his current state. He'd chosen *my* favorite wine in the hopes of lowering my inhibitions and breaking down some walls that had been built up over the last few months. If he wasn't looking for anything from me, he would've grabbed *his* favorite wine, not mine.

I took a deep breath as I hung up the damp dish towel. *Why not?* William was a generous lover and always encouraged me to vocalize what would please me. It wouldn't be the worst fifteen minutes of my life. It'd been months since we last had sex. Even though I'd managed to completely function without it, I knew if I gave in, it would be totally worth it.

However, to a woman, sex is more about the emotional connection than the physical. Don't get me wrong – climaxing one or two times within a few minutes of each other beats any flavor of ice cream. But being intimate with someone who irritates the hell out of me – chews too loudly, grunts every time he gets up from the couch, leaves his shoes at the foot of our bed rather than in the closet where they belong – never seems like a good idea. To me, sex is about commitment and trust. I've never been interested in casual sex or one-night stands. Call me old-fashioned, but allowing someone into my bed is also allowing them into the depths of my heart. I did not take our marriage vows as lightly as William did, and that was why I was having a hard time letting him back 'in.'

I'll never understand how a man can be so detached when it comes to sex. He dips his stick and moves on.

Frank and I had recently argued about this topic during our monthly friendship night out. We were having dinner at a hip, new restaurant that overlooked the city. Twinkles of yellow and orange filled the horizon like tiny flashes of hope. Miles and miles away, they flickered as a breeze blew a tree branch into the view, making it appear like they were winking. The blackness of the night was calming, and the two glasses of wine lightened my mood. All around us, the rooftop restaurant was filled with lovers flirting and teasing each other. Frank and I guessed which tables the married couples were sitting at versus the dating couples. Unfortunately, it was painfully obvious. Touching and long gazes at one another signaled a new relationship, while checking Facebook or staring off into space were telltale signs of a relationship that had aged past the first impressions stage.

I brought up my concern about uncommitted sex.

"Evie, sex without commitment is so invigorating. You leave it all on the table and just go for it. There isn't an expectation of a future. It's just here and now. Very primitive. You should try it. Isn't your crotch hungry?" Frank dipped his lobster tail into a bowl of warm butter and aggressively bit into it, proceeding to seductively lick the tips of his fingers.

A high-pitched giggle escaped from my lips. "Frank, you're a dork. You and I will never agree on principle values because you have no morals. Plus, in case you've forgotten, I'm married."

"That fact doesn't seem to deter William, so why should it slow you down?" Sometimes telling Frank everything did more harm than good, like now, when he threw my insecurities and worries back in my face. Loyalty and defending my honor had become one of Frank's top priorities ever since I texted him many years ago that he was my best friend, and he took that relationship status to another level. His loyalty was a bit on the obsessive side, or at least that was William's opinion.

"He's sorry. We're working on issues." Even though it was only natural to defend my marriage, I doubted my own words. They felt weak with no real depth to them, most likely because it wasn't the first time I'd said them. I wasn't sure why I didn't tell Frank the truth, maybe due to the simple fact that we'd had this conversation before.

"Girl, I'm sorry, but the only issue that I recognize is William keeping his disloyal poker in his heavily pleated pants."

I knew this conversation would lead nowhere. While Frank was my best friend, he wasn't always the most effective cheerleader. He was more like the keeper of knowledge, the librarian who remembered every little fact, and for the memories he forgot, he pulled out his handy little finger file of index cards that detailed the lessons I had managed to overlook. I imagined Frank as the pretentious librarian at the front desk of the stuffy, old library, the one who you wanted to ask a question to but feared the answer. You approached the desk that he sits proudly behind, and he peered at you over his bifocals that are perched on the end of her pointed nose. Your mouth dries up and you can't form a question. Instead of finding what you need, you hang your head and walk away. *Never mind.*

Men and women are wired differently. As the man's pants drop to the floor and the woman takes a sharp intake of breath, she immediately imagines what their kids would look like. *Will they have his dimples? Will they inherit my naturally curly hair? Will we raise our kids with my religious values? Does he believe in God?* Her brain ignites a laundry list of questions. She wonders what they will name their first dog. *Will we get a rescue dog from the pound or pay a hefty fee for a hypoallergenic puppy from a fancy breeder?* He might want to live in the city to stay closer to the office while she would prefer a home in the country where their children can run free in the backyard without the restriction of a fence. How will they compromise?

While for the man, his brain immediately shuts down and concentrates only on the matter at hand, or in this case, in his two hands. *I want to touch that. I want to do that. Her mouth is sexy.* Sex is so different for both parties involved. Frank would disagree with me, indicating that sex was just different in our marriage, but then again, Frank liked to argue. It was his job, and he was good at it.

So, as William offered me a generous pour, I flashed him a smile while I silently contemplated my options. I could fake another stomachache and a splitting headache, or I could give it up and savor fifteen minutes of attention. The poor man was probably ready to explode, and I could admit that I was overdue for an orgasm. Plus, I had promised for the sake of our marriage that I would try - I would try to trust him, I would try to love him again - but trying is hard. Setting up a fallen domino that was in the middle of the domino run required a steady hand.

When I sat down on the couch, I took a deep breath and enjoyed my first sip. I closed my eyes and felt the alcohol trickle down my throat. Letting down my guard would be good, and God knows I could use some TLC.

William interrupted my little reality break by talking about his workplace drama, which normally I was very interested in, but that night our conversation seemed forced and I was distracted.

"You won't believe who is out sick because of Covid." I raised my eyebrows as a signal of curiosity. "Everyone who attended happy hour last week after the big sales meeting: Kevin, Jeff, Rachael, Scott and Gena - the whole gang. It's just me and John working at the office. Of course, John is pissed. He planned on taking his honeymoon next week with wife number five, Sara number two, and has to log a few conference calls from Mexico. How weird is it that his first and fifth wives both have the name Sara?"

In my memory of this conversation, I don't recall William taking a breath until he paused to sip his glass of wine. He was on a roll and very talkative.

Other than my eyebrow raises, I hadn't needed to respond, and even if I could've, I don't think I would've. The names of his co-workers were darting back and forth in my mind while I tried to figure out if he was sleeping with any of them. Previously, William had disclosed how the office accidentally discovered that Rachael often went commando in her very short skirts. Even though William retold the story as if he was appalled, I questioned his words. I've seen Sharon Stone in *Basic Instinct*, and even *I* was slightly turned on and impressed with her confidence and sexuality.

Gena, who was the only other female currently working in his office, didn't like William in the least. This fact was made apparent at the company Christmas party when she stood up in the middle of dinner and yelled at Frank, saying that his white elephant gift of a rooster clock was in bad taste. Frank had forgotten about the gift exchange game so had grabbed the ugly, broken clock from Gena's desk. He threw it in a gift bag and figured the office would get a kick out of his take on the game. No one understood why she kept a clock and especially one that didn't work, but obviously to Gena, it had some sentimental value that they were not aware of.

"Anyway, it's been a crazy week with all those yahoos gone. Most of them feel like complete shit, so they haven't been accomplishing much at home. Enough about me. How was your day, honey?"

Honey? He hasn't called me that for a while.

"Good. Nothing unusual. Proof, edit, type."

"Are you still editing that nonfiction book about the twin who took over her sister's life after she died in that house fire?" He chuckled because he didn't understand why people felt the need to write stories when they can just make movies. William has never been much of a reader and is clueless about things that happen outside of his little bubble. "Ultimate identity theft. Real genius if she could've gotten away with it."

***

Like a snow globe, I shake my head in an attempt to scatter a new memory to the surface. I need a pleasant memory, one when we were happy, and life was simpler. I need to remember how good it felt to be loved and to give love freely. Deep breaths open my nostrils and fill my chest. To find sleep, I must relax. *Think of a happy memory, Eve.*

For our fifth anniversary, William gifted me a restored, antique Brunswick pool table. Hallmark educated William that for each year of marriage there was an appropriate gift to be given based on what it was created from. Wood was the fifth anniversary gift.

"I haven't seen you play pool in years, and that's what drew me to you in the first place. Since you're so busy taking care of me and Hudson, you don't have time for yourself. I thought maybe you could start playing again. Happy Anniversary, Eve."

Because I was so surprised by William's thoughtful gift, tears of joy ran down my cheeks. William put so much thought into his gifts, and he was always excited to disclose the adventure to finding them. For our fourth anniversary, Hallmark advised that the gift should be flowers or fruit. He took the assignment one step further, and cut watermelon, cantaloupe, and musk melon into flower-shaped, bite-size pieces of pure love.

"I found this antique dealer named Jerry who bought the pool table at an estate auction in Omaha, Nebraska. Supposedly, a wealthy family owned it and hardly ever used it. Kept it covered in their basement. That is why it's in mint condition. Do you like it?" He was a puppy bubbling over with excitement. He wanted me to pet him behind the ears, roll him over, and tell him he was a good boy.

The dust had settled into the table and permeated the air in our family room, but it was a welcomed, recognizable smell. Because it had aged alone in a family home, no stale beer or cigarette smoke lingered. The slate wood top and dust gave the indication that it was well worth the money William paid for it. After the movers snuck it into our house while I was out running errands, William removed the cover and tied a huge red ribbon around the table. I ran my fingers across the beautiful, pristine felt. The tips of my fingers tingled with excitement.

"Oh, William, she's a beauty." I swallowed a big lump in my throat. I'd only purchased him a card and a six-pack of beer. I felt like a heel.

"I found your lucky pool cue from college behind a bunch of boxes in the storage room. Wanna play?" As his eyebrows shot up, he handed it to me. It felt perfect in my hands like it hadn't been almost six years since I played.

One thing that Jerry had not told William about was the secret storage compartment under the bottom of the table. Over a hundred years ago, when the game of billiards became popular, some competitive players had a small, locked box built into the bottom of the table so they could hide their pool shark winnings. As a pool shark myself, I knew about this extra bonus section and used it when I needed to keep things hidden.

Great Eve. You managed to tarnish that memory too. You're never going to sleep.

Chapter 12

then

As the second largest city in South Dakota, Miner City sat on the edge of the state line bordering Wyoming. Legend has it that when the miners of the 1874 Gold Rush discovered the piece of land, they thought that they'd stumbled on sacred, holy ground. Because they'd grown accustomed to dust and grime, everything in their line of vision tended to be a soft shade of brown. Therefore, the vibrant colors in this stretch of land were surreal. Instead of a gray haze of dust, their eyes were awakened to the greenest green prairie lining the horizon, resting in between the highest peaks in the hills. Reaching to touch the gorgeous turquoise sky, the evergreen trees stretched tall and were filled with colorful birds that sang songs of joy while perched on the outstretched branches. Miner City, home of the Gold Diggers, was founded in a valley that was blessed with its own small waterfall, which was the reason for the lush vegetation and the draw for wildlife. The water pooled into a small pond at the bottom of the waterfall that the settlers nicknamed, "God's Bath", which became a popular location for baptisms and spiritual awakenings.

The treasure hunters who tirelessly searched for gold in the Black Hills hunkered down and built their homestead over one hundred years ago. They tried to keep their discovery a secret from the rest of mankind, but eventually, people gravitated toward it. It was magical and mesmerized many visitors, like William, who returned only briefly to Nebraska before deciding to build his future in the hills.

Even a hundred years later, the Black Hills of South Dakota was an ideal location to start a family. This area was well-known for its small-town values and a strong commitment to its neighbors. While the heart and soul of the area was solid and dependable, nature's beauty was mesmerizing and hypnotic. Citizens felt protective and extremely loyal toward their hometown.

Not only are there thousands of hiking trails that lead you on adventures to forgotten caves and deserted mining shafts, but these same roads also lead you up and down gorgeous hills decorated with evergreen trees and lead you to encounters with a variety of wildlife. Preserving the beauty and the history of the Black Hills has always been important to everyone who has been a resident. Additionally, they were extremely proud of the history that took place right in their own backyard. Tales of Calamity Jane and Wild Bill Hickok were common topics brought up at family dinner tables as the dishes were cleared and a deck of cards landed on the table.

May 27th was a local holiday that the people of Miner City celebrated because it was legendary Wild Bill Hickok's birthday. This local holiday was celebrated with a friendly game of Five Card Stud after dinner. As the cards were dealt, players silently prayed not to be dealt the dead man's hand - the very hand that Wild Bill was dealt the day of his murder. A pair of black aces and a pair of black eights was a telltale sign of bad luck.

Many residents also liked to claim – but couldn't prove – that they were the ancestors of Calamity Jane. Because she was a woman of loose morals and briefly worked for a popular madam in Deadwood, people loved to speculate about her blood lines. Great-great grandparents were often the main characters in these tales with no documented proof. "In the 1880s, my great-great grandmother lived with a family that illegally adopted Jane's illegitimate child. After the baby, who was wrapped in a blanket embroidered with the initials MJ, was dropped off on the porch, the woman who was dressed like a man quickly jumped on her horse and rode away. They swore it was Calamity Jane whose real name was Martha Jane."

William and I never yearned to leave the land that had become a part of who we were. This was home, and the Black Hills had become our blood. We built our 'homestead' in a community of like-minded people who also enjoyed exploring nature and all the Black Hills had to offer. Most of them were transplants to the area like William and myself. They'd moved here for a simpler, easier lifestyle. No busy hustle and bustle of a big city.

Because we had no extended family that we acknowledged, our friends were our family; therefore, the neighborhood Fourth of July party was a 'family' tradition. We would never miss it. Everyone in the neighborhood attended and looked forward to it. The Kocmick family, who lived at the end of the cul-de-sac, hosted and planned the epic party – they hired a local band, purchased hundreds of dollars worth of fireworks, colored their pool water red, and usually orchestrated one new surprise for their guests every year.

One year, a clown named Messner, who dressed too warmly for an outdoor 4th of July party, was hired to charm the children while the adults enjoyed a cool beverage alone in the pool. Near the end of his first hour, Messner's red wigged curls were drooping from the humidity, and his white painted face was running down his chin and staining his striped shirt. His liquefying face scared the younger children.

That year was fondly referred to as the Elmo year, because after the adults floated on rafts and casually dipped in the water, the Kocmick's two-year-old daughter pointed to her dad as he climbed out of the pool and yelled, "Daddy, you Elmo".

At that precise minute, Larry Kocmick calculated that he had deposited too much red dye into the pool. Everyone's skin had absorbed the dye. We were all different shades of red and different parts of our bodies were stained. Since I had been floating on a round tube, only my butt was colored a nice deep red color. Most of the men had been fully immersed in the water and were red from head to toe. A few women had just their legs dipping in the pool and standing waist high. The pictures from that party were legendary and were displayed in everyone's living room. No one will ever forget that infamous year.

The following year, they hired a comedian to entertain the adults while the children became overheated in a sweaty, stinky bounce house. Even though the pool was a natural water color, everyone was afraid to jump in. Larry had to go first. After that, it became a tradition that Larry made the first cannon ball into the pool to signal that the water was safe and untainted. No one wanted to miss the annual gathering and the surprises that were in store.

One year, there were new faces among the crowd. Mitchell and Becca Black, along with their only son, Clive. They had recently moved into the neighborhood, but because our summer had been filled with following our kids to their numerous activities, we hadn't had a chance to meet the new blood. As I watched them from across the lawn talking to the neighbors, I tried to imagine what brought them to the Hills and what they left behind. I enjoyed my imagination and what it would come up with.

There's no hair poking out from under his Seattle Mariners baseball cap. I wonder if he is bald. William, being a big Chicago Cubs fan, would have a field day with that guy and his terrible taste in Major League Baseball teams. Does he choose to be bald or is it because of a condition? Is he the trophy, or is she? Beer belly or over-eater?

She keeps throwing her hair over her shoulder. Did she not bring a ponytail holder along? It's the beginning of July. Every woman knows her hair won't last an afternoon in this humidity. They must not be from around here. She seems very mysterious. Have I seen her before? Was she that woman from the latest Dateline episode? The one where the mom murders her own children and buries them in her backyard? Perhaps she works undercover for the FBI.

William caught me staring at them, inspecting them. He knew how my mind worked. "Eve, that's creepy. Quit staring. They're harmless, and I doubt they work for some government agency or are from one of your crime TV shows." William knew me so well and how I liked to create amusing stories about strangers. "Why don't we introduce ourselves, then you won't need to stand here and wonder what they are like? You will *know*." He playfully nudged my arm.

"Okay. You're right."

William's eyes lit up. "You know I love when you talk like that." He teased me and raised his eyebrows up and down like he was suggesting we should squeeze a quickie in.

I shook my head. "Are all men one big walking hormone?"

Even though I don't like to publicly admit it, William was right. The four of us hit it off, the conversation flowed easily, Mitchell was charming, and Becca was friendly. While Mitchell was from Seattle, Becca's roots were from Florida. They were transplants too and completely infatuated with their new home. When we discovered that their only son was Hudson's age, we knew we'd be spending more time with them as our lives were bound to cross. Our neighborhood overflowed with female playmates for Hazel, but before the Black's moved in, Hudson was often alone. We decided to invite them over for dinner the following weekend.

Their friendship felt effortless like it was meant to be. I enjoyed my new budding friendship with Becca. Frank had been my only close friend in my adult life, so adding a female to the list seemed ideal. Someone to gossip with about the dramas of our common friends; someone to schedule mani-pedis with; someone who would understand my mood swings and quarrels with my husband.

While Becca and I spent most of our free time together, William and Mitchell discovered that they had a lot in common – sports, sports, and more sports. They played pickleball in a league, flag football with their sons, and watched as many televised sporting events as they could. Mitchell worked in sales, and talking was second nature to him, so every story he told was entertaining. The comfort level and ease of our friendship felt like family– a family that you wanted to spend your free time with.

After a few dinners at each other's houses, we became fast friends, and weekends together became a regular routine. We would hustle through the week in anticipation for the weekends, when we would make memories with our new friends. Friday night pizza at our house was usually followed by a board game, and then Saturday night we'd lay around their pool enjoying whatever meat Mitchell threw on his grill. Clive and Hudson were inseparable, with slumber parties every weekend and walkie-talkie conversations when they were forced to be apart. We all made jokes about how the two boys would need to date a pair of best friends in their teen years because they couldn't do anything without each other.

"Becca, they're only thirteen. Don't marry off my boy already." William poked Becca in the ribs. They had a natural, teasing friendship. William enjoyed her company as much as I did, and for some reason, their closeness didn't bother me even though William and I were in marriage counseling, attempting to mend my trust issues after his first affair. Their friendship even seemed to help William and I find each other fun again.

Giving me a big, over-exaggerated wink, Becca replied, "I got it! Twins! Even better."

Mitchell chuckled his usual hearty laugh that made his round belly jiggle and added, "If those two clowns manage to snag twin girlfriends, I'd be afraid that they would confuse their dates. Nope. Those two would be better off sharing one girlfriend rather than each having one that looked exactly like the other."

As William patted Mitchell on the back, he agreed, "You're so right, man."

While the two men bonded over touchdowns and homeruns, Becca and I shopped for the latest trends; she enjoyed that more than I did, honestly, but I pretended to in order to spend time with her. When the boys were watching Sunday football, Becca, Hazel, and I often had lunch downtown at a small, quaint cafe that served high tea. We dressed in our nicest, brightest dresses and sparkly jewelry. After we'd been escorted to our table, the hostess would supply us with our big, fancy hats and tell us, "Welcome to the Queen's high tea party. Your tea and biscuits will be delivered momentarily by Lord Lance." She bowed to Hazel before leaving the table.

Hazel loved our special lunch dates with 'Aunt Becca.' Every time Becca would speak, she used a fake English accent and demanded that Hazel and I do the same. I had never had a girlfriend that I wanted to share everything with. Highs and lows. Frank was my only long-lasting friendship, and he managed to secure all my requirements...until I met Becca.

Life was good. We didn't know how good those years were until they weren't.

Chapter 13

---

then

Being friends with Becca was like being elected Vice President of the sorority house, and she was the President who was also crowned the Homecoming Queen. Because I'd never been in the popular crowd before, I didn't know how to handle all the attention, even if it was second-hand. Inside I felt awkward and stiff, but on the outside, I smiled, showed all my pearly whites, and spoke when spoken to. I followed Becca's lead as her right hand.

The attention seemed natural to Becca, similar to a child born with celebrity parents. As the center of attention, she shined under the bright, fluorescent lights and soaked up the energy from her many admirers. It didn't faze her or cause her to pause. Her response to the attention seemed effortless. Whatever the case was, I enjoyed being her sidekick. I didn't feel pressure to shine, talk, or entertain. I mainly sat back and absorbed the beauty that was Becca.

And she was a looker. She was five feet, ten inches of a spray-tanned, sculpted body decorated in the finest jewelry and name-brand clothing. Becca was a small-town movie star. To be honest, the first time I laid eyes on Becca was not at our neighbor's BBQ but at a local coffee shop. She was standing in line about three customers ahead of me. As she made small talk with the older gentleman in front of her, she flipped her long, perfectly styled brown hair over her shoulder when she threw her head back and giggled at something the man had said. I didn't recognize the man, but I did recognize the pure joy and instant infatuation that surfaced on his wrinkled face when he realized he had made the goddess behind him laugh. Subsequently following their encounter, the sweet, older gentleman bought Becca her lavender latte. She squeezed his hand a second longer than necessary and placed her left hand over the top of their handshake and thanked him for his generosity. It was as if she had a gift for reading people.

I watched in complete awe. In a matter of seconds, these two had exchanged heartfelt words that had earned Becca a free fancy latte while the man earned a genuine boner that wasn't produced by a little blue pill. The bulge was obvious as he struggled to walk out the front door of the coffee shop.

After she thanked the coffee barista for the best coffee south of the Canadian border, she directed her attention toward a fussy baby in a stroller. As she leaned down and revealed a small tattoo on her midriff, I heard her sweetly comment in a southern drawl to the new mother, "That baby is cute as a peach, and I've seen lots of babies because back in Florida I worked on the labor and delivery floor."

"Awww...thank you. Ava Jean is our first and likely our last baby if she doesn't let her parents get some sleep." The new mother cracked out a tired, weak smile.

"Honey, you look great. I thought maybe you were the nanny. You don't look old enough to have a baby." Her southern drawl was laying on the compliments pretty thick.

I called malarkey, but the new mother of the wailing baby in the stroller looked awful. Not only did she have huge, dark circles under her eyes, but she also was struggling to lose the excess weight from the pregnancy. Her athletic pants were extremely tight – like pulling the fabric too tight – and her T-shirt needed to be pulled down to cover her tummy roll. The poor thing looked like she hadn't taken more than five minutes for herself in months, and the newborn's mother ate up the compliment.

"Oh, my god. Thank you, Miss. It's the nicest thing anyone has said to me in a while." And suddenly the sleep-deprived, worn-out mother started to cry into her coffee.

"Bless your heart. Name is Becca, and sweet pea, hold your head up high because you're doing a great job." She squeezed the gal's shoulder and walked out of the door with a smile plastered on her face and a warm, free coffee in her hand.

Amazing, invisible superpower.

The coffee shop customers were all smiling at the southern belle who had just graced their presence. She possessed a magical ability to hypnotize those that she encountered.

A month later, when we were officially introduced at the neighborhood barbeque, I already knew I wanted to be her friend. I was surprised to learn that her southern drawl wasn't real because it sounded authentic back at the coffee shop. Months into our friendship, I learned that she liked to fake a southern drawl for her own personal enjoyment because as she claimed, "Most men assume southern women are damsels in distress who need rescuing. The southern dialect suggests that I'm a simple woman with a small brain and big boobs that matches my big heart. I'll play along if it gets me somewhere." When she wanted to be fancy or appear superior, she used a British accent. She told me this accent came in useful when she wanted a table in a packed restaurant or a fee removed from her credit card bill. It was very entertaining and self-serving.

I remember introducing Frank to Becca. Because Frank was the voice of reason in my head, the guy I called whenever William and I argued, and the friend who I couldn't wait to tell any good news, his approval was key. Frank was my person. I was excited to have a new female friend, so I really wanted him to like her. We were also couple friends and family friends, and now I wanted the most important person from my past to meet my new friend, whom I wanted to incorporate into my future.

"Stop biting your nails. Why are you so nervous? She isn't royalty, Evie." I'd invited the two of them out for a happy hour drink at one of my favorite breweries. I figured a public meet-up would be less awkward with the other people making noise around us, just in case there was unwelcome silence at our table. I'd overthought all the possibilities. I knew both of them liked beer and me. Otherwise, I had no idea if they would hit it off or not. Of course, I was nervous.

"Bite me, Frank. I want you to like her. Will you please play nice?" I sipped my fresh beer as my eyes scanned the doorway.

"Did you give *her* the same pep talk? Told her to be nice to me?" As he gripped his chest to indicate his heart was breaking, he pretended to be hurt by my request, but he knew it was true. Frank had a bullshit meter, and it was spot on. And if and when the meter was activated, it would immediately alert his mouth. After that happened, there was no holding back.

"As a matter of fact, I didn't need to. Becca is always nice and polite. I didn't need to have this conversation with *her*."

Frank eyed me up and down, looking for more telltale signs of my true emotions. "Okay. I'll be nice. But if she is more than ten minutes late, I can't promise anything. You know I detest when people take my time for granted. Wait. Is this the chick who faked that she was from Georgia to get a free coffee?"

I rolled my eyes and wondered why I always tell him everything. His brain was a filing cabinet full of information. "Yes. But she explained that she talks in different accents depending on her mood. She does it for entertainment. You're making it sound like she is a con-artist, Frank."

"Hey, I didn't say that. *You* did. Just trying to keep the facts straight in my head." He tapped his thinker. "I hope she shows up speaking in a Russian accent. Those accents are sexy. Did you know that when a Russian says 'sheet' it sounds more like 'shit'?"

Frank was a vessel of useless information, but yes, I knew all too well that Frank didn't appreciate tardiness. One too many times, William had been on the receiving end of Frank's wrath when William strolled in late for dinner. He had no tolerance for William's lack of punctuality, believing it was a show of disrespect.

While we waited for Becca to arrive, I distracted him by talking about his mother, my biggest fan. His latest account of his mother and her antics included Vera, a bottle of wine, and a solicitor's phone call asking her to update her credit card information. The phone call ended an hour later with Vera making a new friend, a pen pal from overseas.

Unfortunately, Becca was fifteen minutes late, and Frank had downed his first beer and was ordering another when she breezed through the door looking like a flawless beauty queen without a care in the world, or at least that's how she appeared to me. To Frank, whom I was praying she'd win over with her charm, she was a typical, pretentious, uptight woman wearing designer labels who thought that her shit didn't stink, when in fact, it stunk worse because she sprayed too much hoity-toity Chanel perfume trying to mask the odor. The happy hour didn't go well. He called me afterward to deliver his opinion.

"F.A.K.E. Fake eyelashes, botoxed lips, heavily dyed hair and those boobs. They can't be natural. Every word out of her lipstick-caked mouth screamed phony." Frank uses his talent for imitation to mimic Becca with a high-pitched southern drawl. "'Mitch is too good to me. Last week for no reason at all, he gave me this expensive Gucci purse. He adores me.' Oh no, he didn't! I've met Mitchell Black and he would never step foot in a crowded mall to buy his spoiled, good-for-nothing wife an overpriced handbag. I call bullshit! She bought that purse herself and is telling other people that lie to make her marriage appear better than it is. And does she always talk with food in her mouth?"

"Frank, you're being a little harsh – "

"Are you kidding me right now, Eve? You know that I can see right through people to their core, and I'm telling you right now that I see black, jet-black, in her soul. She's gonna leave a mark, Evie. I don't think it's gonna be good." Besides being a psychic, Frank believed that he had the ability to see directly into a person's soul, and ability to decipher if the person was ultimately good or evil. This gift evolved over time thanks to his job as a lawyer.

"Another one of your predictions, Frank?"

Frank wasn't wrong. I just didn't know how right he was at the time.

The truth wasn't as clear to me because my vision was clouded by pure infatuation. Little things eventually broke up our friendship. She would lie about irrelevant, trivial things that she didn't need to lie about. The first time I truly caught her in a lie that made me take notice was when I invited her over for coffee and she proceeded to give me a huge explanation that her aunt was passing through town on her way to Denver and had only a few hours to meet.

"Otherwise, I'd love to catch up, Eve, but I haven't seen her in years. She recently completed her chemo treatments." Then, as she leaned in closer to the phone receiver, she whispered as if it was profanity. "Cancer." I never understood why people did that. Did she think the cancer would hear her and then hiss and spit in her face?

"It's no biggie, Becca. I will try you another time. Enjoy your time with your aunt."

"Aww...thanks for being so understanding." She hung up before I could even spit out a goodbye.

Instead of enjoying a nice, warm coffee at home, I decided to grab a book and head down to the new little coffee shop. As the door chimed at my arrival and I pulled off my shades to adjust to the light, I noticed the place was buzzing with activity. I wasn't the only one who decided to start my day off with an expensive latte. As I scanned the room for an unoccupied table, I noticed Becca and a couple other moms – boy moms that I had introduced her to the year before – from school sitting in the far corner. They were giggling at something funny Becca said. I wished I'd handled the situation like a cool mom, but I didn't. I stood there as the door hit me in the rear. Mouth hanging open. Staring straight at the group.

She lied. I wanted to shout to anyone who would listen that her boobs were as fake as her smile.

But instead, with my mouth hanging open, I stared at them and felt completely dumbfounded. My brain scrambled to sort through the facts. *Wasn't she supposed to be meeting her aunt? Is she here too?* Instead of marching over to their table and confronting Becca with a snide comment like, 'Shoot. I didn't get the message. But I'm here now. Slide over, Wendy.' Tears pooled in the corner of my eyes, and I felt like a high school girl being dismissed by the mean girls. Before I was noticed, I ducked out of the coffee shop and stormed home.

If considered separately, the rest of the examples of the decline in our friendship wouldn't cause a normal person to pause, but collectively, they affected my outlook and created questions. After the coffee shop scene, I started to analyze other questionable facts.

When we first met, Becca mentioned that when Clive was born, family and friends thought he resembled Mr. Potato Head. With his little pink ears sticking straight out of his large, oval-shaped head, his big round eyes filled with curiosity blinked open as he absorbed his new surroundings. Because his sense of humor was one of his best qualities, Mitchell bought his newborn son a pair of black-rimmed glasses with an attached nose and brown mustache to wear for pictures that they used for Clive's baby announcement. But years later, I discovered that Becca wasn't Clive's biological mother, and that Mitchell's first wife had died in an accident. That was quite a shock, which made me ask the question, "You aren't Clive's biological mother?"

"No. What made you think that? Mitch and I didn't meet until years after Clive was born." She waved off my inquiry while we were sitting on her back deck watching the kids splash in their pool. It was a normal summer day in our cul-de-sac, sipping beers before our husbands returned home from work.

"That's weird. Maybe I just assumed it after you told me the story of Mr. Potato Head."

Without glancing in my direction, she giggled at me and cracked open another beer. "I have no idea what you are talking about, Eve. Maybe the sun is getting to you. Have another drink."

"But I distinctly remember the conversation. You said the local paper published the baby announcement with the Mr. Potato Head glasses. I thought it was hilarious." I started to second guess my memory bank. Maybe it wasn't Clive that the story was about. Maybe I misheard her. However, my friend circle was limited, so I didn't have much sorting to do.

Instead of giving my confusion an ounce of attention, Becca rose from her lounge chair and busied herself with picking up pool toys and laying out damp towels to dry in the sun.

When I was retelling William about our conversation later that weekend and asking him if he remembered the Mr. Potato Head story, the name of Mitchell's first wife came up. "Eve, I think you are overreacting to this. It is a silly story. Maybe it wasn't even Becca who told you."

"But I'm *sure* it was." As I took a bite of my chicken, I questioned my memory. *Who else could've told me that story?*

"Plus, Mitchell told me a while ago about his first wife, Tracie, Clive's mom. The way Mitchell describes it they weren't happy, got married too young, and got pregnant right away. Then he met Becca. Tracie wasn't happy about the affair, especially because she worked with her – "

"Wait. What?"

My interruption surprised William, and his raised eyebrows showed his concern. *Becca has never mentioned that to me.* "Are you sure?" I couldn't figure out why she'd feel the need to lie about that fact, unless it was simply because Mitchell had been married when they started seeing each other. Becca had been my confidant during the mess of William's infidelities. Perhaps she worried that it would cause a wedge in our friendship. Unfortunately, in my opinion, the lies she communicated did the same thing.

He continued to chew his food and then proceeded to talk with his mouth full. "About which part?"

"Mitchell and Becca were having an affair when his first wife, Tracie, died – that part!"

"Yes, I'm sure."

"Mitchell's first wife died due to an accident? What kind of accident?"

"I dunno. I don't remember." William returned his attention back to his food. In his mind, the drama had concluded, but in my mind, the questions had just begun.

Chapter 14

then

Throughout life, milestones are often celebrated and marked by a gathering of family and friends. Babies, graduations, weddings, promotions, birthdays, and funerals were all rights of passage. All were honored with either reflection, tears, laughter, or a few cold ones. Milestones are events in our lives that change the course of our future.

When my childhood friend Hannah got engaged, I received a beautiful, embossed 'Save the Date' postcard announcing her engagement to her college boyfriend. The postcard showed the happy couple kissing under a willow tree as Hannah showed off the big, glistening rock on her ring finger. One day later, the mailman delivered a beautiful gold-foiled invitation to a bridal shower. *Let the celebration of milestones commence.*

In the middle of June, Hannah and Chris exchanged rings in a crowded church where the air conditioner couldn't keep up with the Midwest humidity that had arrived early that summer. Usually, the month of July is when the humidity plagues the plains, but this summer it started a few weeks early. Weathermen were constantly using the phrase, "It's ninety-five degrees outside but feels like one hundred and twenty with the humidity at a record high today." When it is summer in the Midwest, people can count on sweating profusely without even moving their bodies.

Women can rely on humidity to ruin any chance of a good hair day and to sweat in creases they didn't know could perspire. As soon as men got dressed, pit stains soiled their shirts. The only thing that likes the wet, heavy humidity is flowers.

As I struggled to get comfortable on a hard, wooden church pew, fanning myself with the wedding program, I looked around at the festivities. The men were decked out in their pressed, collared, button-down shirts, dress slacks that don't allow much room to overindulge, and pointed shoes. Wearing earrings that sparkled when the light catches them, the women were dressed in floral, summer dresses. Their high heels pinched their toes as they swelled from the heat and pressure.

Throughout the church, Hannah's family and friends gathered for the joyful celebration where the young couple promised to love and cherish each other for the rest of their lives. As I looked around the room, I silently played my favorite game. Based on my observations, I created stories for these strangers. Perched to my left was a young, affectionate couple holding hands and constantly whispering in each other's ears. I wondered how they knew the bride and groom. Perhaps they are the couple who introduced them, or perhaps they are friends from his work. No matter how they knew Hannah and Chris, I was sure they were in love. I looked to my right, and I watched an older woman dabbing the rolling tears from her red, swollen eyes. The strong emotion could be caused from the pure innocence and joy that a wedding brings, or maybe her son was the bride's first love, and the woman was regretful of all that could have been. My overactive imagination made me smile.

From the balcony of the small town church, the pianist began playing the wedding march, drawing everyone's attention to the back of the room. The tone and tempo announced the approach of the groom, Chris. As he ushered his mom and dad on each arm down the aisle, I wondered what

his story was. How did he know she was *The One*? Since Hannah and I
have grown apart, I can only imagine the steps that brought them together.
I wasn't along for the ride on their first date, I didn't witness their first
kiss, and I didn't hear the tenderness in his proposal. I imagined all this
happening, which brought them to this point in their relationship.

Minutes later, with her family and friends proudly admiring her, Hannah strutted down the aisle in her white, sparkling gown as her long train
trailed behind her. She couldn't wipe the permanent grin from her face.
Happiness and anticipation oozed from her pores. When she reached the
altar, Chris extended his hand toward her, offering Hannah a future as
husband and wife. After the ceremony, they signed a certificate, and magically, their milestone was sealed by the church and government. Forever,
the course of their lives had been altered.

Becoming an addict isn't a milestone that is marked by a large gathering
of your closest family and friends. A 'Save the Date' card wasn't mailed to
announce the arrival of something dramatic that would change the course
of our lives. No pre-addiction shower was held anticipating the upcoming
plans for the near future. I didn't mark it with a big, red heart on my
calendar, nor did I cross off the dates leading up to the event. There wasn't a
five-tier, heavily frosted cake to indulge in after the commitment was made.

As the parents of the addict, William and I weren't warned of the im-
pending doom with an official invitation. We didn't sign a legal document
giving our consent for a future of heartache and agony. It wasn't that kind
of milestone. Instead of months of planning and anticipation, we were
brutally slapped across the face with the harsh reality that our lives would
never be the same. It was a sucker punch.

Living with an addict is like living in Hell...fire everywhere that burns
your skin whenever you are within a few inches of the red-hot flame. It's
like walking barefoot on a patch of thistles. Every step is filled with sharp

little needles poking through the bottom of your exposed feet. It's like a thousand angry bees stinging you all at once because you disturbed their hive.

Living with an addict causes your shoulders to slump with the weight of your constant worry. Your neck is stiff and tight from being on edge every minute that the addict is awake. Your eyes burn because they are so dry from the never-ending tears you've shed. Your ears are plugged with the words of anger that he spewed out of his mouth while in a fit of uncontrollable rage. Your fragile heart feels cracked and beyond repair after processing the painful words being shouted throughout the walls of your once happy home.

Never in my life did I think I'd say I hate my child. But I did hate who he'd become. The drugs altered his personality so much that I wasn't sure who he was anymore. I wondered if the sweet, generous, caring boy was stuffed in the corner of the grown man's body. *Where is he? Can I rescue him and bring him back?* I miss the young man he once was – before the demon of drugs consumed him. Not only did it take over his body, but it also stole his personality and sense of right and wrong. The drugs robbed him of the life that we had tried to secure for him.

I can't believe this is my life.

I know I've said this before, but Hudson's addiction didn't happen overnight. It wasn't a bright, neon light bulb that suddenly turned on full power and blinded our family with its bright intensity. We didn't see a blinking yellow turn signal that indicated the change in direction.

Addiction is a hangnail. You don't even realize that it's growing next to your nail until it's sticking out, making itself visible, demanding to be noticed. You decide to bite at it. Use your razor-sharp teeth to cut it out. Except that the germs in your mouth aggravate it and cause it to become infected. It starts to bleed. You finally surrender to using a fingernail clipper which cuts out the excessive skin tag, but it still makes it bleed and your little finger throbs in pain. The long skin tag is no longer poking from under your nail, but you know it'll grow and fester until it rears its ugly head.

We saw the little signs. We grounded him. We took away his driving privileges. We did the normal things that any good, responsible parents would do. We tried to 'clip the hangnail.' We wanted to stop the infection, but some choices are completely out of a parent's control. We can't be with him twenty-four-seven and tell him what he should or shouldn't do. Every child needs to make these decisions on their own. We gave him wings to fly, but what are we supposed to do when his wings fail to support him and he comes crashing down? Who is to blame for his wings not being strong enough? Are we, his parents, to blame that the wind blew him into a tailspin?

When you discover a featherless bird dead on the sidewalk, do you blame the mother for not protecting him from venturing out too young? Do you blame the father for being absent as he collected worms to feed his family?

"Poor little bird. You weren't ready. You should've stayed safely hidden in the warm, cozy nest a little longer."

We couldn't keep Hudson locked in our protective nest for the rest of his life. He needed to spread his wings. He yearned to fly. However, the wind was strong and kept him from flying like the eagles that he admired. He was an ordinary robin that wasn't equipped to handle the hurricane winds that clipped his ability to fly.

Was he overly sensitive? Did he not fit in at school? Does addiction run in the family? Did he run with the wrong crowd?

I don't know. Yes and no. Sometimes. Maybe.

What I can tell you is that we loved him, that he wasn't physically or emotionally abused by us, and that we had no idea it was this bad. The road to addiction can't be avoided by using GPS. There is no road map. No sign warning us of the bumpy road ahead. No flashing yellow caution sign. No orange construction cones.

Does it really matter how we got here?

To other people, it does. Other parents want to know the warning signs, and how to avoid finding themselves on this very path. Everyone wants clear cut answers. People want an obvious sign. A 'Save the Date' card would be appreciated.

If you want an obvious sign, there isn't one. Everything could be going smoothly, like a newly tarred highway, and then, bam, a detour. And if you've followed a detour, you know one detour leads to another one and another one, and before you know it, you are lost. There is no blinking caution light or a wrong way sign down the highway of addiction. You must pave your own road.

Chapter 15

then

I was angry. I was furious with him, my own son, for making my blood boil, for spreading stress hives across my neck, for seeping drama into our nearly perfect family of four. I had big dreams for him- a bright future all mapped out for him.

In my dreams, he was happy and healthy. After graduating high school, he would attend the college of his choice, where he would major in Accounting – he was good with numbers. Then one night during his senior year after his Cost Management final, he'd be celebrating at a small-town bar, and he'd bump into the love of his life while ordering his second gin and tonic. After a romantic courtship, they'd be engaged, and William and I would throw the most elegant wedding for the blessed couple. They would secure jobs in our hometown, where Hudson would be a successful accountant in a thriving company. His bride – Angel – would land a job teaching first grade at a local private school. Of course, the couple would eventually welcome two children who would fondly call me, "Mimi." That was just a mother's dream.

None of these lofty dreams would come true with an expensive, all-consuming drug habit and flunking out of high school. He wouldn't be sipping a classy gin and tonic with his college frat brothers and meeting educated women at local bars. No, my son was sipping tap water from the palm of his hand to flush down the current drug of choice. Upper, downer, or a mystery pill. It didn't matter as long as he could escape his life, his thoughts, and his continuous bad choices. In hidden alleys across town, at some classy golf courses, or even in our backyard, he was meeting drug dealers. Drugs were everywhere. It didn't matter if you were from an upper-class, respected family or if you were scraping by each week, drugs found you.

I wasn't supposed to blame the drugs. It's his choice. His body. Weed was the first drug to enter his system, but it wouldn't be the last. At a high school party, Hudson was offered his first free hit. He was hesitant to try it but was reassured by partygoers around him that they were doing it too. Eventually, it became a normal, everyday occurrence. Not a big deal anymore. Weed relaxed his concern for right and wrong, calming his nerves. People manage to maintain their daily lives while using the drug every day. Weed isn't considered dangerous or risky. So, when his drug dealer suggested something new, an upper, Hudson figured, why not? His friends had been right about weed.

To me, his mother, weed was the gateway drug. Weed invited Hudson through the gate and slammed the door shut, trapping him inside the fenced-in area. He couldn't see a way out. For Hudson, marijuana was not a revolving door.

I never thought I would be a yeller. I've always preferred to keep things light and easy-peasy. I'm never one to participate in any heated discussion, because I don't like drama and drama doesn't like me. Even though I wasn't absorbing the fumes into my bloodstream, weed caused me to become a yeller. For a user, marijuana is a relaxing, tension-releasing drug; however, for the addict's mother, it caused my blood pressure to rise, my hair to fall out, and my wrinkles to deepen. It and all the pain it caused my family infuriated me. Since his first hit, marijuana created havoc and heartbreak for my family. Hudson cared less and less about the things he previously valued in his life – faith, family, friends, girlfriends, sports, and academics – as soon as he agreed to smoke weed. He threw away everything he had going for him. Nothing became as important as his next high.

Hudson was always a rule follower, the kid who raised his hand to volunteer to help and never said an unkind word about anyone. When he wasn't selected for the basketball's C team, he accepted the failure as a sign that he needed to practice more so that next year he would for sure make the cut. But it did happen again, and he accepted it with grace. The poor kid had my ball-dribbling ability, and a basketball varsity letter was a bit out of reach.

When he started disobeying our house rules – coming home late for curfew, failing to complete homework on time – warning bells went off. As any parent would, we wondered if we were overreacting; the teenage years were heavily upon us, and hormones were raging. At first, the changes were subtle, and we let him slide. A slap on the wrist, a warning about next time, a firm talking to– but when he was thirty minutes late for curfew with no explanation, call or text, we grew worried. It had been William's turn to wait up for him, and he explained, once again, our curfew rules and times. Hudson seemed to shrug it off, and according to my conversation with William before he left for work the next day, William said he tried to lean in close enough to smell what was on his breath. All he could decipher was that he was trying to cover up something with a mouthful of minty gum.

The next morning, when he stumbled downstairs late for breakfast, I explained to him that he was grounded for his tardiness, and his reaction to a three-day grounding was over the top.

"Are you fucking kidding me?"

"Hudson! Watch your mouth."

"I was only a few minutes late. You're overreacting." He rolled his eyes and mumbled under his breath.

"You were thirty minutes late, and this isn't the first time."

"Big deal. I shouldn't need to be home by one anyway." His self-righteous attitude poured out thickly. After going to retrieve his phone from the charging station, he shot me a look that could kill. "Where's my fucking phone?" His fist hit the countertop, which rattled the salt and pepper shaker just a few inches from his knuckles.

I took a big gulp from my second cup of coffee, feeling that I might need something stronger to get me through this conversation. I hated when William abandoned me to deal with reprimanding our children alone. He'd made an excuse that he needed to finish up a contract for a new client and left before Saturday morning breakfast was ready. "Hudson, watch your mouth. Your curfew is at one. That isn't negotiable, especially after you recently broke it. You're seventeen. One is plenty late." Signaling that this rule wasn't up for debate, I turned my back to him and continued placing the dishes in the dishwasher.

"Where. Is. My. Fucking. Phone?" He pounded his fist on the countertop again, but this time the tone of his voice scared me because my back was to him and I hadn't seen his arm raised. I jumped and turned around to face him again.

"Hudson, if you use that word one more time, I will add a week to your grounding. I did not raise you to be disrespectful." I was aware that teenagers of his generation are extremely dependent on their phones for entertainment and constant communication. Their hands feel odd without them like the phone is an additional appendage. I understood why Hudson was inquiring about it – he felt it was severed from his arm– but the intensity of his anger was sometimes more than I could prepare for.

Furthermore, I didn't know where it was. For all I knew, he hadn't left it in the charging station when he arrived home after his curfew.

When I looked into his eyes, they were black and completely dilated. His sclera, the white of his eyes, were yellow and lined with a deep blood red. I was looking into a deep, dark hole, because Hudson was a shadow of his former self. Big, dark circles surrounded his eyes as if he hadn't slept for weeks while his cheeks sunk in from sudden weight loss. I'd been too busy to notice. Everyone was moving in the opposite direction. We hardly sat down for a family meal anymore. Of course, I made excuses – we were in a busy season of our lives, we'd squeeze in some family time over the weekend, and kids are naturally supposed to need their parents less and less. Excuse after excuse.

But as I looked into Hudson's empty eyes, my heart seized in my chest. *Where is my Hudson?*

"Hudson? Please take a deep breath. Focus. I don't have your phone, and I don't know where it is. I do know that you're overreacting and lashing out at me." It took all of my strength to remain calm. I knew I wasn't speaking to a rational person.

For some reason, a tiny weakness formed in his pride, and a few words escaped from that crack. These next words would break my heart even more than I thought possible. "All I have is you guys."

"If we are all you have, you would think you'd treat us better." I heard his words, but it was the tone of voice that struck a chord. He was being truthful. He was extending an olive branch asking for some grace. I heard a tiny crack break in his protective barrier, and I needed to tread carefully before he closed it.

The crack opened another centimeter when he admitted, "I can't be happy sober, Mom. I need *something* every day to just get out of bed."

I can't be happy sober. As I thought about those words that he confessed, I thought how sad it sounded...but how much truth was in those five words. Did I want to hear that? No, not ever. Did it break my heart? For sure. Once you become a parent, you understand that all you want for a child is for them to have an easy life. To be healthy and happy. It is simple really. I don't care if he lived in a trailer park or worked at McDonald's. If he was happy, I'd be able to sleep better.

I can't be happy sober. I wondered when he had this revelation. Of course, like I have explained before, I didn't receive an invitation to his addiction. It just showed up. Uninvited, and without a warning. I can't pinpoint on a map where the abrupt change happened, and I'm not sure if he can either.

I can't be happy sober. He hadn't been happy for a while now, I assumed, although I didn't know his definition of 'happy.' I can admit that I hadn't been happy *with* him for at least two years. At first, we figured it was teenage defiance and patiently allowed him to spread his wings. I had to start letting him grow up. It was hard. I admit that I didn't handle it well.

There were lots of things that I didn't do. I didn't follow him when he left the house. I wanted to, but I didn't. Additionally, I didn't google and Facebook stalk his new friends to make sure they were law-abiding citizens. I didn't go through the contents of his room unless he gave me a reason to not trust him, like when he lied about where he'd been or when he smelled like marijuana. I didn't ground him for weeks on end when we did discover that he had lied, snuck out, or drank. The punishment was reasonable.

But what I did that Saturday morning was pull him into a huge bear hug and tell him that everything would be alright. We would figure this out together.

***

After I found the drug paraphernalia in Hudson's bedroom, William and I confronted him and explained to him that in our house we didn't tolerate this kind of disrespect. Drugs were not allowed. Hudson's first response was defensive: "What were you doing in my room?"

"Your mother was putting your clothes away. Clean clothes that she asked you to put away a week ago. Plus, this is still our house. Our house rules. Last time I checked, we are the ones paying the mortgage."

"I'm sorry! I shouldn't have stored them in *your* house. My bad." His smug attitude was uncalled for and a completely new personality trait that we had *not* taught him. As I watched from the sidelines, I was in complete shock of who my son had become.

"The right response is 'I won't do drugs again. Totally irresponsible of me and I know better.'" William's words were sharp and sarcastic because he didn't tolerate backtalk and was completely blown away by how self-righteous Hudson was acting.

"Whatever, Pops. Am I excused?" Hudson's teenage temperament was dialed up high, and on the contrary, our parental meter was elevated as well. Neither party was thrilled to be having this conversation.

"No, you are not, so get comfortable. We are going to have this conversation, and you're going to participate if you want to continue living under our roof - "

"William!" We did not agree on this stance. I never wanted to kick one of our children out of our home for not obeying rules; however, William didn't think Hudson would listen unless he was stripped of all privileges, which included a roof over his head.

"Not now, Eve." He returned his attention back to our son. "What is the purpose of setting a house rule if the people living in the house don't follow the rules?"

"Well, on *Big Brother*, it requires a majority vote to remove a member of the house."

"Are you seriously comparing your life to a reality TV show where a bunch of spoiled brats think they can become famous with no talent? Grow up. We've reached our limit to how much insubordination we can tolerate. There needs to be some major action from your side, or you'll leave us no choice. So, let's start by where you're getting these drugs and how you're paying for them." William's jaw was set in a firm, permanent scowl with his teeth clenched. Hudson had pushed all our buttons, and we felt like we were backed into a corner. Without some solid discipline, who knew where we'd be in a year or if he'd even be alive.

"Seriously?" Hudson seemed appalled by William's question. "You think I'd tell you that? I'm no nark."

"Maybe not a nark, but definitely a drug-dependent failure – "

"William!" He'd gone too far. Name calling and belittling our son wasn't going to get us anywhere near the outcome we wanted with this conversation. "No more, William." I softened my voice and turned my body to completely face Hudson and award him my full attention. William needed a few minutes to cool off. Time to sub in the good cop.

"Hudson, what your dad was trying to explain is that we're extremely worried about you. You aren't yourself. By telling us where the drugs are coming from, we will be able to help you." I paused for a moment since both William and Hudson were trying to control their tempers. In the softest, most nonjudgmental voice I could muster, I asked, "Do we know this person? Is he or she a friend?"

The response I received could only be described as pure, unconcealed honesty. Hudson's eyes, though dilated, widened as if I'd hit the mark. It was someone we knew.

"So, that's a yes, we do know this person. Is it someone from school? Someone you work with?" I wanted to continue my line of questioning to see if I could get a clear response, but I noticed from his facial expression that I was losing his interest, fast. His mask of indifference was sliding back on.

Suddenly, I was seeing *red*.

Always decked out with the latest, most expensive trends.

Newly dyed streaks in his hair.

Loud, thumping music.

Arrogant attitude.

Shiny, new *red* sports car.

"Clive? Is it Clive?" All the images that popped into my brain informed me that I didn't even need validation from Hudson, but I received it anyway. His big, brown, dilated eyes stared at me like a deer in the headlights.

It was Clive. The drug dealer was Clive.

Our family friend from across the street. The boy we've known for years and who was like a second son to William and me. The drugs that were ripping my family apart were coming from across the street.

Chapter 16

now

"Evelyn Sarae Stanton, inmate number 9343162-506. You have a visitor." A rookie guard, who was eager to climb the ranks, bangs his baton onto the metal bars of my jail cell to gain my attention. As he straps it back on his duty belt that circles his waist, he glares at me. No other guard uses the inmate's full name and inmate number, but Brandon is still following all the rules. Jilli nicknamed him 'the cowboy', and I'd asked her to explain.

"Why do you call him cowboy? Does he wear a large belt buckle, or speak with a southern accent? Does he drive a pickup truck and listen to songs about his dead dog?"

"Nothing that obvious, Snow White. We're in prison, and while you're in prison, you need to get with the program and do what the prisoners do – create entertaining slang terms that no one knows the meaning of. It's literally the only control we have." Jilli rolled her eyes at me as if I should know all these unwritten rules.

"Jilli, you lost me."

"Cowboy spelled backward stands for the young, obnoxious bastard we often con." She was proud of her creativity as a big grin rose on her lips.

I spelled out her phrase in my head before I understood. I shook my head in amazement at what my new friend conjured up. "Jilli, you should channel your creativity by writing a book. It could contain all the slang words you made up in jail, as well as your story of how you ended up here."

"No way, girl. I thrive on being mysterious." She flashed me one of her sly smiles. "Plus, no one wants to read about a Black girl's crash in society. White people predicted that back when I was born to an uneducated, low-class mother who already had too many mouths to feed. That story has been told over and over. Ain't no good."

"Not true, Jilli. Everyone has a story to tell, and it just matters how you tell it."

As Brandon bangs the metal bars again – indicating, *I have a visitor, and he doesn't have patience* – I rise from the hard, cement floor where Jilli and I've been sitting. From her lotus pose, Jilli opens one eye and continues her deep, even breathing. We're trying some yoga poses that another inmate taught us out in the yard the other afternoon. I'd never made time to meditate before my arrest, but I'd been pleasantly surprised that I enjoyed it. Jilli gives me a thumbs up for encouragement and returns to her deep breathing exercises.

Even though inmates look forward to the break from the monotony of our prison life, visits are mentally exhausting. The visits from family and friends initially lift our spirits and fill our buckets. We yearn for the allowed bear hugs at the end of each visit, the genuine love and concern in their eyes, and the accounts of their lives outside of this hell. But when the visit was over and the bear hug ended, we were shoved back into our hard, cold cell to be reminded of our many regrets and stiff punishments.

As Brandon's and my footsteps shuffle down the hallway and he repeatedly uses his keys that are also stored on his duty belt to move us farther and farther away from my confinement, I wonder who my visitor is. I knew better than to ask because the guards don't know or care. They simply answer a phone call that alerts them that my presence is requested.

I'm relieved to see that my visitor is Frank, even though lately he's all business and seriousness. I know he still loves me, and his friendly face is a welcomed sight. And following my fifteen minutes of yoga, my mood is relaxed and light-hearted.

"Hey, Buttscab. It's nice to see you."

"Buttscab? Dang, Evie, you haven't called me that in years." His smile reaches the corners of his eyes. Our nicknames used to turn heads because they were a bit odd and politically incorrect. He directs his smiling eyes and big grin at me. "I must say, Boobie, you're looking mighty fine and perky in orange today."

"Well, now, I know you're lying." But his term of endearment for me makes me giggle. I have missed this easy, no-nonsense banter.

"Evie, I've got some bad news." He's back to all business. My eyebrows rise, and Frank notices that he has earned my full attention. "They have pretty damning evidence that suggests you were at the scene of the crime."

After the words pour out of his mouth, I understand his disheveled appearance. His button-down shirt is wrinkled and appears as if it had been worn the previous day as well. Frank's hair is messy and greasy, and signs of a five-o'clock shadow appear on his normally clean-shaven face. My head tells me not to ask, but my heart stops beating for a few seconds before starting back up at a ridiculously fast rate.

"What evidence?" Obviously, there has to be some evidence in order to arrest me, but I'm very curious about the proof that I need to discount.

"Your phone."

"How?" This can't be good. "Someone must've stolen it." As soon as those words come out of my mouth, I think about how Hudson always blamed everyone else for his problems.

"Eve, there's a text sent from you during the time of the accident." Neither of us can call it murder yet. "I read it. It's not good."

"Enough with the mystery, Frank. This isn't an episode of *Dateline*. Just tell me."

"You sent a text to William at 1:06 in the morning saying, 'The problem has been taken care of.' It pinged your location in the Black's backyard, and then you must have dropped it and walked home."

"First of all, let's quit assuming I did this."

"Sorry, Eve."

I knew this would happen– evidence that I would need to break down and squash so that I didn't look guilty. I tell myself, *stay calm. Relax. You can do this.*

"Frank? This can't be real."

"Eve, I'll be your friend no matter what happens. As your legal counsel and best friend, I will defend you to the grave. As your lawyer, I will defend your innocence and search every haystack for that sharp needle to the full extent of the law. As your friend, I will always love you but will tell you the harsh truth – it isn't looking good. Imagine two parallel lines on a smooth, blacktop road. One line is the truth, painted with a crisp white and perfectly straight line. The other line is your case and the evidence against you. That blotchy, messy line is painted by a drunk driver. And it is wonky. As your lawyer, I need to straighten out your line. Paint over the messy blobs of paint. Maybe cover a portion of the line if I can find the perfect match. Help me paint you a straight line, Eve. Let's talk about who else knows how you feel – felt about him."

A deep breath of resignation and defeat leaves my lungs. "Again, Frank, with the assumptions."

"Honestly, honey, I don't care if you did. I wouldn't blame you one bit. If you had confided in me all the crap that was happening in your house, I might've rang the kid's neck too, but we need to provide reasonable doubt to the court. Create suspicion that shows that it could've been someone else. Until then we'll discuss everything that led us to the accident. You know how I think. I paint the picture – visualize it in my head, so I can do what I do best – color and scribble outside of the lines." During our college years, I would help Frank study for exams. Studying cases in hindsight created tools for seeing holes and predicting a pattern. He learned so much more through discussion rather than reading from a book. It proved to be beneficial for both of us. While Frank excelled in his studies, I gained knowledge on how to evade the law. We both took notes but for different reasons.

"That's a lot of art analogies, Frank."

"Shush, I know." His eye roll indicates to move past that part of the conversation. "The prosecution is gonna look under every rock, in every crack. This evidence may not be much alone, but all the pebbles under a rock and the width of all the cracks added together will create quite an earthquake. So, humor me. Tell me about Clive and Hudson. Pretend I know nothing."

"What's there to tell? I hate – hated Clive. Once, he was like a son to me, but then he brought drugs into our lives. He was the devil living right across the street wreaking havoc. Before I knew it was him, I pictured some vile criminal with scars and tattoos all over his body, tricking Hudson into ingesting these 'harmless chemicals.' Wearing a black, stained hoodie, he was the creepy stranger who owned a black van with boarded up windows, and as he drove in circles around the playground, he preyed on the inno-cent and naive. However, the reality was worse than my imagination. The drugs were supplied by his childhood best friend, our neighbor, someone I trusted and cared about. I invited him into our home. Clive is to blame for everything that went wrong in Hudson's life."

"Eve...really? You're going to blame him for all of Hudson's choices? Seems like an easy cop-out."

"If you remove Clive from the picture, Hudson wouldn't have had to choose between right and wrong. If Clive wasn't there to ask the questions, there wouldn't have been a choice to make."

"Fair, but seriously, Eve, don't pretend to live in a fairytale. Drugs and alcohol would've tempted Hudson no matter what. He's a teenager. Temptation is everywhere. Nowadays drugs are probably easier to find than alcohol. And kids are resourceful when they want to be."

"Frank, I'm tired. I don't want to debate how and when your godson would've found drugs if Clive hadn't entered the picture. These are the facts. I want to get out of here and be with my kids. This nonsense banter isn't helping."

Frank ignores my whiny voice as his head starts to create the picture he needs to see. "Your phone couldn't have gotten into their yard by itself. We need to consider how it got there. Who would want to make it look like you did this? Who had access to your phone? Where do you keep it when you go to bed? When did you notice it was missing? Talk to me, Eve."

"We've been over this, Frank. I drank too much that night. I don't remember anything after my third glass of wine..."

"Okay, talk me through it. Wait – three glasses of wine and you blacked out? Definitely not the chug-it girl from our college days."

"Frank, those days have been long gone for years. Three glasses and its lights out Eve. Well, not usually, but I must've been drinking on an empty stomach, or maybe I had more, and I can't remember. William and I were enjoying each other's company for the first time in months, so when he poured me my third glass of wine, I didn't hesitate."

"Still three glasses and you blacked out? Hmmm..." Frank starts to frantically write on his yellow legal pad. "Three glasses of wine wouldn't even make the tiniest of women blackout, let alone a seasoned drinker like you. No offense."

"None taken."

In order for Frank's brain to focus, he likes to move. He jumps up from his hard conference room chair and begins pacing. He is a hamster on his hamster wheel. "So, while that's odd in itself, it's not enough. For argument's sake, let's pretend you were totally drunk and don't remember anything. If you were that sloshed, wouldn't your footprints in the snow, I don't know, be sloppier? Haggard? A drunk person might even trip or slip. The evidence photographs showed perfect, evenly spaced-out boot impressions in the snow. Evenly spaced out like they were planned and precise."

Frank is having this conversation with himself like he did in our younger years when we'd cram for finals. He claimed that I was his sounding board when he wanted to think things through, but I never needed to contribute much to these late-night conversations, which was fine by me since the legal jargon and theories flew right over my head.

"Would Hudson have been able to sneak out of the drug facility?"

"It isn't a drug facility. It's an addiction care center, and no. It's locked down at night. Furthermore, he could never have done this." I remind myself that Frank is just doing his job, but I'm annoyed that he even suggested that Hudson might have killed Clive.

Suddenly, his constant chatter stops along with his nervous pacing across the small conference room. He stares at me.

"William poured your last glass of wine?"

"Yeah, I think so. Why?"

"Eve, do you *trust* William?"

"What do you mean?"

"With your life? A trust-fall with your life?"

I pause, and in that brief second of consideration, Frank had his answer.

"Okay, Eve, do you completely trust me? Trust-fall trust me?"

"Of course, Frank. I've known you my whole adult life. You're truly the only one right now that I do trust."

"Then trust me when I advise you *not* to tell William where we are going with our questions or our discussions. I'm not asking you to lie to him, just tell him I'm working on reasonable doubt. Because right now, I think you and I need to play dumb. Pretend we're in over our heads. I'm not sure why yet, but I need you to trust-fall trust me and my process."

Frank has been my best friend for so many years that I could read him like a book. He was dead serious. His little self-chatter motivated his brain into working overtime, and he needed some time to process before revealing his knowledge. I knew his process, and in most cases, Frank landed on top and right on the money with his thinking. It was the reason that the majority of his cases never made it to trial. My head and gut knew that he was right. They both instantly agree with him, but my heart seizes in my chest. If I couldn't trust my own husband, how would I be able to sleep knowing my children were under his care? He is my one and only lifeline to my family. Things have been difficult between us lately, but that is understandable and bound to happen considering what we went through. But for him to not be my support seemed heartbreaking. Plus, he is paying Frank's attorney fees.

I nod my head and lower my gaze so that Frank wouldn't notice the tears pooling in my eyes. However, he knows me as well as I know him. He reaches across the table with his first two fingers and lifts my chin.

Our eyes meet.

"Eve, honey, I got you. I don't think William is involved, but I don't know for sure. So, for now, I want to be safe. After you and I do our thing and brainstorm together, we'll sort out the rest of this mess."

I nod because what else can I do?

After Frank left, all I could think about was what he said about not telling William just yet about our questioning the evidence. *Does Frank know more than he's letting on? Does he suspect William?*

I'm too afraid to ask Frank these direct questions, mainly because I'm afraid of the answers. When deep, dark feelings are given a voice, those hidden insecurities that once were safely trapped inside of your soul become real. I knew I wasn't ready to hear what Frank's suspicions were. I still counted on William for financial support, communication with our kids, and, of course, love and commitment.

But the little voice in my head, whom I refer to as 'Witch', likes to cause drama and point out heartache. It reminds me of several odd occurrences that happened in the last couple of months. Things that, if looked at independently, don't amount to much, but collectively they do seem suspicious. Doubt set in. It just didn't add up.

Chapter 17

then

The night that Hudson side-swiped a parked police car was the night of the beginning of the end.

We'd recently held a family come-to-Jesus meeting where we informed Hudson that he needed to focus on getting clean and healthy. We'd do whatever we could to assist him in achieving that goal. Drug rehab, a new school, or counseling. We'd help however we could.

Our children grew up aware of our no-tolerance policy when it came to drugs. *Disobey that rule and find a new home.* We were so naive to think we could outline a rule and assume our kids would follow it without any objection. Now, Hudson's defiance felt like we were simply slapping him on the wrist for disobeying a minor rule. It was a double-edged sword. We started with a neon sign that brightly lit up, "No drugs!" to a homemade sign written in crayon, "stop using drugs... please." *Hypocrites.*

The adaptation of our rule didn't make sense even in our minds, but we didn't know what to do. We loved Hudson. We were terrified that if we kicked him out, his drug usage would skyrocket and he'd end up dead. On the other hand, by not asking him to leave right away because he disobeyed our no-tolerance rule, it was as if we were condoning his choices. No one seemed to win in either situation.

On the night of the accident, Hazel asked her big brother to take her out for some celebratory ice cream, because our family always celebrated any good deed with ice cream. She had earned all As on her exams, and since she idolized her big brother, she wanted him to join her in celebrating her accomplishments. Even though Hazel strived to make her own high marks, she adored her brother, whose legacy pushed her to always try harder. She yearned for his attention and approval. When Hudson attended one of her events, she was sure to perform at the maximum level. Hazel loved Hudson and looked up to him. Always had. Their adoration for each other was mutual. Hudson would do anything to hear Hazel giggle or earn a big, cheesy grin from her. She didn't identify his drug use. She didn't notice the change in his attitude or personality. Her admiration for her brother was clouded by a pair of rose-colored lenses.

In our defense, we'd lost sight of the real Hudson as well. We recognized that some days he slept until noon – but what teenager didn't? We noticed unprovoked mood swings – teenage hormones, right? His weight and appearance fluctuated - but didn't all growing, young men eat at weird hours of the night? Maybe these were all excuses, but hindsight is twenty-twenty. The perfect lens.

We wanted to focus on the good. Yes, we were those parents who couldn't believe it could happen if we were involved parents and loved our kids with our whole hearts. When time allowed, we held Sunday night family dinners where we discussed our upcoming plans as well as the highs and lows of the previous week. We listened. We cared. We loved.

Drug addicts were supposed to be the people who were raised in dysfunctional families, broken homes, and emotionally or physically abusive relationships. There was supposed to be a clear-cut reason for the defiance. *Right?*

When I heard Hazel ask Hudson to drive her to her favorite ice cream shop, The Parlor, my heart fluttered. My ears perked up to listen for his response as I watched them out of the corner of my eye. They were both standing in the kitchen looking for something sweet to eat.

"Hudson, please, pretty please!"

He giggled his normal, polite chuckle. "Don't beg. You're acting like a diva right now, Hazel." He'd been home since school dismissed, so the odds were in our favor that he was sober, but even though he disobeyed our rule about using drugs, he'd never *do* drugs in our house, under our nose. *Right?*

"I finally earned a perfect score like my famous, big brother. Stop! It's Hazel time!" Pretending her thumb was a small microphone, she began singing the song that she had appointed as her own. "Stop! It's Hazel time. Oooh oooooh. You can't touch this." William had introduced Hazel to MC Hammer and the rest was our family history.

Following behind in her brother's wake did bother Hazel. Hudson had a glowing, flawless high school record – An honor roll student, active in sports, and popular with his teachers. So far, the problems we were having with Hudson at home hadn't bled into his academic career.

They were four years apart in age but five grades apart in school, which did help Hazel shine a little brighter while she was in a separate school building. However, no matter the distance, Hazel was always compared to her starting quarterback, Honor Roll, 160-pound state wrestling champion, and medal-winning long jump brother. Unfortunately, Hazel had big shoes to fill, and she was loudly and proudly setting out to accomplish just that. No matter who her famous family was, Hazel wasn't about to sit back in the shadows. Nope, not our Hazel. Her spirit burned so bright that it was almost impossible to contain her. She wanted to be noticed, but for her own achievements and accomplishments, not because she lived under the same roof as the all-star athlete and the guy all her friends drooled over. Hazel was tired of being referred to as Hudson's little sister. She wanted to create a name for herself.

So, that night, we took a collective deep breath and silently encouraged the sibling ice cream date. Hazel's smile and enthusiasm were contagious, and I silently prayed that her positive energy would transmit to her big brother.

Rather than simply walking out the front door, Hazel skipped and looped her arm through her brother's. Hudson's dimpled, half smirk appeared on his lips – a rare occurrence lately. But Hazel was magical. She had a way of getting people to do what she wanted without them questioning her intentions. Her dad and I were often victims of the Hazel Charm. "Just one more episode of *Grey's Anatomy,* and I'll be an angel all day tomorrow. Not grumpy, I promise." Or..."It's only one more friend to sleep over. We'll be better behaved if Peggy *and* Lindsey stay, Mom. Three is better than two. The more the merrier, right?"

Watching our two children smile at each other felt like a dream moment when your heart overflows with love. The two little humans that we created were enjoying each other's company. Arm in arm, they paraded out the front door to celebrate Hazel's achievements.

William and I collectively breathed a sigh of relief. A moment alone in our house together. A few years ago, we would've torn off each other's clothes during the first second of solitude, but unfortunately, years of tension and comfort have dulled our attraction for one another. I wasn't sure when our desire evaporated, but it had. We were simply coexisting in our five-bedroom home. Each earned their fair share of the income that covered the bills and a little more for our retirement nest egg.

All those future plans seemed ridiculous at this point in our relationship. Even though we shared the same bed and adjoining bathroom, we rarely touched each other fondly. If I rolled over too close to him in bed, my body jerked back as if I had touched something freezing. My body recoiled in response. Somewhere in the fight to stay afloat, we lost the love and desire for one another. We were simply existing next to each other.

As the front door closed, William switched on the oversized TV. After clicking on the game, he sat back on the cushions of the couch to get comfortable. His plans for our time alone had been determined. I pulled out my novel that was tucked into the side of the couch in my usual spot.

In the years before this pattern worked for us, I would attempt to watch a football game with William and Hudson. Football was a fast-paced game, and I enjoyed tracking the ball after the center shuffled it to the quarter-back. But sports and I never seemed to click. My brain didn't seem capable of retaining the rules of the game.

Scientists believe the brain filters and sorts information depending on a person's own brain development. The left side of the brain becomes the 'interpreter', deciding what information should be kept and filed and what information should be discarded. My brain's interpreter did not believe in the importance of retaining sports terms or regulations. Therefore, what little sports facts I had retained were a jumbled mess. I didn't understand the need for different terms per sport; therefore, phrases like this often escaped my mouth.

"The umpire is making some terrible calls." Pride swelled my chest as I contributed more to the conversation than simple comments about the team's matching outfit – more times than I care to count, I'd been told it was called a uniform. But this time I was paying attention to the basketball game, and I had actually understood and recognized the incorrect call.

"See that big orange, round object? It's called a basketball. He's a referee, Mom, not an ump. This isn't a baseball game. Totally different sport."

Hudson rolled his eyes and shared a giggle with William as they returned their attention back to the TV.

After one of Hazel's softball games where her team was mercy-ruled, we crawled into the car feeling very defeated; however, I wanted to remain optimistic and didn't want the loss to ruin our evening. "You scored two points tonight, Hazel. I'm proud of you, honey."

Hazel was slightly more patient with me and my lack of sports knowledge. When she leaned forward from the back seat of the car, she touched my forearm gently and shook her head. "They were two runs, Mom. We don't call them points, but thank you."

My family's favorite memory that showcased my lack of sports understanding was the time that uncontrollable excitement overtook my body and mouth. We were at Hudson's baseball game, and I leaped out of my bag chair and yelled, "Touchdown!" as he slid across home plate, which is not actually a plate but more like a triangular stepping stone that was nailed into the earth. So confusing.

Eventually, I gave up pretending that I understood. I attended all my children's events, kept my mouth shut, and smiled during their achievements and defeats. No matter the score, I was silently supportive.

I'd become a pro at keeping things bottled up. I never complained about all the hours William watched March Madness, which, to my dismay, is not a sale at the mall but a basketball tournament. I stopped asking him, "Do you want to go for a walk instead?" or "Another game? Would you rather sit around the firepit?" or "Want to watch a movie instead?"

Maybe I was afraid of the answer he would've given. "No, Eve, rather than have another pointless conversation with you, I'd like to forget my life and watch *any* game."

I glanced up from my book and noticed William was smiling at something he was reading on his phone. Then his fingers frantically typed a reply. He set his phone back down next to where he was sitting on the couch, and he must've felt my eyes on him. He looked up at me. Due to the length of our marriage and our shared history, I recognized his expression. His lips were pinched in a tight line, and the color drained from his face. Guilt. I caught him. He was doing something he wasn't supposed to. I'd seen that look before.

Unfortunately, I wasn't in the mood to hear his lies or excuses so I returned my focus back to my book. Whatever he felt guilty about, I was sure that I'd find out soon enough. William wasn't the most loyal and honest husband, and he was an even worse liar.

After we'd settled into our routine of ignoring each other, my cell phone lit up with an incoming call. The caller id indicated that it was our neighbor, Jackson Fode. We didn't have the type of relationship as neighbors where we'd often chatted on the phone. More of a wave of the hand and say, 'hey', as I walked the dog kind of neighbor. Jackson and his wife, who was an emergency room doctor, lived around the corner from our house with their five children.

"Hey, Jackson, what's going on?" My words sounded casual, though I felt anything but casual. My mother's instincts were on high alert. I held my breath and waited to hear the reason for his phone call at nine in the evening.

"Hi, Eve. Sorry to bother you, but Hudson hit my patrol car – "

"Oh my god..." His words burned in my brain as my heartbeat intensified. Blood seemed to rush to my brain as I stopped breathing. My thoughts raced and bounced around in my head. *What? Huh? Why didn't Hudson call? Why is Jackson the one phoning me? Is it because his wife, the doctor, is working on my son's body?*

Suddenly, my imagination conjured up possible images of the accident. On the wet, black pavement, Hudson's white Ford Focus was lying on its top with its wheels still circling. Clouds of dark gray smoke rolled out from under the hood of the car as emergency personnel rushed to pull Hudson from behind the wheel. Loud rock music continued to blare from the speakers. An EMT yelled over the chorus of 'Smells Like Teen Spirit' to her co-worker that there was a female in the passenger seat. *Oh my god, Hazel was with him!*

These fictitious images were quickly erased, and I was pulled back into the present. "Eve? Are you still there?"

Luckily for me, one of my positive attributes was that I was well aware of my own personal limits. Because I wasn't sure if I'd be able to handle the rest of this conversation, I handed my cell phone to William without saying another word.

Our neighbor then informed William that our son had sideswiped his parked police car not far from our home. Jackson had been parked on the side of the road to oversee the traffic surrounding a new stop sign that had recently been installed. When he called, he'd pulled out onto the road and started following Hudson and Hazel into a nearby parking lot. Everyone was fine. No one was injured.

Everything was not fine. Hudson was arrested for the first time for sideswiping a police car and failing to stop to report the accident. In addition to the traffic accident, he also tested positive for marijuana. Our legal fees and Hudson's record as a criminal had just begun.

Chapter 18

---

then

Reading the screen of my phone, which announced 'Custer County Jail', ranked as the worst caller ID that I've ever received. I assumed that it ranked as the world's second worst caller ID to receive, right after 'Mortuary.' I was blindsided.

When that phone call happened, my stomach dropped, my mouth instantly dried up, and the throbbing in my head began. I've always been amazed at how the body physically reacts to thoughts in your brain or feelings in your heart. Fear and dread consumed me.

"Mom, ummm...I'm in jail." *Again?* The sting of his first arrest by our neighbor felt fresh. Hudson's voice was tentative and vulnerable and pulled at my already fragile heartstrings. "Can you come get me?"

"Where are you?" But the harsh, blunt voice in my head shouted, *'Are you kidding me?'* It was taking more than a moment to sink in. A mother is never prepared to hear the words that her child is waiting behind metal bars, that he is handcuffed and forced to remain in a cold, cement cell. Strangers, the law, and people employed to keep citizens safe had to intervene in order to make things happen or not.

"I said jail. I got pulled over." His snarky, self-righteous tone of voice was back.

"What are you in jail for?" While my head needed to know the answer to this question and I needed to hear it coming from him, my heart wanted a sudden deafness to take over my eardrums. I was unsure if I'd be able to handle the truth. While my heart wanted to protect me and keep me in a bubble, my brain demanded an explanation that would help this shocking event make sense.

"Speeding, open container, and resisting arrest. A whole bunch of crap. But I wasn't drunk. Oh, and they *illegally* searched my car and found drugs, but they weren't mine. I'm totally gonna sue them when I'm out of here. They didn't have a warrant. Treating me like total dirt. This mess isn't my fucking fault." *Of course, it wasn't. Never is.* Hudson was rambling and didn't make a lot of sense.

In hindsight, as I recall this conversation, I can more clearly hear his words without the shock of this situation clouding my reaction. I understand his tone of voice. My son, my Hudson, was gone and was replaced by a drug-induced shell of a person. He had no concept that he broke multiple laws in one evening. He didn't understand that just by paying his bond, this nightmare was not over. There was no going back to erase this mess that he'd created. He'd be forever clouded by this huge mistake. With his current attitude, all he could focus on was the here and now. The future was irrelevant, and dreaming of what was to come was pointless.

"You have to pay my bond."

"What is a bond?" I knew what a bond was. Hazel and I loved watching crime TV, but I was stalling for time. I was unprepared to have this conversation.

"Seriously? You don't know?" He chuckled a little as if he had the upper hand, standing next to a cop while making a phone call to his mother from a phone attached to the jailhouse wall. Instead of begging me to help him or crying in remorse, my child was rudely demanding my help and making fun of my ignorance. *Where did we go wrong as parents?*

"Ummm...no, I don't. Why don't you tell me?" I returned his impatience with a little of my own. My jaw was clenched and the tension in my shoulders tightened. This was not the son I raised.

"It's like a big fine to get me out of here."

"I have to pay the jail so you can go home?"

"I know, right? Fucking ridiculous. It's like a bad episode of Cops, and I'm the fucking victim." Hudson misinterpreted my outrage. He believed that I was angry about the fact that I was buying his freedom, when in fact I was flabbergasted that he believed that after what he had done, I'd want him to come home. My son had lost all sense of right and wrong. He referred to himself as a victim, not a criminal.

"How much is it?"

"Two thousand dollars." *Crickets.* "Mom?"

"And where is the car?"

"Where is the car?" I assumed that he directed the question to the officer that must've been standing next to him as he made his one allowed phone call. "I don't know. Some towing company, and I heard it's fucking expensive to get it back. Fucking stupid. What a joke."

"Did you get in an accident?"

"No. I told you I was pulled over for speeding. Should I say it slower so you will understand?" He was in full rage mode, and I'd never been so glad that he wasn't home or anywhere near his family. Angry at the world, he blamed everyone else for causing the accident, similar to how he had blamed everything else when he sideswiped the police car. The streets were too narrow. Jackson's cruiser wasn't hugging the curb enough. It was the car's fault for being so wide that he couldn't tell how much room to leave on each side of the car. It was Hazel's fault for wanting ice cream. It was the moon's fault for not shedding enough light in the right direction. It wasn't the fact that he was distracted or the fact that he was high. Nope, according to Hudson, it wasn't *at all* his fault.

"Who were you with?"

"I can't tell you that. The phones are probably tapped."

"Why would the phones be tapped?"

"Mom, you live under a goddamn rock. The government is always listening."

"I need to talk to your dad."

I need to talk to your dad. It was a total cop-out. I was his mother, but I wanted him to suffer, to pay for what he was putting us through. After months of harsh words, slammed doors, and tears of frustration, I was glad for the calm and the quiet. I wanted him in jail until he sobered up and realized how much pain and anguish he was causing our family. But how long would that take? His brain was so messed up that he couldn't see anything past his goal to secure his next fix. As his mother, even though it broke my heart that my kid was in jail with other criminals, I was relieved that I knew where he was. We would not lose sleep tonight worrying about where he was or what he might be doing.

After I hung up and my blood pressure reached a new limit, I sat down and pulled out my laptop. I didn't call William right away. I needed to think. I needed to educate and calm myself. I read about the rules of intake for a criminal, I read about the daily schedule, and I read about the rights that an inmate has.

If the police indicate that they are arresting you, do not resist. That fact alone shows defiance. This charge is the most important for the judicial system because it shows that the criminal will have a harder time rehabilitating and conforming to the rules. And according to Hudson, this was one of the charges against him.

When in jail, your rights are stripped down to the bare minimum. You have the right to humane conditions – a bed, somewhere to relieve yourself, cleanliness, and safety. You have the right to nutrition – it doesn't have to taste good; it just has to fit into the basic food groups. If you are injured, you have the right to medical treatment. And according to Hudson, he was not in an accident.

The freedom of communication is the one that baffled me. Did you know you can text an inmate while he is in jail? He can only call you collect from the shared phone; you can't call him. But on his individual, text-only iPad, you're able to text back and forth night and day for a small fee, of course, with a prepaid calling card. It's twenty-five cents per minute for a phone call and nine cents for a text with a character limit of one hundred sixty. It seemed odd for an inmate to be given such a privilege, but honestly, my dismay was for selfish reasons. I didn't want to hear from him every hour asking if we were coming or not. When my phone pinged with an incoming text, a feeling of dread filled my chest. *What does he want now?* I didn't want to hear from him unless it was to apologize for the last few months of hell that he put us through, and I truly doubted that that specific text would ever see the light of day.

No, I never wanted or thought I would say I would prefer my child be locked in jail than tucked in at home. That sounds like a terrible mother. That was the *before* mother. The *before* the drugs, *before* the defiance, *before* the arrests. Hudson's new mother learned to never say never.

Chapter 19

then

Deciding to talk to Mitchell and Becca about the fact that Clive was selling drugs out of their family home was obviously not going to be a quick or easy conversation. Even if we were close friends, no one wants to be the bearer of *that* kind of news. Any respectable parent dreads even the Elementary teacher's email informing them that little Johnny punched a kid on the playground or that little Johnny pulled the chair out from a girl as she sat down next to him. As parents, we are tasked with the important job of teaching them manners and tools for everyday living. For most parents, it isn't an easy task.

We didn't blame Mitchell and Becca. They were involved parents. Clive wasn't raised to break laws and create addictions, just like William and I didn't choose to have a son addicted to mood-altering chemicals. Our goal was simply to talk to our good family friends and make them aware of the illegal activity happening under their very own roof. In the best case scenario, we could devise a strategy to free both of our children from this illegal and painful choice. Additionally, because we also wanted it to stop, in our ignorant minds, we thought that if Clive wasn't supplying Hudson with drugs to curb his hunger, the hunger would go away. Simply be erased. Obviously, we knew nothing about the power of drugs and the power of addiction. We were very naive.

We decided it would be better to pop over unannounced so it wouldn't appear like we were planning an intervention or finger-pointing. We wanted to appear like we were searching for help, not blaming anyone. The conversation would be between four friends as we sat down to solve a mutual problem – a problem that they weren't aware of yet. We had no idea how ignorant our plan was.

When we walked down our driveway to the street, I yearned to steady myself and hoped William and I would portray a team. We were in this together. As I reached out to hold William's hand, he jammed his hands into the pockets of his pants.

Our footsteps echoed down the quiet street as the street lights casted shadows on the pavement. It was the weekend, and the hum of neighborhood activity had dulled when the sun set. We knew the Blacks were home because their lights were lit throughout the house and several cars were parked in the driveway.

As the doorbell chimed its familiar song down the long entryway hall, I heard a set of heavy footsteps making their way to the front door, where William and I stood nervously. I quickly glanced at William hoping to receive an encouraging thumbs up or a small supportive smile, but instead, I was greeted with a scowl of annoyance. His message was clear.

Great. This is not going to go well.

When the heavy, oversize wooden front door creaked open, Mitchell, who was sporting a wide, cheesy grin, greeted us. He was dressed in his favorite palm tree swimming trunks, bare chest and bright turquoise flip-flops. In his right hand, he held an empty crystal glass full of ice with a splash of an amber-colored liquid.

"Eve and William? Hello. Come in! I didn't know you two were coming too. I assume that since you don't have your trunks on, you thought swim trunks were optional." Mitchell always liked to keep things light and skinny dipping was one of the topics he liked to joke about. Sometimes, I didn't think he was joking.

Since we weren't expecting a half-drunk, half-clothed Mitchell to answer the door, it took a moment for us to gather our bearings. William was the first one able to comprehend that this wasn't what we were expecting with our drop-in. He cleared his throat and said, "Ummm...Eve and I were hoping to talk to you and Becca, but since you have company right now, we can come back another time."

"Nonsense! Stay. Come in. We have plenty of food and drinks." He was gesturing us into his home with a gentle push on William's shoulder and closing the door behind us. "Plus, it's Wendy and Glen. You know them too. It'll be fun. I was just about to mix us all a drink. Old fashions for the posh, fancy men and some strong Margaritas for the smokin' hot tamales."

William and my eyes met. We felt trapped and off kilter. This wasn't our plan, and furthermore, we were not in the mood for socializing. Our son was spending the night in jail because, when he was pulled over for speeding, he tested positive for marijuana. There was a whole list of charges. Throwing back a few cocktails, creating fake smiles, and making small talk wasn't in the cards for our evening plans. William planned on drinking himself into a stupor alone, while I planned on having a good, hard cry alone in our bedroom before picking up our son the next morning from the slammer.

And to add more salt to the wound, we were no longer friendly with Wendy and Glen. Wendy and I had met at a local gym, both trying to lose the baby weight that plagued our tired mom bods. Even though we were never close friends, our paths crossed quite often, and we found ourselves spending time together – watching our kids' sporting events, working a school fundraiser, or attending mutual parties. However, soon enough, I realized that Wendy had been spreading rumors behind my back, telling mutual friends lies that hurt my reputation and earned me a few snotty side glances. When I finally realized that she was behind the backstabbing, I confronted her, and it did not end favorably.

A few years ago, I introduced Wendy and Glen to Mitchell and Becca at a local golf club, but I felt the need to warn Becca right away. I didn't want my new friend to go through the drama I had endured years before.

Under my breath and out of the side of my mouth, I told her, "That's her. That's Wendy, the one who I told you about." Because my friend knew I was trying to be subtle and deliver the comment to her ears only, Becca peeked up quickly and nodded slightly in Wendy's direction.

"That one? The one with the gigantic nose and mile-long buck teeth?"

Girlfriends are the best. Wendy's nose wasn't that big, and her teeth hardly stuck out over her bottom lip. In fact, Wendy was actually quite attractive, but Becca was being a mean girl and staying loyal to me, her best friend. I loved her for that.

"In the tight, bright red, V-neck shirt that is too low for a school event? Yes. That's her."

"And we hate her because she couldn't handle that you had other friends besides her?"

Still, in a hushed tone, I answered. "Well, yes, among other things. Like she talked about herself ninety-nine-point-nine percent of the time. Never paused to listen to anyone else, took credit for other people's work, and created more drama than a tornado stirs up dust. Plus, she started the nasty rumor that I plotted to fire the kids' third-grade teacher, Mrs. Lisa Shade. Supposedly, the rumor claimed Mrs. Shade ran a brothel back in Minnesota before she moved to Miner City."

Becca's eyebrows shot up as she questioned me. "Did she? Run a brothel? I haven't heard that word used in a decade." She sounded out the word again for her own amusement.

"I'm not sure. The rumor mentioned that her ex-husband, who was a pastor, was the pimp daddy to the whole scandal. But not the point. I didn't start the town's gossip, but she told everyone I did."

"Got it. Avoid tight V-neck and camel-toe-wearing hoe bag. Check." She looped her arm in mine, and we moseyed up to the bar.

***

Behind Mitchell, Becca's high-pitched giggle bounced off the walls.

As Mitchell ushered us down the long, narrow hallway, our feet shuffled under duress as Jason Aldean was bellowing the chorus to "My Kinda Party." We smelled the perfectly seasoned steaks on the grill and witnessed Becca in her black string bikini giggling with her camel-toe-wearing friend Wendy dressed in her signature color – a red one-piece swimsuit. Standing in the corner of the kitchen, tossing a salad, was Glen, the tall, lanky husband who everyone believed Wendy married for his money.

When we saw Becca's pained facial expression as we entered their warm, brightly lit kitchen, it was obvious we weren't welcomed. The next hour before we were able to politely escape was painful and strained.

After our unannounced visit and failed attempt to talk, I tried to get a hold of Becca with a short text. "Becca, sorry we crashed your party. Not our intention. Can we talk?" Crickets. That text went unanswered, so I sent an email. "Becca, there is something I need to talk to you about. Can we meet?" No response. One afternoon when I watched her park her car in the driveway and walk through her front door, I slipped on my shoes and strolled over to her house. I rang the doorbell and heard the chime sound in the house, but she never came to answer the door. Maybe she was in the bathroom. I politely knocked on the door just to let her know I was still waiting. Nothing. I stood there dumbfounded for ten minutes.

I didn't need any more of a sign to know she was avoiding me. I recognized the subtle hints that Becca was pulling away from our friendship. She didn't return my texts, phone calls, or emails. She ignored me altogether. Honestly, I wasn't sure what I did besides pop in unannounced that night; perhaps she felt me pulling away when I hadn't been confiding in her about the pain my family was going through. Without being able to talk to her, I had no idea what was happening to our friendship.

I was hurt and a little surprised, because just a few weeks before we had enjoyed a Saturday lunch date. We laughed, we threw back a few cocktails and munched on our salads. I couldn't fathom what had changed in our friendship when there were no warning signs. In my messages to her, I never alluded to what I wanted to talk about, and the only conclusion that I could come to regarding her sudden change in behavior was that perhaps she knew about Clive's drugs and allowed it. Why else would she ghost me so abruptly?

Chapter 20

then

I tried to do what was right. I used the knowledge I'd absorbed from years of reading self-help books. I took the bull by the horns. I faced my problems. I tried to take the high road. Instead of complaining about the problem to anyone who would listen, I faced the problem. Or tried to.

But where did that get me? After attempting to discuss the issue of Clive's drug dealing with his parents, we managed to become alienated from our community and rejected by our friends. It was like I received a pink slip, rather like a subtle, 'your presence in our lives is poison.' It was obvious from the sideway glances, the quick turnarounds when headed in my direction, and the lack of response to texts or messages. The message was loud and clear – Becca told everyone that I was an itchy, infectious rash. Touch me and the toxic drama will soil your family too.

As I sipped my first glass of white wine and thought about how much had changed in the past few months, I gazed out the window at our neighborhood, and a shiny, red car grabbed my attention. That little brat loved and cherished his car. Clive and his cherry-red Corvette. From behind the wheel of his flashy sports car, his arrogance was enough to make me vomit in my mouth. Following the break of our friendship and the revelation that the little punk across the street continued to sell drugs in our neighborhood, I wanted to simply slap that cocky smile from his face.

But first, I tried prayer.

I folded my hands and knelt down next to my bed. *"Dear God, please help Clive find the error of his ways. Please guide him back into your loving embrace. In Jesus' name, we pray. Amen."*

As the numerous prayers to save his soul went unanswered, I started wishing that Karma found him and concluded that Clive was due to pay some unsettled debts. I reasoned that God recognized something in Clive worth saving so, He sat back and continued to keep a watchful eye over him, or maybe his soul was too far gone for God to do anything miraculous. But on the other hand, Karma must have enjoyed watching Clive mess with other people's lives. Karma popped some popcorn, pulled the lever on her recliner, and sat back to watch the show. Both God and Karma were more patient than I was. How could I, now that I knew where Hudson's drug supply was coming from? A kid who he used to call his best friend and who I referred to as my second son. A kid who enjoyed slumber parties under our roof. If he had a bad dream, I would have rushed to Hudson's room, and I would've been the one to console him.

In my distraught brain, I reasoned that the next responsible step would be to punish Clive anonymously. I reasoned that I tried to be an adult and talk to his parents, and look where that got us. As a Christian, I prayed for his soul. And before all of that, I had tried every avenue I could think of to deter Hudson from going down this path. Nothing had worked.

Finally, I'd had enough. I couldn't take it anymore. Honestly, it felt gratifying to be taking back a little control. For so long, everything was happening without my permission. Clive was destroying our family and I could do nothing to stop it. So, I decided to ruin something of his to cause him some extra grief. Eye for an eye, or maybe my little jab would be like a little poke in the eye?

Before I could second guess my decision, I slid on my tennis shoes and grabbed Milo's leash. We walked out the side door of the garage, but not before I pocketed a big, rusty nail from William's workbench. I dropped it into my pocket. Every day when I walked past their house while exercising with Milo, my heart would beat twice as fast as usual, as my anger boiled to the brim just thinking about the pain that he was putting my family through. I didn't blame his parents, Mitchell and Becca – they probably had no idea that a drug *dealer* lived under their roof just like William and I had no idea a drug *addict* lived under ours.

My first payback was a rusty nail that I placed under the tire of his precious car. Nails are always causing a few flat tires here and there. Might slow him down on his way to school. Make him late. Annoy him. Make him miss an appointment to collect his weekly drug distribution. I didn't care. Anything to deter him away from his job of ruining other people's lives. Stop him from meeting a client. Stop him from profiting from the illegal substances that he shares with his peer group. Stop him from getting another unsuspecting, innocent victim addicted.

That little nail caused a spring in my step, knowing that I was making his life slightly more stressful. Made me smile. Lifted some worry. Brought focus onto something I felt I could control. I didn't care how big the inconvenience it caused him; I just knew it felt good.

***

The nail in the tire was the first of many retributions that I justified in my brain. I was working undercover for Karma as her accomplice. Punishing the unjust. Fulfilling the fate of punishable acts. It felt good to take some control back.

A few nights later, I got into an argument with Hudson when he came home two hours past his curfew. I yelled. I cursed too, but none of it could even penetrate his brain. He couldn't even fake an apology.

After he retreated to his room, I noticed a light being switched off in the Black's house across the street. Clive must've just arrived home as well. His car was parked in the driveway. Rage fueled inside of me, and before I knew it, I'd marched over to their house with a pocket knife and stabbed the small, sharp blade into all four of Clive's tires. As the air gushed out of each expensive tire, I felt the stream of my anger rolling out of my body. Rage had controlled both my brain and body, and before second guessing my decision, I'd just committed a crime.

Slash the tires on the thing he loves most. That'll teach him.

But it didn't. The next morning, before I'd crawled out of bed, Clive called a local mechanic, who promptly arrived and installed new tires on his car as it waited patiently in the driveway. When I strolled over to my bedroom window, I watched the mechanic's vehicle pulling away.

The high of my new-found righteousness didn't last long. It dissipated like every good high eventually does, and then the yearning to reach a higher level overtook my sense of right and wrong. Disobey the law, and take the task one step further. If I had paused long enough to comprehend what I was doing, I would've seen how my revenge was similar to Hudson's addiction.

Before this year of my life, I'd been a normal, law-abiding citizen who took pride in following the rules of society. As a religious person, I also wanted my merciful and charitable actions to reflect my belief in God. I believed that I was making Him proud by giving generously, loving unconditionally, and forgiving easily. However, a dark, sinister voice suddenly possessed my common sense and spoke to me as if He owned me. I was the faithful one, I had served Him, and now it was my turn for His help.

I wanted another human to pay for not following God and conducting immoral actions. He owed me, and I was cashing in my chips.

I knew in my heart that this wasn't how God worked, but with my anger and desperation reaching a new limit, I couldn't comprehend the voice of reason. I named this voice, Witch, and her voice was soothing and sympathetic. She always knew the right things to say.

But no matter what the rational side of my brain tried to tell me, fury boiled over and consumed my body. Honestly, I must've blacked out because the next thing that I remember is looking down at my hands and wondering what I'd done. I'd smeared Milo's fresh dog poop all over Clive's car.

Chapter 21

then

Have you ever noticed that when bad things are happening in your life, you feel like you're running downhill? Gravity pulls you down to the bottom while your legs can't seem to keep up with the rest of your weight. You know what's going to happen, but you can't get your bearings fast enough to stop it. Down, down you tumble without being able to save yourself.

After failing to discuss their son's drug distribution, William and I solemnly returned home with our tail between our legs. Of course, William blamed me for the uncomfortable situation I'd put us in by dropping by unannounced. He had stomped and pouted all the way home, and after making himself a stiff drink, he slammed the door to his home office, and I didn't see him again that night. It was for the best. I needed to formulate a new plan. When control was lost, organizing and plotting helped me regain my sense of direction.

As devoted and loving parents, we tried everything to knock sense into Hudson. We grounded him, we took away his driving privileges, we threw away anything drug-related that we discovered, and we removed any of his extra privileges. And after each sentencing was completed, a temporary honeymoon period would settle over our household before he'd start back up again. Law enforcement was aware of his name now, and I felt that it was only a matter of time before he killed himself or someone else. I didn't see another option besides chaining Hudson to his room, and unfortunately, the local police and social workers 'frowned' upon that. Nothing can prepare a parent for this heartache. There are no textbooks that lay out the ground rules for how to handle each situation that parenting throws at you. Even if there was a book, it wouldn't work for every child. Nope, this nightmare was one-of-a-kind.

I didn't think my level of anger and heartbreak could withstand much more; however, when I discovered that the drugs were being supplied by someone who my family loved and trusted like a member of our family, my heart literally cracked into two pieces. Prior to this discovery, I'd imagined Hudson meeting some shady, rotten-toothed, shifty-eyed, needle-supplying, asshole in a dark, dangerous alley in the roughest part of town. My imagination never even considered the possibility that the drugs that were destroying my family were being supplied from across the street in our safe, upper-class neighborhood, where our close friends lived. That was a complete shock.

Since confronting Mitchell and Becca had only led to additional stress in our friendship, I decided that it couldn't hurt anything more by standing up to the problem himself – Clive. In my Mother Bear brain, I didn't see another choice.

Even though he'd earned the new title of drug dealer, I wasn't afraid of Clive. He'd been in our lives for years. I rubbed his back after he had a nightmare during a slumber party with Hudson. He was the lost, angry teenager that I picked up on the side of the road after he ran away from home. When he'd gotten into a fight with his parents, it was our house that he walked over to and begged to stay for supper. Clive was the boy who I'd hugged after he gifted me my favorite necklace that the 'SM' – second mom – charm dangled from.

So, years later without him enlisting my help or my advice, I vowed to be a supportive adult and steer him back on track. That's how I viewed my role, or at least tried to convince myself that that was what I was doing. I'd help him see the error of his ways, and we'd all return to our normal, sober lives. Maybe we'd even laugh about this gigantic mess years later. Since I was a problem solver and I didn't give up easily, I thought if I managed to control the situation, I could convince Clive to stop.

I assumed Clive would be home from school within the hour while Becca and Mitchell would still be at work, so I scheduled the afternoon off from work. I didn't want to overthink the conversation, but I wanted to make sure that the scene would provide us with some uninterrupted time. I had a plan and this was an important step in that direction. Additionally, it was a perfect afternoon to enjoy one of the amenities of our house – the front porch.

When the kids were little, I'd begged William for a swing on our front porch so we could rock our babies to sleep while listening to the noises of the hills as a natural lullaby. I loved my swing. As I waved at the random car that drove past our house, I was sure I appeared to simply be a woman who was thrilled with the sudden change in weather and decided to plop myself down on my front porch and enjoy the surprisingly warm afternoon. If only life was as simple as it appeared to a random bystander.

Fall in the Black Hills of South Dakota was Mother Nature as a moody teenage girl. In the early morning hours, with her face in a permanent 'I hate mornings' scowl, she poured heavy, wet snow out of the sky, causing the innocent residents to curse as they called in late for work because their commute was taking double the time. But by lunchtime, Teenage Mother Nature had a change of heart, and she splashed on the charm and pressed her bright, yellow sun rays down, causing her fresh, white creation to dissolve as quickly as it started. It was just another one of Mother

Nature's mood swings. The residents adjusted to her mood swings and didn't question her generosity.

Instead of spending the day shoveling hefty snow like the residents had planned, our neighborhood was alive with playful activity. A small breeze blew through the air leaving a faint scent of burning leaves from the night before. I could smell mouthwatering barbeque ribs smoking on a nearby neighbor's smoker. The quick melting snow dripped down the overstuffed storm drains as the water sprinted down the sides of the streets. Even the birds were singing with gratitude for the beautiful day.

As I situated myself among the pillows and wrapped myself in a cozy blanket, I listened to the noises of our neighborhood. To the south of our house, the Kocmicks were playing a lively game of basketball on their driveway. To the north, Mr. Johnson was cutting a tree branch that was hanging dangerously low over the street. In the bushes that lined our front porch, I'd trimmed a four-inch-by-four-inch peephole to provide me the perfect, unobstructed view of the Blacks' front door that was kiddy-corner across the street.

In between my sips of coffee, I inhaled several deep breaths to relax. I wanted this conversation to go well so I could save my child as well as the Black family. My words would be power. As an editor, I completely believed that words could be very persuasive given the right timing, tone of voice, and audience. I knew Clive would be defensive as soon as I brought up the drugs, and I was sure that he wouldn't willingly admit his wrongdoings or that he was dealing drugs. Furthermore, I didn't believe that I could talk him out of his drug dealing job right off the bat. My initial goal was to erase Hudson from the equation and leave Clive with some things to think about. I hoped that he'd be able to see beyond the immediate gratification to the big picture. Small steps.

My eyes felt heavy as I rocked myself in a steady, calm rhythm. The sudden change in weather had even helped my outlook on the conversation I was about to have. I was feeling optimistic.

Suddenly, the peaceful neighborhood was overtaken by the deep bass of a teenager's car stereo.

Thump...thump...

Because the bass was so piercingly loud, the singer's poetry was muffled and unintelligible. I'll never understand teenage boys and their need to shatter their eardrums or announce their arrival to every living, breathing thing. I straightened up in my seat. That god-awful noise was my cue that Clive was almost home.

Thump..thump...

I stood up, smoothed out the wrinkles in my clothes, and verified that the contents in my pocket were secure. It was a small baggie of a white crushed substance. By the thumping of the music, I estimated that Clive was approximately a block away. After I tossed the blanket onto the swing, I started walking toward the Blacks' house. If I timed my arrival just right, I'd be able to catch him before he entered his garage apartment.

By the time my feet reached the end of their driveway, Clive's car was idling inside the garage and the deep beat of his music pounded the pavement. *How can he stand that noise?* It bounced off the walls of the garage, and I swear I heard a window crack. When the ignition turned off and the music stopped as Clive opened the driver's side door, I was standing at the entrance of the garage, just behind his car, his pride and joy. It was a cherry-red Corvette that he'd been given for his eighteenth birthday, decked out with all the bells and whistles. There wasn't a dent or scratch on it. Clive was often witnessed waxing it in the driveway.

I didn't want to scare him. That wouldn't be a good start to this conversation so I slightly shifted my balance to my right hip and quietly cleared my throat.

As he stepped out of his car, I saw his stark white sneaker followed by the leg of his jeans. With the ease of his youth, he climbed out of the car dressed like a typical high schooler – ripped jeans and a gray hooded sweatshirt that supported his home team, the Gold Diggers. His dark hair was perfectly styled without a strand out of place. Clive was a mini version of his father, Mitchell, but there were two major differences. What Mitchell lacked in hair, Clive flaunted on the top of his head. Waves and waves of thick, blonde hair. The other difference was Clive's arrogance and blatant disrespect for authority.

We hadn't seen Clive except for his silhouette in the window of his car as he drove by. I wasn't prepared for his over-the-top confidence. Before our eyes met, I heard his question, "Why are you here, Mrs. Stanton? There are no refunds."

"What?" I had no idea what he was talking about. *Refunds? Refunds on what?* "Clive, I'd like to talk to you for a minute." My presence hadn't shocked him. I didn't scare him; maybe nothing scared him anymore.

"You got one minute. Go." He looked down at his watch as he started to time our conversation. *Snot-nosed punk.*

It required every ounce of my patience to not reach out, grab him by the neck and shake the arrogance out of him. Gone was the sweet, vulnerable boy who my son had grown up with and whom I'd looked after like my own family. He was replaced by a smug teenager who was too cool for an old lady.

I reminded myself that the young, sensitive boy whom I loved like a son was still in there. Somewhere deep, deep in there. Clouded by drugs and poor choices. I just needed to reach *that* kid.

Here goes nothing.

"Clive, I'm aware of your new occupation, and unfortunately, I'm not very happy about it. I think you are better than that." I cleared my throat and cast him a motherly glare – my glares were legendary when my kids were young and used to work wonders. A bit magical maybe, but that was a long time ago when they believed in magic.

"Mrs. S, I'm not interested in your approval or your opinion. Neither means shit to me."

"Clive, I've known you since you were a boy. I know you better than you think. You care."

"That was years ago. I'm not that pathetic, acne-faced, little boy anymore." And to prove his point on the *little* adjective, he took a couple of long strides toward me so that he had to bend his neck to look at me. He was at least five inches taller than me and had at least sixty more pounds of muscle. However, I told myself that size didn't matter, and deep down was the young boy who had once fondly called me his second mom. *Keep going, Eve. You can do this. Give him the chance to redeem himself. Don't give up. Do it for Hudson.*

"I'm simply telling you that I know what's in your heart." I gently poked his chest since he was standing only inches from me. "And your soul. You wanted to be a sports reporter just a few years ago. Are those dreams gone? Because being a freelance pharmacist will not look good on your resume if you ever want to land your dream job." I was trying my hardest not to point fingers or make him feel defensive, but looking at his smug expression was baiting me and my nasty tongue.

"Free-lance pharmacist?" He half-laughed at my synonym for his current career choice. "Good one."

"Clive, you're young and you think the choices you're making right now don't matter, but this one – the one to sell drugs – is huge. It's a huge mistake. You're too smart to make this detrimental decision that will affect your future. You're getting messed up in something very dangerous. I'm worried about you. I'm worried about your safety and concerned for your future."

Again, he awarded my acting skills with a weak attempt at a laugh. "Mrs. S, you've always been a little naive and a little late to the ballgame. But you're right that I'm too smart. I don't dabble in my merchandise. Dude, drugs can mess you up. Addicts have no fucking self-control over their habit, so they sacrifice everything – family, friends, their jobs, their future, *their marriage* – just to get high." I noticed a slight eyebrow raise when he said the word, marriage. "Nope, you're right, I'm too smart for that shit. It takes an idiot not to understand how bad this shit is."

"Well, I'm glad to hear that you aren't using, Clive." To be honest, I was surprised about that revelation and didn't fully believe him. How many drug dealers are worried about telling the truth?

"But you aren't here to talk about *my* usage, are you?"

"You're right. I'm worried about Hudson. I know he is getting the drugs from you, Clive. I'd like to ask you *not* to sell it to him."

"You're here about Hudson? *Only* Hudson? But wait, isn't he in jail right now?" In Clive's tone of voice, I detected some fake concern.

"Actually, he isn't in jail any longer. He was transferred to a rehab facility where he is getting help for his substance abuse. But I'm still concerned about Hudson. He is going to need all the help he can get. I don't know or care who else you sell to. Just not to Hudson."

"Ahh...okay." Well, that conversation went easier than I'd imagined. A little too easy.

Chapter 22

now

Fall is my favorite time of year. Pumpkin Spice lattes, cozy sweatshirts, and cooler temperatures – sign me up! If there was a city that sustained the season of fall all year round, I would proudly be its mayor, marching up and down its streets, spreading my uncontainable joy and gratitude to all the residents. "Good day, fine residents of Autumn Pleasure! Isn't it another perfect day in our little corner of heaven?" I wish I could bottle the fulfilling feeling that a fall day provides and sell it as a natural mood enhancer to people who needed assistance finding happiness in their day.

Sure, springtime in May is hard to beat with the fresh scent in the air after a good, hard rain and the fact that the bugs have not yet woken from their slumber, but in my opinion, no time of year can compare to the sensory overload that fall delivers.

The sights. Everywhere your head turns, a kaleidoscope of color entertains your eyes. Each tree contains its own unique, vivid array of colors, from brilliant burnt orange speckled with a deep maroon to the sun-kissed yellow and even the deep worn-out brown. Just like a snowflake, no fall infused tree is the same. While your vision is seduced by the brilliance, out of the corner of your eye, you notice two furry squirrels playing tag between the trees, and a brown, fluffy rabbit scurries into a bush for shelter.

There is life all around. Even the late morning sunrise pleases the eye with the blend of colors painting the beginning of the beautiful day until the harvest sunset bleeds across the horizon and makes even the busy farmers working in their fields pause to bask in its hues. My heart bleeds for the colorblind boy who can't witness the colorful beauty on display.

The sounds and smells. Following the rhythmic sound of the sturdy, metal rake collecting the fallen leaves, the crackle of burning leaves fills the still, crisp air. Because the air is thinner, neighbors overhear conversations from across the street as well as the dogs barking in the fenced yard. Teenage boys grunt and harass each other as they toss around a football while their dad coaches from the sidelines in his lawn chair. When you walk into any coffee shop or restaurant, they advertise a variety of different options featuring pumpkin. Pumpkin pancakes, pumpkin pie, pumpkin spice lattes, and even pumpkin scented candles.

The feels. The brisk, chilly air feels like a welcomed break from the choking, wet humidity that plagued our state for three months prior. When the wind shifts from the south to the north, an invigorating fresh breeze rolls in, causing noses to turn red because of the lowered temperature. Fuzzy sweatshirts and soft socks are pulled out of storage. In the Midwest, fall warns the residents that soon they will be fighting the heaviness and bitter cold of winter. Mother Nature says, "But before I cast frostbite and blizzards on you, I'll bless you with the season of fall."

However, this fall I won't be able to enjoy my morning walks with Milo through the neighborhood while basking in the beautiful colors Mother Nature has created. I'll miss watching the innocent trees fight off the changes that are happening. Under my feet, I'll miss hearing the crunch of the dried up, discarded leaves. I won't giggle at our dog, Milo, as he chases a leaf that has been forced to tumble in a light breeze. I'm missing my favorite time of the year. I'm missing everything.

As I lie on my prison cot, I think about the tall, colorful sugar maple tree that stands proudly in our backyard. She's – Hazel nicknamed her Maple – a backdrop to many of our family pictures because of her eye-catching beauty. Every fall, I'd dress my family in coordinating cool tones as we used the timer on my camera to capture the perfect picture. Maple stood tall and proud as she hovered over us. Not only was she gorgeous, but she was also dependable and strong. She provided an abundance of shade to our back deck where we would sit for hours entertaining our friends. Always the silent and sturdy friend, she never judged a secret or snickered at our dreams. Maple was a staple.

But now as my heart feels crushed and broken by the events over the past year, I remember Maple and how she must feel throughout the year as each season influenced her. Years and years ago when she was planted, her roots were short, fragile and weak, but slowly over time, she willingly accepted the gifts of soil, water and sunshine as they were offered to her. As a result, long, thick branches stretched out from her trunk and were covered with vibrant green triangle-shaped leaves. Each year she grew stronger and taller, and we flocked to her and enjoyed the shade and protection she provided us. She had a purpose, and with this important responsibility, she flourished. Not only did she feel needed and useful, but she also felt loved and cherished.

Suddenly, one fall morning, she woke up and noticed that on her sturdy outstretched branch, one of her precious leaves had turned yellow. Maple felt ashamed and frightened, so she shook the odd colored leaf off. It grace-fully floated onto the grass below. She breathed a sigh of relief; however, she saw it laying on the ground beneath her as if it was taunting and teasing her. She would never forget.

The following morning, there were more yellow leaves sprinkled among her outstretched branches. She panicked, but this time she decided not to shake them loose; maybe that was the mistake she made last time. One was plucked and a bunch grew as replacements. Instead of paying attention to the inconsistencies of her leaves, she focused on what she could control. She stood tall and shaded the backyard for her people. She had a job to do and was determined to hold her head high.

Day after day, her branches were splashed with apricot-orange, golden yellow and cocoa-brown colors. Maple became accustomed to their sudden appearance and stopped panicking like she did at first. Even though her people still gathered around her and enjoyed her protection, she felt disappointed in herself for not being stronger and more resilient. She knew that should a strong breeze blow, her fragile leaves would shower the grass below without so much as a second thought. She'd become bare. Naked. Useless.

Before she knew it, every remaining leaf betrayed her. Maple was tired and defeated by the things that she couldn't control. They changed her. Even though she only wished she could remain strong, healthy and green, she realized these golden leaves were battle scars. Each golden leaf told a story, and Maple was both smarter and wiser for having survived the season. These disloyal leaves portrayed pieces of her being stripped of her youth, innocence and naivete. The golden leaves are parts of her that have been harmed or tarnished by the things she can't unsee, unhear, or not feel. The golden leaves changed her. Once the last green leaf had succumbed to the golden color, Maple felt prickly and very fragile. With the fall winds picking up power, Maple doubted her ability to withstand the chilly, high winds that would eventually strip her bare. She knew she won't remain green with youth and innocence forever, yet it was still hard to accept.

Maple sighed a weighted, deep sigh. She yearned to return to the season before everything changed, before *she* changed. But her wish went unheard, ungranted, so she stood as tall as she could against the brisk wind as she watched as her leaves, her offspring, glittered the ground beneath her.

As I lie on my back and tears roll out of my eyes – one after another – I realize I'm Maple.

Chapter 23

now

In a six-foot-wide and eight-foot-long jail cell, laying on my back on top of my thin mattress, I typically have a lot of free time on my hands. Before I was caged up like an animal, interruptions were annoyances that I cursed and sometimes avoided. Work emails, phone calls, random conversations, household chores, and TV commercials. Distractions remind me of the news bulletin that comes across the TV screen, "And now we return you to the regularly scheduled program," which was either work, downtime, or family. But inside the walls of a jail, distractions are welcomed. The only thing I can count on for distraction is my overactive imagination and random thoughts.

Mailboxes. Innocent concept but very old school.

While our modern society is more often times worried about being electronically hacked – personal banking accounts, Facebook or any social media or email account – our personal letters from family and friends, phone or utility bills, advertisements that disclose where we shop, and orders from various companies are delivered daily by federal employees to an unsecured, tin box literally right outside of our own front door. This information that sometimes sits unattended, unlocked, and unclaimed outside of our home contains essential information that would disclose so much to a hacker if they got their hands on that right piece of mail. For example, the birthday card from your mom that has her hyphenated name on the address label – provides your mother's maiden name and your birth date. The alumni newsletter from your alma mater revealing your college mascot. The list goes on and on. Intimate information is delivered to a rectangular box with our name and house number listed on it. People want to remain anonymous, yet their name is written on their mailboxes. Or even carved into a giant boulder in their landscaping. "Smith, established 2000." The back window of the family minivan parked in the driveway has a picture of a dad, mom, two sons and a dog. All of those personalized signs scream, "I live here! Here is my personal information!" Where is the anonymity in that?

Years ago, when the Black family had moved in, I innocently peeked in their mailbox one afternoon while I was walking Milo. I couldn't remember their names after meeting them at a neighbor's potluck. William and I had hit it off with them and wanted to invite them over for supper; however, we both are terrible at remembering names. The act of snooping was completely innocent.

But during that quick snoop, I learned a great deal about them – besides their names. With one pull of the little latch that closes and seals the contents, I was able to get a glimpse into their lives. Mitchell subscribes to Playboy magazine while his wife, Becca – I discovered her name by looking at the second piece of mail piled in their tin box – received a coupon for an online boutique. Mitchell also received a hand-written card in a lime green envelope from someone with the same last name who lives in Montana. And from the cute, bright sticker of a birthday cake on the back of the envelope, I understood that it was Mitchell's birthday. The fourth piece of mail was addressed to Becca, indicating her voting preference as democratic.

As I slid the mail back into the box, I realized that I'd collected some essential information about Mitchell and Becca without even having to open a piece of mail. I was innocently just interested in getting their first names. Before we invited them over for supper, I knew that Mitchell had just celebrated his birthday and Becca's political preference.

However, years later, when our friendship began cooling off and their kid started selling my kid drugs, I stole things from their mailbox to interfere with their lives. Because I knew enough about them, I wasn't interested in new information. No, I simply wanted to cause them some stress like their son was doing to mine, and my recent vandalism of Clive's car wasn't making any sort of impact. At first, I stole a phone bill and then a water bill. I took them home and shredded them, hoping that they would be charged a late fee, or due to their lack of payment, cause a break in their service. My vengeance was innocent enough. Nothing murderous.

But the third time I removed mail from Black's tin box, I decided against shredding it. I opened it instead.

The bill was from a company called Poo-B-Gone. I blame the name of the company because my curiosity got the best of me. As I slid a knife over the back of the sealed envelope, I discovered that the Black family paid twenty-five dollars a week to have the employees of Poo-B-Gone pick up their Yorkie's dog poop. *Are you kidding me?* That yippy, oversized rat's poop is probably no bigger than a tootsie roll, and they needed to hire someone to pick up tootsie rolls from their manicured lawn, which by the way, was also hired to maintain.

Another piece of mail indicated that they possessed a retirement fund with Fidelity. And as I unfolded the statement, it showed they'd earned five hundred thousand dollars in the last quarter. My family was struggling to pay for my son's lawyer, all his traffic violations and fines, and mounting credit card debt. I was cutting coupons and buying generic brand groceries.

Our lawn was crunchy and brown as it suffered because we stopped constantly watering it. At night, we turned off the air to simply try to save a few dollars while just across the street, our neighbors, who used to be close friends, had a half million dollars sitting in a fund and increasing every day. Furthermore, their delinquent son was selling my delinquent son drugs as they partied in their olympic-size pool. *What the fuck!*

My intrusive, lawbreaking adventure which at first created a surge of joyful, innocent-enough adrenaline, was now causing me a tremendous amount of stress and resentment. *How could life be so wrong? Where was Karma? Why did they seem to prosper as I watched my family sink? How is that even fair?*

If Karma and the universe were unwilling to do anything to correct this ridiculousness, then I was sure glad that I was up for the task. I had the balls. I just wasn't sure at the time what game my balls were going to play in. After I shredded the poop bill, I hid that investment statement in the secret compartment built into the bottom of our pool table. I needed to overthink this bit.

***

Hours later, as I'm still laying in my jail cell, I listen to the other women around me loudly snore and occasionally scream in their dreams. Sleep is playing a game with me. A game of tag in which I'm always just an arm's length away and I can't quite catch her. She always seems to be just inches from my grasp.

I shake my head. I'm only human. I make mistakes and do things I regret.

My Witch voice inquires, *but do you really regret it?*

She has a point. I don't completely regret it. Even as I sit rotting in a smelly prison cell, I feel like my actions were warranted.

Sometimes, I need to ask myself if it was worth the jail time, and I hear the Witch respond for me, *totally*.

I'm overthinking what I did with the investment statement that I stole. The bold dollar amount at the bottom of the statement caused great turmoil in my soul. Life wasn't fair. But since I wasn't a complainer but more of a doer, I decided to do something about it.

That night after I stole the statement, guilt and a little something else was festering in me, and following my third glass of wine, I looked over at William. He was sitting in his usual spot in front of the TV, and I was in my usual spot with my nose in a book. The kids were out socializing with their friends.

I cleared my throat. After being together for so long, William recognized that I was attempting to get his attention. He swallowed a sip of his whiskey neat before replying. "Yes, Eve?"

His voice had a bit of an edge to it, an irritation like he didn't appreciate his attention being pulled away from his game. However, the whiskey was softening his edge. It was his third glass as well.

"So, I did something. Something I kind of need to talk to someone about."

"You aren't catholic, Eve. You don't need to confess your sins to me or anyone else."

"But I want to. I need to. It isn't so much of a sin as a wrongdoing that I want to finalize." I sat up a little straighter. I had his attention, and I needed his help. Normally, I confided in Frank. Frank was the one who knew all my secrets, but this secret wasn't for my law-abiding best friend. I'd saved this secret for my less than moral husband. "I stole a financial statement from the Blacks' mailbox. It's a lot of money and if anyone knows how to steal someone's money, it's you, William."

"I'm not sure if that is a compliment or not. But more importantly what the hell, Eve? Why would you steal their mail?" He muted the game, which implied that I'd earned his full attention at the moment.

"I don't know why I did it. And that isn't the point. Removing it from their mailbox is complete, but what I want to discuss is what to do with it now. I thought maybe you could slide some of it out of their account and into ours. They owe us, William. Clive is the reason Hudson is doing drugs. Their family should have to pay for all the shit that we're going through. It isn't fair."

He shook his head and took a sip out of his rocks glass. "First of all, that's completely illegal. And secondly, it would be traced in a matter of seconds. No thanks." I knew William was furious about all the money Hudson's addiction was costing our family, from the legal fines to the lawyer fees. If anything made William upset, it was money. He was greedy, and I knew my suggestion got his wheels spinning, even if it *was* illegal.

Perhaps it was the alcohol or the fact that he was finally paying me some long-overdue attention, but in that moment of vulnerability and asking for help, I decided our dry spell was over. I needed his help, and I knew he needed me. Sex would convince him. Wild, uninhibited sex would persuade him to cooperate with me. I stood up from my corner of the couch and slowly, seductively dropped my sweatpants to the floor revealing William's favorite pair of black, lace thong underwear. When I pulled the sweatshirt over my head, I wasn't wearing a bra. Very slowly, I pulled out the ponytail holder from my hair to loosen my messy bun, and I shook my hair loose like I'd seen sexy models do during expensive car commercials. The energy in the room changed as William's eyes were glued to my naked, exposed body. I gained his *full* attention.

I swayed my hips to the left, then to the right in a thrusting motion, earning an eyebrow raise. After I swung my ass toward him, I bent over and picked up my sweatshirt with my fingertips. Looking over my left hip, I flashed William a seductive grin. He swallowed a large lump in his throat.

Confidence was sexy. That was the first lesson I learned from one of William's notorious Valentine's gifts.

"Pole dancing? What the hell! What makes you think we even *want* to learn how to pole dance?" Becca was the first to vocalize our shared opinion. She was appalled. Mitchell and William had given Becca and I both gift certificates for pole dancing lessons at a local strip club.

For how intelligent and successful our husbands were in the business world, they were the exact opposites at home. Normally, William followed Hallmarks' rules on gift giving, and I was sure the CEOs of Hallmark had not suggested pole dancing as an appropriate Valentine's gift. They had no clue what Becca and I would deem acceptable Valentine's Day gifts. "I can't even dance the two step." I wasn't exaggerating.

Previously, the husbands had advised us not to make plans for that evening because they had a surprise for us. Becca and I had giggled that we were being whisked away to a warm beach where the four of us would enjoy a kid-free weekend. Of course, that is what we would've planned or suggested had they asked. But instead, we were asked to dress nicely and be ready by six o'clock. The kids would stay at our house, babysitting and supervising each other. Mitchell had grilled us a delicious steak dinner while William ordered and purchased a three-tier cake and chocolate covered strawberries. As the candles flickered on the dining room table, bottles of wine chilled in a crystal ice bucket. The lights were dimmed, and Zac Brown sang a ballad throughout the in-home speaker system.

Looking back on that night, the men were bonding and trying hard to influence how we reacted to our gift. The purpose of the romantic atmosphere was to influence our acceptance of their gift. I assume they knew it might not be completely well received. However, even though we were initially appalled by our husband's self-serving gift, Becca and I did schedule our pole dancing lessons at 'Howdy' and enjoyed every Tuesday night with our instructors, Tad D. Wild and Cinnamon Sweet. We arrived two hours before the lesson to have dinner and down a few drinks to loosen our inhibitions. After filling our bellies and throwing back some very strong Vodka Tonics, Becca and I would stretch, sweat and giggle for another hour as we learned to back bend, chair spin and flamingo pose.

Obviously, William and Mitchell purchased those gifts for their own selfish sexual fantasies, but after Becca and I got over the hump – pun intended – of being deceived by the romantic candle-lit dinner and grossed out by imagining the insides of the local strip club, we had a blast. Those talented women made pole dancing appear easy and effortless as they gripped a steady pole and twirled magically around it. The pole seems to do all the work. *Incorrect.* My core was never tighter than after those eight lessons. My thighs lost a few inches, and my confidence level increased. William and I have never had issues connecting under the sheets, but now we connected in the bathroom, once in the garage, and several times on the floor in the living room. Those lessons were invaluable.

Even now, looking back on that evening when I convinced William to disobey the law, I'm awed by the influence a naked woman's body has over a horny, middle-aged man. This wasn't the first time and wouldn't be the last time that I used sex to get what I wanted, but it was the first time I realized how easy it was to manipulate men by using sexual favors. Sex is powerful. I used sex to convince a man to disobey the law and do something that, if he were caught, would get him fired and most likely end up in jail. So, yes, sex is power.

When I'd finished giving William the blowjob of his life, I wiped the spit from the side of my mouth and laid my head on his hip as he continued to breathe deeply.

"Dang, Eve. Why don't you do *that* more often?" I was completely amazed that my bright, intelligent husband couldn't see what I was doing. Even more reason to drive straight ahead with my plan.

Honestly, it didn't take much convincing for William to jump on board with the illegal bank transfer. I think that after his fifth whiskey neat, he was feeling invincible and kind of wanted to see if he could pull it off. In under an hour, he created a fake charity account overseas. It would appear that the Blacks donated a large sum of money to Sisters in Arms.

"Wait, we don't know their password."

It was as if he was daring me to see how far I was willing to go. I always picked dare.

"I'm sure we can figure it out. They were our best friends for years. It'll probably be something obvious." And I was right – it was Clive's birthdate. Furthermore, the security questions were just as easy for someone that knows and listens to their friends. Mitchell's high school mascot was a mustang, and his first car was a Ford pickup truck. It was almost *too* easy. Using my half-full positivity, I read it as a sign that it was meant to be.

Before he pushed the 'transfer now' button, he voiced one last reservation that he had about what he was about to do. "I'm not saying I don't wanna do this. I do, but stealing his parent's money isn't really hurting Clive. Slicing him up and chopping his body into a million pieces sounds more of a fair consequence. However, I have no idea how to get away with murdering someone, but I do know how to steal money." Not all of William's clients were upstanding, honorable citizens.

After we transferred the money from the Fidelity account to a charity overseas, I waited for the guilt to set in, but it didn't come. I cared more about the untraceable fact and wanted Mitchell and Becca to feel some stress, worry, and pain. It was completely vindictive, and that's why I was surprised when the guilt never arrived.

For weeks and weeks after that night, I'd recreated the mind-blowing blow jobs, and since my knees were getting rug burns, I had to stop removing my sweatpants. He didn't seem to mind. He was getting what he wanted, and I righted a wrong. Win-win.

***

So, I overthink. There are some things that I'm willing to admit that I did. I'm totally guilty of stealing thousands and thousands of dollars from our friends. Additionally, I can admit that I vandalized their property more than once. Okay, probably at least a dozen times. The poop smearing still makes me giggle. Wish I could've seen Clive's face when he realized that his precious Corvette was covered in poo. When he opened his car door to race to the nearest car wash, his fingers would've slid into the hidden shit caked under his door handle. Wish I could've seen that!

Lastly, I can admit that I enjoy revenge. It evolved into an addiction. *My name is Evelyn Stanton, and I'm an addict.*

Chapter 24

now

"Hello?"

"Eve, it's Mitchell." His deep, husky voice surprises me.

When a guard interrupted my game-show-watching marathon, I assumed the phone call would be from Frank with some trivial news about my case. I welcome the distraction but am taken off guard by Mitchell's voice.

I don't know what to say. When I'm put on the spot in any situation, I freeze. I don't blink, breathe or move while willing myself to go back in time to the *before*. Of course, I realize that freezing just puts off the inevitable, but it allows me a brief second to comprehend what is happening. And in this case, I listen to the heavy breathing of the father of the son I'm charged with murdering. This is the definition of awkward.

"Eve, I'm not an idiot. I'm aware that my kid was no saint. The crowd that he spent his time with recently didn't have the cleanest records. Clive was messed up and involved in some bad shit." When a big, strong, muscular man starts to cry, all your defenses go into shock. I hear a loud painful sob, like a lone coyote in the night. During our years of friendship, I don't recall Mitchell ever showing any emotion but joy and amusement. He'd always been so happy-go-lucky; he never seemed stressed or anxious about anything. This was a side of Mitchell I've never seen. "But, Eve, I know you didn't kill him. You couldn't have."

"Wow. Thanks, Mitchell. I'm not sure what to say." I'm being completely honest with him because I can't be anything but honest when I hear the pain in his voice.

"He loved you. You were like a second mom to him. Probably more of a mother than Becca ever was." I notice he used a past tense verb, but I assume it's because Clive was dead. He sniffs back a large wad of snot from his nose into the back of his throat. "There's no way you could've done this."

"Mitchell, hearing you say that truly means a great deal to me. I'm so glad to know that after all the crap we've been through, that you and Becca know me well enough to arrive at that conclusion."

He clears his throat before he responds. "Eve, I know you've been locked up for a month or two so you probably don't know this, but I have no idea what Becca thinks. She left me. She told me that I was a different man after Clive's death. I was no longer the man she married. No fun anymore. Depressing." Instead of the sadness that I heard at the beginning of the phone call, I detect a hint of anger and hurt coming from his voice. "Well, of course, I am. My only son died. It would be completely heartless of me *not* to be changed by this excruciating experience which led me to question her about why *she* didn't seem upset or heartbroken. And you know what she said? *'Well, he wasn't my kid.'* She was his stepmom for God's sake! She was the only mother he remembered. I thought she loved him. Do you know that a week after Clive died, she asked me to join her and the Anfinsons for dinner? And after I refused to go, she was pissed because she had to cancel. She screamed at me that no one cancels with the Anfinsons, because they were influential pillars of the community. It was unheard of. A month later, she packed her bags and moved out." I hear sobbing on the other end.

"Wow, Mitchell. I had no idea. I'm so sorry. You've been through a lot in a very short period of time. I wish there was something I could do or say to make you feel better."

Hearing someone on the other end of a phone break down makes you feel about as helpless as an elephant in quicksand. If I was sitting next to him, I would've draped my arm over his shoulders or pulled him into a hug. When you aren't physically together, giving support is difficult. Mitchell is a giant teddy bear who likes to have a good time. He is always in a good mood and could find the positive in any situation. As his old friend, it's hard to hear him so vulnerable and sad.

"Did you know she didn't love me, Eve?"

I'm surprised by his question. "What?"

"Becca. Did you know that she didn't love me? I don't think she ever loved me or Clive. When we got engaged, my siblings warned me not to marry her. They thought she was marrying me for my money, and I guess they were right." He blows his nose before he continues. "There is about one million dollars missing from one of our investment accounts. I didn't even notice. It happened before all this crap, and I didn't see it. Did she ever mention anything to you, Eve? I know you two were close."

"No. Mitch, I had no idea. She never said a word to me."

"I didn't think so. You guys just stopped hanging out with us, so I figured maybe she'd hit on William or something. She was an enormous flirt. Clive even told me that she came onto him a couple of times. I never believed him, but now I wonder if he was telling the truth. I guess I'll never know." He sniffles some snot into the back of his throat. "She can have the money. She always cared more about money than I did. I just want my old life back. I want Clive back. I miss my son. We had some good times, the seven of us, didn't we, Eve?"

I can hear a slight ounce of positivity return in his voice. "Yes, we did, Mitch."

"Well, there is another reason I'm calling today, and I wanted you to hear this from me, Eve. As soon as Clive's death was considered suspicious and not a suicide anymore, the police issued a warrant for his phone and its records. His messages, texts, emails, everything. And there were some very worrisome messages from William."

"My William?" I don't know why I feel the need to clarify this fact and add possession to my husband's name.

"Yes, your husband, and my former best friend. The messages were deleted and had to be retrieved from the phone company's records. The first few messages revealed that William purchased several packages of gummies, a few joints, and then a few uppers. His usage steadily increased. The week before Clive died, William ordered a date rape drug, a roofie. After that order, William sent some very threatening messages to Clive. From both his phone and email address, he fired off some frenzied messages. He told him he was going to kill him and chop him up into little pieces. It was very descriptive. It didn't make much sense compared to the rest of their exchanges, but drugs change people." There is a small pause in our conversation as I allow this news to seep in. Mitchell takes a deep breath before he tells me, "I'm sorry, Eve, but I delivered this information to the police. I truly hope this will help you earn your freedom, but it focuses the investigation on your husband...my best friend. I can't believe this has happened."

Chapter 25

then

After Clive was found dead, the local police knocked on every neighbor's door, asking routine questions. But no matter how ordinary the inquiries were, the rumors spread like wildfire that afternoon. You could almost hear the buzz bouncing off the wet pavement in the cul-de-sac. Whispered conversations were shared over picket fences, text messages blew up phones, and phone calls to family near and far spread the shocking news of a local tragedy that had taken place in our own quiet, little neighborhood.

He died from carbon monoxide poisoning. I wonder if the police think it was suicide or an accident.

He's always been a troubled boy. Growing up in that household where his parents hosted party after party. It's a wonder that he lived as long as he did.

Why was he living above their garage in the first place?

As soon as Clive's death was considered suspicious, the police returned to each house and asked the neighbors to write a formal statement. We needed to include the last time we saw Clive and what we were doing the night that he died.

Evelyn Sarae Stanton, age 45. I live kiddy-corner from the Black Family at 1234 South Elgin Road. My husband was home with me on the night in question.

I was supposed to give facts, not opinions. Descriptions without personal insight.

*I didn't see Clive Black on October 19, 2021; however, I did hear his car
stereo thumping to the beat of his music around three that afternoon. I'd been
working in my home office when he arrived home from school. I did not visibly
see or talk to him.*

*Before my daughter, Hazel, left to stay overnight at Peggy Hunt's house, I
fed her supper, homemade Chicken Parmesan. She left around five. You can
verify this information with Peggy's parents. My son, Hudson, has been a
patient at Tallgrass's Addiction Care Center for the past three weeks. He was
there that evening. You can verify that information with the clinic.*

As soon as Hazel headed out for the evening, I'd plopped down in front
of the fireplace to read my book. A few hours later, when William arrived
home, he was in a chatty, upbeat mood. Since he was a little later than usual,
I assumed that he'd be annoyed that he had to work late on a Friday night.
Because I had checked his location on our phone GPS, I noticed that his
last client meeting had taken him clear across town, which would give him
an extra thirty minutes to commute home. But I was wrong – the traffic
and working late didn't dampen his mood. William walked in, happy as a
clam. Humming was the telltale sign that he was in a good mood, and I
recognized the beat of a Justin Timberlake song. Something had pleased
him immensely. Maybe his late client meeting had gone well.

"Hey, honey. Sorry, I'm late." He removed his overcoat and hung it in the
entryway. "Just started snowing. Guess I'll be shoveling in the morning.
Did you hear we are supposed to get three to four inches?" Fall in the
Black Hills is often sprinkled with a white blanket of snow. It never sticks
around long, so no one is too concerned. But when December arrives,
winter becomes a whole other monster.

My husband, William, arrived home from work around seven. He had a client meeting after work. I'm not sure which client, but you could check with his secretary.

"Dinner is in the oven." I wasn't sure what had brought on his chipper mood, so I was leery. He hadn't been visibly happy in my presence for months. Our marriage seemed to be at a stagnant stage, and we were more like roommates than spouses. Neither of us sought each other out for company. I blamed all the drama on dealing with Hudson's addiction as the culprit. We were mentally exhausted from all the stress and worry. When we didn't have to focus on it, we shut down. Took a break from feeling or pleasing anyone. It was how we were remaining sane. I identified it as a chapter in our lives. Not an ending. We'd turn the page soon and things would improve. I needed to be patient.

The floor plan in our home allows the people sitting at the kitchen table to see and communicate with the people relaxing in the living room. It was one of the features that we loved about this house when we bought it. When he sat down to dig into his meal, I commented on his working meeting. "Your meeting must have gone well at Crave?"

As he took a bite of his Chicken Parmesan, he almost choked. Worry and shock filled his eyes. I jumped out of my chair because I misinterpreted his expression as he was choking on his food. He quickly regained his composure as I aggressively swatted his back.

"I'm okay." He tried to shrug me off. Relieved that it was a false alarm, I walked to the kitchen to retrieve him a glass of water. "Sorry about that. Must have gone down the wrong pipe."

"Drink this glass of water just to get things moving." I placed the glass in front of him. He looked into the clear glass of water and then back at me.

"You didn't drop some poison in here, did you?" He flashed me a grin to suggest he was joking, but I knew that it was a legitimate concern.

"Don't be silly." I waved off his joke and turned to the sink to wash my hands. "What client did you meet at Crave? And I'm surprised you didn't eat supper there. It's your favorite restaurant."

He returned his eyes back to the small TV that he had turned on in the kitchen.

"Yeah, it was a quick meeting."

"You were there for two hours. How is that quick?"

"What's with the third degree?" His tone was sharp. I had touched a nerve.

Around four o'clock, I'd looked at his location to see if I should hold off on dinner. Hazel and I were hungry, and the recipe indicated that I needed an hour for prep and baking. I wanted her to be fed rather than arriving hungry at her friend's house for a slumber party.

"No third degree. Just a typical question that any caring wife asks her husband when he returns home after a hard day at the office. Unless he has something to hide?"

His eyebrows creased. He didn't like arguing, and I apparently stomped all over his good mood. "Sorry. I didn't sleep much last night so I must be edgy." He stood up and walked toward me. As his muscular arms wrapped around me, I leaned into the familiar embrace. It had been a long time since we had touched, but it felt comforting and natural. "Sorry, honey. Let's relax tonight. I don't want to fight. Where's our Little Storm?"

"She's sleeping at Peggy's tonight."

"Oh, that's right. Good, just you and me. Want to catch up on Yellowstone? Let me get you a fresh glass of wine while you find out what episode we left off on."

We sipped wine and snuggled on the couch like a couple of normal forty-year-olds.

My husband and I watched two or three episodes of Yellowstone before going to bed around eleven that night. I didn't wake up until the next morning when I heard the sirens next door.

Chapter 26

now

Dear Hazel,

I want you to know that I love you. Things are extremely difficult right now. I don't know if anything could've prepared our family for this, and I totally understand you hating me for causing this immense level of drama. I hate myself, too.

If you ever need to talk or vent your frustrations, grab a pen and paper. Scribble it all down. I promise it will help.

xxoo – Mom

***

Writing a letter to Hazel is painful. There were numerous drafts. I want to say I'll always be there for her, but I can't promise that. I want to tell her that I'm only a phone call away, but that isn't true either. I want to tell her to text me, but William refuses to pay for the texting service because he thinks it might do more harm than good. Not being able to communicate with my children breaks my heart, but a small part of me understands. Plus, I know everyone that I love is livid with me, hurt by me, and disappointed in me. Even though I know I don't deserve to be here, it pains me to think about what they are going through. I don't completely blame them. The evidence must point somewhere, and the majority of it currently points in my direction. Someone must take the blame. That's how our society operates.

Honestly, Mitchell's phone call sparked a painful awakening that I was not mentally prepared for – my absence from my normal daily life and how my loved ones would cope without me. What could happen, what would be said. However, even the most detailed and well-thought-out plans have holes. You can't predict how other people will react. As a planner, I forecasted reactions based on past experiences and my own knowledge, but there is always room for interpretation. So, Becca's walking out on her marriage isn't something I'd banked on. I hadn't predicted that coming. And even though it's out of my control, I need to think about how I can use this new revelation to my benefit. Many developments are happening without knowledge or planning.

So far, I have missed Hazel's first high school fall formal dance that she had planned on attending with a boy named Phil Loving from her algebra class. During the second week of school, he had asked her to be his date before she even knew there was a fall dance. Of course, because she was giddy and beyond excited about the dance, we started dress shopping before the temperatures dropped below ninety. That was all *before*.

"Mom, do you like the sound of Hazel Loving? Peggy thinks it sounds like a stripper name. I wonder if hyphenating it would help it roll off the tongue better. Hazel Stanton-Loving. Yep, hyphenated." Her constant chatter filled up the space and time in between dress shops. Between paying attention to my driving and trying to keep up with the conversation, I was at a loss.

"Mom, do you think I should wear my hair up or down?" Hazel pulled down the passenger side visor so that she could visualize her inquiry. She gathered her curls into her hands and twisted her hair into a bun. Then she smiled at her reflection and pressed out her pouty lips. Before I could even think about uttering a response, she answered her own question. "Wait. It'll depend on my dress. One shoulder, hair down. No sleeves, hair up. I learned that tip online. Maybe I'll ask Phil for his opinion. But I don't want to be the girlfriend that does whatever her man tells her to do. Nope. That ain't me."

She paused long enough for me to ask, "You're his girlfriend? When did that happen?"

"Oh! It isn't official yet. We're just talking, but if he plays his cards right, he'll be my first boyfriend."

"Lucky guy." I rolled my eyes at her constant chatter. Teenage girls and their train of thought were hard to follow.

At the time, I thought it was going to require a fair amount of patience to listen to my teenager talk nonstop about her first crush. The end of October seemed like a long time away. But now, realizing that I missed her epic first official date because I'm living behind bars, my heart breaks.

***

Dear Mom –

You're right – I'm mad at you, but not for the reason you think.

I know you said Frank advised you not to talk about what happened, but I need to.

At first, I was too shocked to process what had happened. My mom, my own mother, was arrested for murder? It felt like a horror movie, and even though I never signed up for it, I was cast in a starring role.

In my heart, I knew you couldn't have done it, but everyone, even Dad, was telling me that you did it. I felt like my sense of reasoning was completely botched. I had a hard time believing anything my heart felt; my eyes and ears were telling me that my heart couldn't be trusted. I started to believe it. When I saw you in the courtroom that day, I couldn't look at you. My heart broke hearing the charges against you. I felt abandoned by you. You were charged with something so unforgivable that I couldn't trust you anymore with my heart. Told myself to move on. Forget you. You and the drama weren't worth the heartache.

Dad seemed to be doing the same thing. Because the media was insanely focused on this crime, he started working a few days from home. We didn't want to leave our house. We pulled the shades, kept the lights off, and kept our heads down. Honestly, at first, it was good for both of us. We leaned on each other and survived together. And Becca...she helped too.

I've been forced to learn so much about the harsh reality that is real life. Although I felt I needed to 'turtle' to protect myself after your arrest, I also learned that I was only delaying the inevitable. I need to hurt, I need to feel the loss, and I need to use all my senses.

And I did. I started seeing, hearing and feeling the truth. It was hard and painful. But with knowledge, there is control.

Mom, I'm just mad that you aren't here.

I do love you – Hazel

***

When I finish reading Hazel's letter, so many feelings pour out of me. I'm relieved that Hazel is now questioning her initial reaction, but I don't know what to think of Hazel mentioning that William believed I did it and her subtle mention of Becca. I ask Jilli to read the letter. Sometimes, an outsider can read between the lines better than someone living in it. It is always good to obtain another perspective.

"Who's Becca?"

"Becca is Clive's stepmom, our neighbor. We were good friends before everything happened and I ended up here. Probably broke Hazel's heart when she stopped coming around. She was like an aunt or second mom to Hazel."

"Hmmmm...a second mom wouldn't just abandon a kid or her family when the shit got deep. My momma used to say, 'don't make excuses for nasty people. You can't put a flower in an asshole and call it a vase,' but she also claimed that she drank Vodka because it was filled with vitamins. So, what the hell did she know?"

I've always told myself that I shouldn't ask for someone's opinion if I wasn't looking for the truth. If I want nonsense, I'll scroll Facebook and believe that everyone's life but mine is all roses and daisies, filled with celebrations, positivity, and affection. On social media, there are no family quarrels about whose turn it is to take out the trash or wash the dishes. No one yells profanities when they feel unappreciated or unvalidated in their role. No, I appreciate Jilli's candor, even if she's right and recognized something I didn't.

Jilli rests the letter on her lap and gives me a focused stare. "You know it isn't your fault, Snow White. You didn't cause his addiction, and you can't control it." Jilli is wiser than she pretends to be. While she portrays a hard, rigid exterior, she is so insightful as my friend and confidant.

"Jilli, I really appreciate your kind words. But that's it – they are just words."

"Maybe so. They are just words until you believe them. Then they are powerful."

Chapter 27

now

"Evelyn Sarae Stanton, inmate 9343162-506, you have a visitor."

Because Frank had been to visit the day before, I doubt that he was my visitor. Plus, he had informed me of his weekend plans: binge-watching all of his shows, filing random motions on my behalf, and drinking too much – again on my behalf. Even though he tried to make it sound like a lame, boring weekend of mundane activities, I'm envious that he can make choices on how to spend his free time. That liberty is stripped from me.

I jump down from my top bunk, where I was reading *The Outsiders*, for the third time, and slip on my jail-issued flip flops. Jilli had already been summoned to the visitor's lounge, so I was enjoying some alone time in our box.

As I follow Cowboy Brandon, who insists on the formalities of his job, I decide that he must have a type A personality - extremely organized, punctual, and a driven rule-follower. He doesn't participate in small talk or smile, which I assume he believes are insignificant tasks. Additionally, I'm sure he probably prefers only right angles on his desk. He doesn't like to lose and never disobeys rules. By-the-book-Brandon. On the outside of this cold, hard building, we would've gotten along well.

When I enter the visitor's lounge, I don't recognize anyone, so I glance back at Brandon for direction. He's whispering with the guard stationed in the room. After their short conversation, he takes a few steps toward me and turns to me to explain, "Your visitor is using the restroom. She'll be right back." He clears his throat and returns his attention to his co-worker. He's over my dilemma.

I stroll to an open table to wait for my *female* visitor to return. As I glance around the room, I witness a sample of every possible emotion. In a small corner on the opposite side of the room, I notice Jilli sitting with an older, gray-haired man. She doesn't get many visitors, so we were both surprised when she was summoned. Hopefully, she'll fill me in later. She catches my eye, and I give her a little excited wave, which I realize as soon as I do it isn't appropriate jail behavior. As her eyelids forcefully close, she shakes her head at me. I've received that same look from my children when I've done something to embarrass them. Her male visitor glances in my direction and gives me a polite nod in acknowledgment. I feel like they've been talking about me.

Sitting at the table to my right is a woman that everyone refers to as 'Pebbles,' because she always wears her long, auburn hair in a ponytail on the very top of her head. I don't even know her real name, but I think that is why inmates like nicknames. They don't want anyone to know the real them. Pebble's face is covered in blotchy red spots as her nostrils flare open and close. She is doing everything in her power not to explode. Whatever her male visitor reported to her has upset her and had the guards watching her table with a keen sense of interest. Silently, I pray she'll be able to keep her temper in check because if she doesn't and she loses her shit, the guards will usher us all back into our cells. Closing the visiting hours early.

To my left is a lifer, which is a jail term defining an inmate that will never be allowed outside of our cement walled and barbed wire facility.

Suzy-screams-in-her-sleep is serving back-to-back life sentences for driving drunk and killing a family of four. I'm not sure if her real name is Suzy or not. Before her imprisonment, she was a physician assistant and engaged to Kevin Costner's son, whom she met while he was staying at his dad's place in the Black Hills – that's the rumor, anyway. Her famous ex-fiancee's father influenced her nickname, which stems from his movie, *Dances with Wolves*. No matter her name, she is visibly broken as big, heavy tears fall from her eyes. Her visitor looks a lot like her, same button nose, sky blue eyes and big toothy smile so I assume it's her sister. They are both crying uncontrollably.

Directly in front of my table is Big Betty, who is surrounded by her four children. They all are laughing obnoxiously. Even though her table is disruptive and a bit over-the-top, no one messes with Big Betty. Everyone turns the other cheek and allows her a moment to forget where she lives. *Giggle, Big Betty. If you can find something to giggle about, do it.* I still don't know what she did to end up here. She seems like everyone's grandmother.

When the ladies' restroom door opens and I'm able to comprehend what my eyes are revealing to me, my breath catches in my throat. It's Hazel.

In the month or so that I haven't seen her, I could swear she grew. She's all legs. At fourteen years old, she is full-blown in the awkward teenage body stage where different parts of her body grow before others. For her, her legs are currently sucking up all the growth hormone. She is a natural beauty, which I'm relieved that she hasn't realized yet. She isn't interested in makeup, tight crop tops or doing feminine things to impress and attract attention from the opposite sex. William and I had been grateful for that fact. Hazel is drama-free. The next thing that I notice is the sadness that lines her puffy eyes. They're lined with dark circles, while the white of her eyes are pink. She's been crying, and unfortunately, I'd passed down the ugly crier gene to my daughter. Her lips press downward into a depressing frown.

It requires all of my strength not to leap from the table and run to her with my arms outstretched as wide as they will go. Every fiber of my being wants to squeeze her so tightly that all the agony she feels pours out of her and into me. My eyes dart to where Brandon remains standing. Even though he is a rookie and doesn't know me well, he knows what I'm thinking and shakes his head. I remind myself that I can hug her at the end of our visit – that is, if she allows me to.

For her first visit to the jail, Hazel is dressed casually. Her curly brown hair is pulled into a high ponytail; a pair of small dainty daisy earrings decorate her earlobes. The oversized, heather gray sweatshirt that she is wearing is a hand-me-down, or, as Hudson claimed, more of a stolen-from-your-brother sweatshirt. Across the chest, it reads, 'Gold Diggers Baseball.' She chose her favorite ripped jeans and a pair of Nike tennis shoes. A classic, low maintenance Hazel outfit. During my absence, I'm glad that some things haven't changed.

Finally, our eyes meet as she scans the room looking for me. A quick, fleeting half-grin rises on her lips before it quickly fades away, making me feel as if I imagined it. As she strolls towards me, I straighten my back. If I stand up – which would be a normal, polite gesture outside of jail – the guards will read my action as a sign of aggression, so I remain seated. I hope that they informed her of the hugging and touching rule. I don't want her to feel alienated from me, her own mother. While all these worries and concerns speed through my brain, I try to remember to smile. I'm sure it looks like I'm having a stroke as one side of my face cooperates, and the other side is still processing the shock of seeing her.

As soon as her butt is planted across from me on the hard, cold metal chair, her beautiful sparkling eyes look straight into mine. Because I thought she was angry with me and the situation we were in, I'm not expecting to recognize her unwavering love and support. Her hand-written letter had indicated a change of heart, but I've always believed that actions speak louder than words. I'm caught off guard again. My daughter, who has always been wise beyond her years simply because she was born with an old soul, now has a cracked, damaged heart. Her young life has been scarred by tragedy and pain. This realization causes a large lump to form in my suddenly dry throat. Parents only want their children to lead happy, healthy lives protected in a glass, bullet-proof case where no harm can penetrate. So, sitting across from Hazel and seeing her visibly upset by our situation hurts me. The corners of her eyes grow tears that gently race down her cheeks and land like raindrops on her sweatshirt. My body and soul want to reach across the table and wrap my arms around her while whispering that everything and everyone will be okay. My hands want to stroke her soft, wavy curls, petting her into a calmer state. *Everything will be okay, honey.*

But I'm not allowed to touch her yet. If I do, we'll be publicly humiliated – if you consider the commons area in a jail public – as our embraced bodies are torn apart and removed from the visitor's room. The misery that it would cause us both isn't worth disobeying the rules. I'd never imagined how this situation would hurt her. All this time I'd only been visualizing the end result. I take a very deep breath and pray that the words that seep out of my mouth will bring her some comfort, because the pressure I feel in my heart is so intense that I struggle to choose the most effective words.

"Hazel..." Because I can't say things like, 'don't talk about anything incriminating' or 'they might be recording this conversation,' I must convey these sentences by my tone of voice and my solid eye contact. My body language must convey what I need her to understand.

"I know, Mom." She acknowledges my concern with a quick blink and a head bow, but she doesn't let me finish. I am again reminded that I don't give my own kids enough credit. She is smarter than all four of our Stanton family members combined. "They told me all the rules, but I need to talk to you about something that's bothering me." Under her breath to emphasize the next statement, she whispers, "It has nothing to do with your case."

However, the fact that she says that sentence makes my ears perk up, which I'm afraid will also alert the staff that reviews these taped conversations. But maybe that is her point.

This time I rush forward with what I need to say. "Hazel, even though you look like an adult and are wise beyond your years, there are some things that you aren't ready to hear." I feel the normal, motherly need to protect my girl from the harsh realities of adulthood. No child is ever prepared to hear that someone they love and worship is flawed. Hazel has always been a few steps ahead when it comes to maturity for her age. Adults found her vocabulary and knowledge entertaining, but as her mother I wanted her to remain naive, to never lose her childlike innocence. So even from behind bars, I want to protect her as much as I still can, even more so than ever. I try to gently steer this conversation towards a light-hearted mood. "Tell me something new."

"Like the fact that Dad's having an affair?" Those six words escape her mouth with great pain. As her voice cracks and a tear races down her cheek, I observe that she is trying with all her pride to be strong. Well, there goes my good intention of sheltering her. It lasted about a hot second.

Before I could process an appropriate response, these words pop from my lips, "What? How do you know?" I'm not surprised by *what* she said, I'm surprised that she knows. William and I have been having marital problems for most of our marriage, but we grew even farther apart when Hudson's addiction escalated and the tension in our household was bursting at the seams. Instead of bringing us together as a united front, the drama pushed us apart. However, for my only daughter, who is devastated that she had to be the one to break the news to me, I mustered up a pained expression.

"Hazel, please don't worry about your dad and me. You need to concentrate on yourself right now. Your dad and I will figure it out after this mess is behind us. Okay, honey?" I should know my own daughter; she isn't about to let me distract her to another topic. "I want to hear about the school dance with Phil Loving."

She ignores my inquiry. "But it's not just that. I think he's seeing Becca. Becca Black." Tears trickle down her cheeks. She's trying so hard to be strong for me. My poor, sweet daughter.

"Honey, if I could hug you right now, I would, but I can't. We must wait until the very end of our visit, and it must be quick, but you know I'd love to hold you and comfort you. I'm sorry you're hurting."

"Mom, did you even *hear* me? I think Dad is sleeping with Becca. Your friend, Becca. Why aren't you more hurt, angrier, or more surprised by what I'm telling you?" As Hazel's voice rose an octave, she earned the guard's attention. I smile at him to assure him that everything is okay at our table. His eyes meet mine before he continues scanning the room for suspicious behavior. I suppose this is the type of conversation that happens in this room, so the rise in her voice didn't surprise him much.

"Hazel, of course, it breaks my heart that your dad found another woman to comfort him during this turmoil, but being an adult is messy. It's not always black and white." After those words leave my mouth, I almost giggle at the use of 'black.' *Ironic.* Frank will get a kick of that when I tell him about my conversation with Hazel.

"When I mentioned my suspicions to Hudson, he admitted that he already knew." *That* fact surprises me, and unfortunately, my facial expression reflects my shock. I shouldn't be surprised since my children have been raised to be aware of other people and their feelings. They're quite sensitive and thoughtful. Hazel's index finger points straight at me. "*That* tidbit received more attention from you than me telling you about your own husband sleeping with your best friend. Seems odd, Mom. Do you care to explain?"

"What did Hudson say exactly?" This is one of the few times that I wish my daughter wasn't so perspective, and that she was more of a self-absorbed teenager.

"He said that one time, when he was leaving Clive's garage apartment, he caught Dad and Becca swapping spit. Really messed him up. He told me that he couldn't even look at Dad anymore. Totally lost respect for anything that came out of his mouth. And, Mom, I found the highlighted credit card bill that you hid in your closet." In a few short minutes, my first conversation that I've had with my daughter in weeks has escalated to the point of no return.

Months ago, I'd highlighted some charges on William's credit card bill because I was curious about them, but I had no concrete facts that he was cheating on me. I hadn't confronted him. That little nagging voice in my head kept repeating, 'if it quacks like a duck, it's a duck.' I had forgotten and obviously got a little side-tracked with my current situation to dwell on that.

"Isn't that what you were thinking when you highlighted the one-hundred-dollar charge to Flowers by Tiffany and the three-hundred-dollar charge to a hotel?" The worry and concern grows on her face, replacing the hint of resentment that I recognized as she sat across from me.

"Oh, honey. I don't know. I didn't know anything for sure, and then everything happened with Hudson, and I forgot about it. It doesn't matter anyway. Your dad and I will figure it all out. One hurdle at a time." I realize that I'm downplaying my husband's infidelity to my daughter, but as her parents, we are her foundation, and to her, everything was crumbling. Someone was murdered across the street from where she lived, her mother was arrested for that crime, and now she learns that her parent's marriage is a sham. Hazel might be the smartest, strongest, and most stubborn member of our family, but she still needs stability to thrive. I didn't want her to worry, and I was being truthful when I said that I needed to focus on my arrest and charges before I even questioned William. Plus, I couldn't stand to lose him right now. I still needed him on my side.

Have you ever wanted to adjust the time on your timeline when you gained knowledge about something that changed the course of your life forever? Just move the dial back three minutes so you could choose a different path? One that would not lead to this conversation. A path with the least amount of pain. A pain that allows you to stay in your naive but happy place. That is exactly where I was sitting. Smack dab in the middle of the road like a deer who suddenly chooses to dash across the highway only to be startled by the bright, blinding headlights of the oncoming car. I was frozen in fear, forge forward or step back to safety. Deer in the headlights. When I found those odd charges on his credit card bill, I willed myself to move.

But instead of taking the easy way out and running from my fear, I shoved the shadow behind me. I moved forward without allowing myself to learn from the new knowledge. To face the challenges of the day and not drown in the pain, I wiped my tears, put on my big girl panties, and smiled as if everything was alright. My children needed me. I'd take care of William's betrayal after I figured out how to save my son.

Subconsciously, I knew it was true. Otherwise, why would I have high-lighted and then hidden the questionable credit card bill? The seeds of doubt grab a hold of distant memories that have been tucked away in my memory vault. They float to the surface begging me to reconsider their filing titles as 'my imagination' or 'she was just a friend' or 'that text must've been from a client' or 'you are being ridiculous.' Now, those filed memories are being scanned under a different eye, a more critical one. He'd been sending and receiving more text messages, which made him excuse himself for privacy. It was the smile that he couldn't conceal. Why is he smiling when he reads a work message? He claimed it was John from work. I'd met John, and he was anything but funny. No wonder he was on his fifth wife, the second one named Sara. William never found him humorous or funny before.

Then there was the time he offered to go grocery shopping.

"Don't seem so shocked. I know where Cub Foods is." He didn't return for two and a half hours that afternoon, with a spring in his step and a big smile on his smug face. My gut clenched, but I didn't have a reason for why.

"You seem proud of yourself."

"Yep, I found everything on the list without even having to call you. It took longer, but I did it."

"It took an extra hour." I know I should be thankful that he helped complete a chore on my never-ending to do list, but I was skeptical. *Where had he been?*

"Yeah, but I found the thyme, whatever the hell that is." He dropped the bags of groceries on the kitchen counter, and then flashed me a grin. "I'm gonna take a quick shower."

He literally showered just before he left. I knew because I had just picked up his damp towel off of the bathroom floor.

***

"Mom, there is one more thing." By using her I-know-more-than-you-know voice, she's trying to draw me back into the present as the memories cloud my vision. I blink several times in a row to bat away the memory fog. "I called one of the merchants that you highlighted on that credit card bill."

"Hazel, how did you know how to do that?"

"CSI shows, duh. They do it all the time."

"How were you able to get any information?"

"Mom, I love you, but you aren't very sneaky. I know your mother's maiden name, your birthday and your favorite passwords. It wasn't very hard."

"Okay, wow. That's a bit scary. Maybe I should use your help in *securing* my information better, but we'll discuss that later. I want to know what you found out. Even though impersonating your own mother is wrong on so many levels, I'm honestly quite impressed."

"Thank you, I think. The credit card company sent me a screenshot of the receipts so I could verify the charges and see the signature. I gave them to Frank. The flower shop shows that the flowers were delivered to the hospital, where Becca works."

"Why did you give them to Frank?" My head is spinning. This isn't part of my plan, b*ut it could work to my benefit, right?* Hazel is trying to help. I know her heart is in the right place, but I can feel a strong migraine coming on. Her first visit, my first time seeing her in weeks, is far more stressful than I'd anticipated.

"Mom, this throws doubt on your case." The first smile that she has formed during our visit grows on her face. Hazel is proud of herself.

"Yes, but it throws suspicion on your dad." I chose my words carefully. I don't want my kids to choose sides between their parents. I'd never make them choose. If they come to the realization on their own, that's different.

"But if he didn't do it, then it wouldn't lead anywhere. It doesn't look good if Dad sends flowers to a woman whose son just died and his wife is arrested for the murder of that son. Even to little old me, it looks more like Becca or Dad have more to gain from Clive's death than you do." Hazel still believes the innocent notion that the truth will set you free. She hasn't seen that sometimes the truth can lock you up and throw away the key.

"I'm sorry, Hazel."

"Nothing for you to be sorry about, Mom, I'm just trying to help you."

Chapter 28

now

"I have this gut instinct."

"Are you sure you aren't just hungry, Frank? You get like this when you're hungry." Frank and I are sitting in the conference room reserved for inmates and their lawyers. We both have a white, Styrofoam cup of lukewarm coffee sitting in front of us, untouched. The room is windowless and void of any color, just a white plastic table, gray walls, and one slightly grayer door, with two black cameras on opposite sides of the room pointed at the table in the center of the room.

"Can you be serious for a minute, Eve?" His face is set in a rigid, stiff expression, and his tone of voice doesn't reveal any positivity either. He is determined to get his point across. "I'm not hungry, Eve. I'm nervous...anxious...leery of something that I can't quite put my finger on. And I need you to trust me."

"I trust you, Frank. Honestly, I do. It's just that you've had these" – I used air quotes – "feelings before, and they don't always pan out the way you envision them."

When we were roommates, Frank claimed that he had a premonition that our apartment would be broken into. Because he had a vivid dream about a home invasion and felt very strongly about it, we double-bolted our doors, propped chairs up against the handles, and slept with baseball bats next to our beds. Frank's dream had been a little off. No *human* intruder broke into our tightly locked apartment; however, a wild bat did invade our living space the next night. We aren't quite sure how he snuck in, but he made a lot of noise trying to get out. When the tiny, flying mouse flew straight into our windows, walls, and cabinets, the ruckus woke us from our guarded slumber. From our separate bedrooms, Frank and I both jumped out of our beds, each grabbing our baseball bat, and ran toward the noise, only to find the helpless creature frightened for his life.

Frank claimed that the bat incident must have been the invasion his dreams were warning him about. Of course, I was skeptical and laughed off his ability to see into the future and interpret his dreams. Instead, I teased him about it every year by celebrating the bat premonition anniversary. One year, I sent him a hundred frosted, bat-shaped cookies to his work. The following year, I paid a local radio station to dedicate the Batman theme song to him every hour, and the next year he begged me for a truce after I'd mowed the shape of a bat into the grass of his immaculately manicured lawn. Pranking Frank was one of my favorite hobbies.

"Evie, I know I told you many, many moons ago that I adored your sense of humor and personality, but somehow you've managed to change my opinion. Your bat themed jokes are getting preposterous. I think you have way more fun planning these shenanigans than I do in receiving them."

In between my uncontrollable giggle fit, I admitted that he was right. "I'm fucking hilarious."

"Even though I don't enjoy this anniversary that you've invented, my neighbors look forward to your pranks. It's marked as a holiday on their family calendar. They can't wait to see what you come up with. My neighbor Jen's all-time favorite bat joke was when you purchased and distributed thirty bat costumes of all sizes to the neighborhood kids. Then you persuaded them to pretend it was Halloween and come knocking on my door. She thinks you need to publish a prank book. She thinks it would be a bestseller."

But even I had to admit that his gut instincts had a small ounce of foreshadowing. It reminds me of a fortune teller in the movies and how the strange, little lady dressed in the violet tapestry announces to you that a loved one who has recently died wants to communicate with you. Usually, the words from beyond are vague and could be interpreted in several ways, very similar to Frank's visions.

A few months after the bat episode, Frank persuaded me into playing hooky from my part-time waitressing job at a local restaurant, Hillcrest Lounge. Even though we lived together, we'd been so busy lately that we only passed each other coming and going from our little apartment. No quality time. Life had gotten busy, and he encouraged me to slow down and have some fun.

That evening as we were relaxing on our old beat-up couch, sipping on some beer, and playing a game of Monopoly, Frank promptly sat up and grabbed my hand as I'd reached for a handful of popcorn. "Evie, I selfishly wanted to spend some extra time with you, but for some reason I feel relieved."

I glanced down at the board game to see what property he had landed on.

"I'm not talking about the game. I feel like I saved your life."

"Another intense feeling?"

"Yes."

"Are you sure you didn't see the next card in the pile? Is it a get out of jail free card, Frank?"

"I'm serious, Evie. My gut tells me that something dreadful would've happened to you if you hadn't stayed home tonight."

We brushed off his 'feeling' and returned to our board game and snacks, not taking much stock in Frank's sudden comment until the next morning. As I clicked on the TV and poured myself a cup of coffee, I heard the local news anchor announce that the Hillcrest Lounge had been robbed the prior evening.

"The armed suspect didn't simply take the money and run. After the restaurant's manager handed over the money that was locked in the till, the unidentified man shot her in the back of the head and fled the scene. Local law enforcement are searching for the man responsible for this crime. If you have any information, you are asked to call the phone number at the bottom of the screen."

At precisely the moment the journalist started talking about the robbery and murder, Frank had shuffled into the kitchen in his stocking feet. "Eve, that could've been you," he gasped.

Our eyes were frozen in a shocked stare. We couldn't believe it.

On our small TV that rested on the kitchen counter, the cameraman zoomed in on the outside of the restaurant that was wrapped in yellow crime scene tape. Last night when I faked my pounding headache, I'd talked to Sally, the manager. She told me not to worry about it. "It'll probably be a slow night. Tucker will be here later. It's all good, Eve. Get some rest and we'll see you this weekend."

Sally was dead, and Frank's gut instinct had begged me to stay home from work that night. And even though I had a hard time admitting that he may have been right, I felt relieved that Frank and his premonition had saved me.

Here, we were again listening to Frank's gut and trying to interpret its meanings.

Frank clears his throat directing my inattention back onto him and the present. "Honestly, when William invited me over for dinner, I was optimistic. I've always been a little on the fence about the guy – "

"We were married for twenty years, and you're just telling me this now?"

"I know, Evie. I brushed it off because I figured that deep down, I didn't think anyone was good enough for my best friend. I shoved those feelings far in the depths of my heart, where all my real feelings are. The Black Pit. Anyway, when he sent me a text inviting me over, I thought he'd have ideas to bounce off me. Possibly some evidence to exonerate you. The naive part of me thought maybe this colossal mistake would bridge the gap in William's and my friendship. We'd bond over our mutual task to save and clear your name. And if that didn't pan out, I was hoping to see my godchildren at least." Frank pauses a moment to take a big drink from his coffee. When his eyes return to mine, concern and worry line them. "Eve, he thinks you did it."

All I can do is return his stare. When I blink, my eyelids feel weighed down, like a drug induced movement. With each blink, I will time to stop and back up before those painful words escaped Frank's lips.

My head knows that Frank wouldn't even have mentioned anything that would worry or upset me. I could only imagine the battlefield that played in Frank's consciousness as he had to decide whether to tell me or not. He must've been pretty sure of the facts that he had gathered.

Even though my head knows, my heart wasn't prepared. Meet the emotion named Hope; she is a heartbreaker. She plays with your heartstrings, begging you to give her a second chance, pleading with you to not give up. With her tentative smile, she plants dreams of a brighter tomorrow. With her soft voice, she whispers positive messages into your ear. However, when Hope fails you, be prepared for a firm slap of reality right across your face.

When I hear the actual words that my husband has lost faith, my heart cracks. I knew there would be a few people that would question if I was capable of murder, but never thought in a million years it would be my own husband.

"I was feeling apprehensive about confiding in him regarding the direction of your case, but I thought maybe a relaxing evening with him would help ease my worries. It didn't. Evie, he suggested that I drop the case. In his words, 'You're in way over your head, Frank.' I informed him that no one would fight harder to free you than me. He shook his head and announced that he couldn't and wouldn't pay me what I would need to represent you. What husband would do that unless he was guilty of something himself? Evie, you know I don't care about the money, right?"

I can only nod. I'm incapable of forming a sentence, let alone a sound.

"He told me about how you'd been vandalizing the Blacks' property. He said he has proof and that he warned you to stop before it got out of hand."

William, what the hell? Last time he visited he'd been distant, uncompassionate and cold, but I shrugged it off because we were in an awkward, difficult situation where neither of us knew what to do. What were the proper emotions for visiting your spouse who is in jail? Were there any?

But now, when Frank informs me of William's withdrawal of support, the rose-colored glasses that I'd been wearing slide off, and I can view the scene more clearly.

He'd been working me for information to use against me. He hadn't visited me out of love and respect for our marriage. He'd been here to see how weak and vulnerable I was. It was a tactic he used often on his clients. The man was a con-artist, and he was very good at his job. He read situations and scoped out weaknesses for a living. I just wasn't used to being a victim, a pawn in one of his schemes.

Frank recognizes the look of despair on my face as my eyes become wide and start to tear up. My mouth drops open in shock.

"He also mentioned that neighbors have witnessed you trespassing on the Blacks' property. Jodi Johnson confessed to William that she witnessed you peeking into the Blacks' front window, early one morning before the sun came up. He had asked her how she knew it was you if it was so dark outside, and she told him that she recognized Milo. You had him on a leash. She included this information in her statement to the police."

Damn it! Jodi is always running her mouth to someone about something, and unfortunately, this time it was about me and was factual. It made me rethink nicknaming her the 'gossip queen.' Maybe some of the stuff she was spreading around the neighborhood was true after all. *Crap!* What else did she know?

It's time to come clean to Frank, well, at least partially. I'd looked in their windows plenty of times but obviously one time too many. It's similar to how everyone has premarital sex, but only a few unfortunate souls have to live with the consequences for the rest of their lives. But Frank doesn't need to know that it was a regular occurrence.

"In my defense, Hudson hadn't come home the night that Jodi witnessed me peeking in the Blacks' living room. I thought maybe he crashed at their house, so I looked in the window to see some sign of him, maybe his shoes at the front door, his jacket, his backpack or maybe even see him passed out on the couch." I hung my head for effect. "I know it looks bad, but I was desperate."

"You're right. It makes you look very bad, and very guilty, especially since you were arrested a few months later for killing someone who lived in that house." Frank shakes his head and jots down some notes on his legal pad. Probably notes to follow up with a time and date for the peeping Tom event.

"Eve, William never used the word guilty. It was more in the way he was trying to talk me out of representing you." Frank looks up at the camera in the far corner of the room before catching my eye. "I really want to hold your hand or comfort you somehow, but you know I'm not allowed. Now, don't freak out when I tell you this, but I agreed to consider helping him find you a new lawyer. I told him I questioned your innocence too."

I can only imagine what my facial expression reflects to Frank on the opposite side of the table. I only know what it feels like. The blood leaves my face to assist with the overbeating of my heart as I feel it breaking into two. My best friend doubts my innocence too. My throat dries up and a tiny, helpless sob escapes my throat as I can no longer control my emotions. This wasn't part of my plan.

"I wasn't serious. I would never abandon you. Don't cry, Eve. Be strong. I need you to have faith in my plan. And I need to have William trusting me as well." As he was packing up his file folders, he looked me in the eye and asked me one more question. "William also mentioned that my crazy mother had been to your house. What the hell, Eve? What was she doing at your house?"

Chapter 29

now

Frank believes William killed Clive and set me up to take the blame. Wow. That is quite an accusation, and I'm not sure if he could manage to pull it off. But then again, crazier things have happened.

With doubt planted in my heart by Frank's concern over William's lack of faith in my innocence, I'm not at all surprised that my foggy brain doesn't allow sleep to consume me. As I stare at the cinder blocks that surround me, tears slide out of the corner of my eyes and soak my flat pillow. I don't know how to process this new information or even if I need to process it. *Is it a relief? Is it fear of the unknown?* What good does questioning the loyalty of my husband do when I've hardly had any contact with him since being locked up? I've never felt so completely helpless. I feel like I have no control over what happens next in regard to my marriage to William, who can decide to divorce me at any time.

With Frank's warning that I can't trust William, I feel like an ant under a big, flat shoe as it's about to squish me. I scramble to move. As the shadow of his foot hovers over me, all six legs scurry, but I can't move fast enough. Seconds before being crushed, I narrowly escape, and another dooming, heavy shoe casts its shadow over me. It's never-ending.

When fear or doubt has a voice, it becomes more real, or perhaps it is the fact that someone else outside of the relationship recognizes the flaw, too.

William and I are broken, beyond repair. I've known about it for a long time. In my heart, my love for him has evaporated and disappeared without a trace. However, hope still lingered in the dark, blackened shadows of my heart, like the last fallen drop of rain in a desert. Without hope, I would've automatically turned into the vengeful, determined woman I have become. It would be like whiplash. One quick jerk. Hope grounded me, helped me stay present in our family. I fear that without hope, I would've taken a blade to his throat years ago when he first broke my heart in two. This sounds like a threat and makes me appear murderous, but I hate blood. In fact, blood makes me weak in the knees and brings vomit to my mouth. I have never fantasized about a job in the medical field because my fear of bold, brick-colored fluid scares me. Nope, no chance you would ever find someone else's blood on my hands.

Sure, I'd been questioning his faithfulness to me for months, but I didn't want *him* to question *my* innocence. I know that sounds strange, but it is almost as if I separate our marriage from our friendship. William broke our wedding vows, again. He proved that he didn't respect our love or commitment. With Frank's warning of William, our friendship, the part that is the real me, is also at stake. Not only has William disrespected our love for one another, but he has also shown disrespect to my true self by not believing in my innocence. He thinks I'm a killer. If this is true, there is no hope left for any part of this relationship. Hope has finally been abandoned.

Validation is wonderful, but at what length? Sure, everyone likes to be told they were right, but at what cost to your soul?

After you've been stabbed in the back so many times, you stop *feeling*. You don't forgive, and you will never forget. You muster up all your patience and wait. In my case, I sit in a jail cell that I knew would eventually house my body, but my heart is with my children, and my faith is in Frank.

William...I have nothing left to give him now that he's stolen my trust and security.

***

Frank wouldn't understand why I hadn't said anything or left William if I thought he was cheating on me again. Since Frank was a student of the law, he liked everything to be right or wrong, black or white, straight or gay. He would never lie, cheat or steal. But I was dealing in the gray area. Divorce seemed easy, but if I left William, I would share time with my kids, split incomes, lose the house, and everything that was stable in my life. I needed to think about all possible outcomes.

Furthermore, Hudson had finally started seeing the light, the error of his ways. He'd been at Tallgrass Addiction Care Center for twenty-seven days. With Hudson sober and on the mend, I could focus on the mess that was my marriage.

There were a few incidents lately that made my Spidey senses tingle.

William had lied about where he was – he said he had a work dinner, but his GPS location indicated he was at the Lodge in Deadwood, thirty miles in the opposite direction. I didn't question him when he arrived home. Maybe because I wasn't ready for the truth or the lie. Isn't that why there is a word called denial? Or avoidance? I felt it but didn't want to see it, hear it, or know it for a fact.

One afternoon, William's phone rang while he was mowing the lawn. Over breakfast that morning, he mentioned that he was working on closing a big deal, so when his phone indicated an incoming call, I instinctively answered it, thinking that it might be his secretary or someone from the office with news.

The caller ID read 'unknown.'

"Hello?" I heard breathing. I knew someone was there, on the other line. I assumed that they might have been surprised by a woman's voice, which was the reason for the delayed response. "Hello? Sorry, this is William Stanton's wife, Evelyn. Can I help you?"

The Russian accent replied, "Oh, sorry. Wrong number." And before I could say another word, she hung up. Odd. I never even mentioned the call to William.

A few days later, a small package was delivered to the house. I didn't even look at the return address label. I had assumed it was something I ordered and forgot about. As I cut into the box, I was surprised to discover a set of wooden Matryoshka dolls wrapped in bright white, tissue paper. The outer doll, traditionally the mother, had been painted with beautiful, sparkling blue, oval-shaped eyes and perfect ruby-stained lips. Her historic Sarafian was painted in a floral pattern in a rainbow of colors. When I screwed off the top half, it revealed the next doll with an identical face; however, her hood was pulled down and seductively designed off her shoulder to reveal a bare shoulder. The next doll was the same woman, but the Sarafian had been dropped to her midsection, where the doll twisted in half. The third, hollow wooden doll bared her perky breasts as her smile widened and her eyes squinted in a sexy, alluring way. Of course, by now I realized that this gift was not intended for me, but curiosity controlled my sense of right and wrong. Quickly, I screwed off the third doll to reveal the fourth doll who was completely naked. The details that the artist used were impeccable. I could even make out a tiny belly button ring and a faint tramp stamp on the back above the illustrated butt crack. *I've seen that tattoo before, but where?*

I dropped the last doll onto our hardwood floor, and she cracked into several pieces. Inside the naked Russian Matryoshka doll was a condom, as if to indicate that the gifter did not intend to have a traditional baby doll. This gift was thoroughly planned and very detailed. Even though it broke my heart because I knew this gift was intended for William by another mistress, I was also slightly impressed.

Ribbed for her pleasure.

Chapter 30

now

Who would've thought all those years ago in college, when Frank and I brainstormed his cases, that we would be doing the same thing for a murder investigation that included my involvement? The idea would've thrown us into a fit of giggles.

I'm sure the conversation might have gone something like this: *"Eve charged with murder? What did you kill? A ladybug?"* Frank would've clenched his stomach muscles as a giggle cramp would've formed from his continued laughter.

Unfortunately, even though it's hard to wrap our minds around, it is my current reality. As I look across the hard plastic table, worry lines have formed around Frank's eyes. "Let's discuss the evidence against you, Eve. But let's pretend it isn't *you* and just play our old game when you would be my devil's advocate." Frank's normal, easy-going nature is replaced by his 'I'm-in-charge' lawyer voice. My nerves skyrocket. My throat is dry, and my palms start to sweat.

"You didn't call me a devil's advocate back in the day. What was it that you called me again?"

"Fucking pain in the ass is what you've always been."

"Come on. You had a cute nickname for me when I would help you prepare for trial. I can't remember what it was." I remember, but hearing him say it would be nostalgic, and we both need to smile if only for a moment. My case and the evidence against me are overwhelming and stressing us both out.

"You were my CP." A small smirk climbs up his face. All law students find someone that they can practice their ideas on, and Frank coined the term among his classmates. He called me his Clawless Parapuss. "You were a lioness without any claws. A paralegal with no qualifications or degree." He shakes his head trying to erase the memory so that he can concentrate on the matter at hand. "As I look over the evidence that was supplied for your arrest, I have a few questions for you, Eve. Some things that make your innocence look questionable."

"Shoot." I flash him a little smile as Frank peers at me over the top of his bi-focals, a new addition to his already bookish and aging appearance.

"Good one, Evie." He uses my nickname whenever we are playing around, and thankfully, he recognizes my weak attempt at humor. His eyes return to the file folder filled with loose papers.

I know we need to do this and discuss the evidence stacked against me, but I don't want to. It will just make it more real. Stating your fears out loud and putting them out in the universe rather than keeping them locked up tightly in your heart takes courage and a willingness to put yourself out there and be vulnerable. These are all things I don't think I'm ready for. Sure, I'd rehearsed it all in my head – that's what an overthinker does. However, I feel like a cutter who'd been asked to pull up her sleeves and make visible her self-inflicted scars, her latest cuts for others to judge and gawk at. Plus, Frank is my person, my biggest supporter, and I hate to disappoint him.

I realize Frank is waiting for me to give him my approval to continue. My small smile evaporates, and I nod slightly and immediately cast my eyes downward like a scolded child.

"First on the list are these weird footprints in the snow that are still puzzling me, Eve. They are made with your boots for sure, but just the toes are showing where the pressure was applied. This means that the real killer practically had to tiptoe the entire time while wearing your boots, distributing their weight only to the front." He is worried and asks a lot of tough questions. I don't blame him. It's his job. If I was in his position, I'd ask questions too. But as my best friend, I wish he'd have a little more faith in me. Additionally, I was having a hard time pretending that this was just a case for us to brainstorm about.

From the evidence file folder, he has pulled out the photographs of the boot prints. He turns it upside down, facing me, and continues talking. "The thing that seems odd to me is that the footprints looked like you'd been tiptoeing in the snow. Look here." He points to a closeup of one print. "It looks like more pressure is applied to the toes, which would be difficult to do when you're drunk." Even though my only reaction is my eyebrows raising, which doesn't make any noise, Frank knows me well enough to look at me after those words come out of his mouth. "Don't look at me like that. I had to see if my theory was true, so I proceeded to get sloppy drunk last night – all for you – and tried tiptoeing in the snow. It's harder than you think it would be."

"Well, that's weird. So, what you are saying is that someone used my boots to make sure that the prints would be traced back to me, but the boots didn't fit their feet?"

"Exactly! Maybe that's it. Someone else was wearing your boots. Perhaps they didn't fit, so only their toes were putting pressure on the boots. Genius, Eve! I feel like I'm having deja vu."

I didn't want to break it to Frank that this, in fact, was how he got a client off during grad school. I remember the case and our brainstorming sessions clearly. It was a robbery, and the perp had worn his roommate's shoes that were two sizes too small. He had to literally tiptoe because he couldn't fit his heel in the shoes. He'd been too high to realize that they weren't his own shoes. He left a muddy footprint on the floor in front of the register. Luckily for the detectives on the case, the tread on the shoe wasn't very popular, so they were able to trace the name brand and which stores carried the shoe. However, the perp didn't own a pair of those shoes, his roommate did. During our brainstorming session, Frank slipped on a pair of my discarded shoes to reenact the scene when we came up with the idea that perhaps the perp wasn't wearing his own shoes.

Frank's boss concluded that he was a genius for coming up with the idea. To celebrate, Frank had taken me out to dinner, where we toasted to our crazy, insane brains that seemed to complement each other.

Thank goodness for me Frank hadn't remembered that case from twenty-odd years ago. For once, luck was on my side.

"If the shoes were too big, a person would need to shuffle and would have a hard time keeping the shoes on their feet. However, if the shoes were too small, a person would need to tiptoe because they wouldn't be able to walk heel to toe. Eve, do you think someone could have been wearing your boots that night?"

"Possibly, Frank. Anything is possible. I didn't have them on while I was in bed." His hand flew across the page of his legal pad. His writing is so sloppy that I hope his assistant will be able to decipher Frank's chicken scratches.

"We need to show doubt. And this shows a sliver of doubt. But let's keep talking."

Talking is what Frank and I excel at. We could discuss any subject, argue both sides of the coin, and even switch sides just for argument's sake. Our individual intellects flattered each other, and it was like a game to us. An evenly matched game of checkers.

"Now, let's brainstorm ideas about your cell phone. We've already discussed that your phone was discovered at the scene of the crime along with a damning text. Does William know your password?"

"I'm sure I've told him. Whether he remembers it or not, I don't know."

"Do your friends or kids know it?"

"Do *you* know it, Frank? I don't know. It isn't like I wrote it on the back of the phone case, but if you know anything about me, you could figure it out. It's the date of our wedding so with the right guess, my family and friends could figure it out, I'm sure."

Frank ponders this. When he does his deep thinking, his eyes always glance up to the ceiling, and I've read somewhere that that means he is imagining or creating. When his eyes glaze over and he looks up to the ceiling, I need to stay quiet and patiently wait for the words that will pour out of his mouth. He comes up with his best ideas after his little disappearance into his imaginary cloud.

"Let's imagine this scenario for a moment, Eve. Someone with a slightly larger foot than you slips on your snow boots and tiptoes across your yard to the Blacks' house. This person also steals your phone and sends a cryptic text. Then he or she drops it in the snow next to the victim's home. All just to frame you. What we need to do is find holes, things that appear one way but could actually be another, like the tiptoe boot prints. Not only does this person need to know where you keep your phone at night, but also your phone's password. This person wants to frame you for murder, but what does this other person have to gain by Clive's death? Then we'd have a motive."

I keep quiet knowing that Frank is processing his thoughts. He's good at his job. Sometimes, I think he should've been a detective instead of a lawyer, but this way he gets to do both things he loves: be a savior and investigate a crime.

"This person knows you, Eve. You know this person. We need to come up with a list of possibilities and cross out the ones that have solid alibis." He sits back in his hard plastic chair, removes his new glasses, and looks at me. "Yesterday, the results of the prints from around the Blacks' garage window came back, and they are positively yours, Eve. They were all over the windowsill. Can you think of a possible reason that your prints would be there?"

Because I pause too long for the silence to be comfortable, Frank adds his own observation. "It looks like you closed the garage window to keep the fumes in."

I notice the worry lining his eyes. Frank loves me and is trying to do his very best to represent me, but I wish that I didn't see so much doubt in his eyes.

I take a few seconds to appear surprised by the question. My eyes scan the ceiling because I also read that that gesture shows that you are processing, trying to search for the answer.

Suddenly my eyelids spring open, I have my answer. "Earlier in the week, I'd visited Clive and shut the window because it had just started to snow."

"You were visiting Clive? What the hell, Eve? Why would you go to see Clive? Please tell me what's going on."

"Frank, relax. It was totally innocent -"

"Nothing about this situation is innocent, Eve."

"I know, I know. But listen. I was just trying to help Hudson. I decided to confront Clive about his drug dealing. He'd just gotten home from school, so I followed his car into the garage. I closed the window because snow was accumulating on the windowsill. Ask Jodi Johnson's husband. He saw me walking over there. He was trimming a tree and waved at me when I crossed the road. He'll remember seeing me. Those two are into everyone's business." That alibi works to my benefit.

"Help Hudson? How would talking to Clive *help* Hudson? This isn't an elementary school problem. We're talking about a drug dealer and his client. You didn't seriously think you could simply *talk* him out of selling drugs, did you?" Frank seems appalled by my explanation. Not at all the reaction I thought I was gonna get. He hasn't written down Jodi Johnson's name on his legal pad yet.

"Yes, I was trying to *help* Hudson. It's what any good mother would do. What could a few words hurt? I'd already alienated us from his parents with my big mouth, so I figured what harm could a little conversation with the problem himself do?"

"Well, I guess we know the answer to that question now, don't we?"

Our friendship has many layers. From the layer that I'd always wished he didn't prefer the same sex for intimate relationships, to the layer that we focused our attention on – being best friends. The last layer was the one where he was like my older brother and scolded me for anything questionable that I did. Like now.

I know the best response is no response, so I simply hang my head. Since I need him on my side, I will accept his scolding.

"Evie, this is bad." My best friend is back. "You know this is bad, right? It doesn't make you look innocent. All these little things add up and point directly to you."

"I'm realizing that, Frank, but there's a logical explanation for all these little, questionable things. Just because those answers were easy doesn't make them right."

"Of course, I know that, Eve, but I'm your lawyer, and I'm telling you that it doesn't look good. As your lawyer, I need to lay out the facts of the case. The cold, hard truth. I was really hoping for more than weak explanations. I thought we would be able to find some cold, hard facts that would prove it wasn't you."

"And as my friend...?"

"As your friend, as your best friend, I'm worried too, but my opinion doesn't add up to jack shit. I will do whatever is necessary to help other people see your innocence."

"That is all I am hoping for. If you believe in me, Frank, I know others will too." I decided now is the time to tell him about the money- the Blacks' money. I wanted to wait on laying down that card, but it seems like I'm running out of options.

As soon as he finishes feverishly writing down some notes, he looks up at me. "Evie, you look like you are gonna throw up. What's wrong?"

"Frank, there is something I need to tell you, and it isn't good."

Chapter 31

now

When I strolled into the conference room, I didn't expect to find Frank sitting with two other suited men. Yesterday, Frank had indicated that the evidence was piling up against me; therefore, I wonder if my legal team is growing because Frank is unequipped to handle such a nightmare of a case. During our last conversation, I recognized the doubt in his eyes about my innocence. Frank wanted it to be black and white. Guilty or not guilty. Did I make a mistake by telling him about the money William had helped me steal from Mitchell and Becca? Of course, but I painted the picture to Frank a bit differently. I'm not a complete idiot.

Sitting in three folding chairs shoulder to shoulder across the table, the three grown men are buttoned up to their necks in starched, three-piece business suits. The fact that they sat next to each other on one side of the table while a lone chair on the opposite side waited for me, made my stomach flip flop. They stand at attention when I'm escorted into the room by Officer Brandon. After my time behind bars, I'm surprised by the formality and small gestures of politeness.

"Please take a seat, Mrs. Stanton." The older of the two strangers address me. As I plant my butt into the hard folding chair, my eyes search Frank for a clue as to what is going on, but he won't look directly at me. He keeps his head buried in his files. Instantly, my throat dries. *What is going on?*

Without Frank to reassure my worries, my focus dashes between the two men. The younger man clears his throat to earn my attention. "I would like to get right to the point, Mrs. Stanton, and not waste any more of your time. Considering new evidence that has been discovered, the state is dismissing all criminal charges against you. Your attorney, Mr. Baker, has some paperwork that we need you to sign so that we can release you as soon as possible. Please accept our sincerest apology."

I glance at the older gray-haired man, and he simply nods his head.

What? I want to say this out loud, but the two men said their peace and were already making a beeline for the door. I'm too shocked to respond. My eyes darted back and forth from the exiting, suited men to Frank, back to the men again, and then to Frank begging for answers. Again, my ability to communicate has been hindered by my inability to comprehend what is happening around me.

As soon as the door closes, Frank raises his head and looks at me with the biggest Cheshire cat smile. He did it. I am free! Almost.

"Frank?" I need him to repeat it, say it again, make it feel real.

"Evie, I'm breaking you out of here."

"Frank – "

"Well, not technically *breaking* you out of jail. I've assisted with releasing you of any legal wrongdoings. It isn't all me. The evidence speaks for itself actually. And some of it, I don't even know where it came from." He is rambling because he knows I want to jump across the table and give him the biggest, tightest bear hug ever.

"Frank! You did it! Am I really going home?" Again, I need to hear him say it.

"Yes, Evie. Just sign on the dotted line, and we'll ditch this joint." Even though I'm giggling hysterically, tears fall from my eyes and create a small puddle on the table. As he slides the file folder full of papers toward me, I recognize the orange game card from our favorite board game that reads, "Chance: Get out of Jail Free. This card may be kept until needed or sold."

***

As my tears make water droplet stains on the legal papers, my eyes scan the document, and my signature flies across each page.

"I've read it all, Evie. It's fair and legit. Your signature confirms that you won't sue them for wrongful arrest and imprisonment. As your legal counsel, I advised them that you would not. Considering that some of the evidence pointed directly at you, I couldn't totally blame them for thinking you could've done this." Frank is flipping each piece of paper as soon as my pen leaves the paper. I want out of here as quickly as I can. I can't wait to hug my kids again. I want to hear all about Hazel's new boyfriend, Phil Loving, and I won't roll my eyes at her endless, giddy chatter. I want to tousle Hudson's hair as he sits slumped over on a bar stool eating breakfast, and I won't complain that he doesn't put his dishes in the sink when he is done.

When I have finished, Frank organizes the stack neatly and files them into a manilla file folder that is labeled with my name and inmate number. He folds over the top of the file and clears his throat. "Evie, I don't want to cast shade onto this glorious celebration, but I need to tell you something before we blow this popsicle stand."

I can tell that he is serious, and honestly, I'm tired of Stiff Frank. I can't wait to get my old friend back who likes to joke around and tease me. However, I look up at him and nod my head for him to continue. "Let's hear it."

"Although the new evidence that the police discovered proves that you didn't kill Clive, it led them to consider William. He was arrested an hour ago. I'm sorry to be the one to tell you this, Evie." He reaches across the table to hold my hand. I guess that now that I'm technically a free woman, touching is allowed.

I search my heart, my brain, and my soul for the right response. *Is there one?* I've been given the gift of freedom, but at the price that someone I love – loved – will take my place. My eyes watch Frank to see his reaction to the news, but he is blank. He is waiting for my response so that, as my best friend, he can respond accordingly. If I'm sad, he will be sad too. If I'm heartbroken, he will be hurt as well. But I am relieved, and selfishly, I am not concerned about William being arrested. I have patiently waited for this day to come, and it's finally here. I'm not sure I care who had to pay for me to receive my freedom, least of all William.

A tiny smirk plays on my lips. I don't want Frank to worry about anything. I want him to feel like he accomplished a great task as a lawyer and my best friend. He deserves to be happy. He deserves to feel relieved and proud of himself for earning my freedom.

"Can you tell me what happened, Frank? I need to know." I want to be prepared for what comes after I leave this cold, harsh building. I need to understand what my kids are learning and how they are coping, but first I need the facts, because knowledge is power.

"A few things have happened in the last couple of days. First, after you explained that you couldn't remember much from the evening of October 19, I decided to check your refrigerator for the leftover bottle of wine. To my utter dismay, you hadn't drunk it all." He winks at me. He is trying to tease me, but I don't bite. I want more information. "It totally seemed unusual to me that you would've blacked out after only three glasses. So, I had the wine tested. The lab came back finding small traces of Rohypnol in the bottle of wine." When he recognizes my confusion, he adds, "Roofie."

To Frank, my excess blinking is my attempt at fighting off tears, but to me, I know it is simply because my eyes are dry. I knew this would happen.

"And Hazel explained to me that she found a credit card bill where you previously highlighted some suspicious activity by William. Of course, it's not against the law to have an extramarital affair, but it does paint him in a questionable light, especially because of the affair with the victim's stepmother. Very peculiar indeed." Frank shifts his focus from my face to the file folder that he has in front of him. "Although William's cell phone pinged him across town later that night, the police still believe he could've had time to start Clive's car to spread carbon monoxide. Becca's phone was not pinged across town, but William had texted her that night to ask if she would meet him at his office. She never responded. The police are questioning if William did that on purpose to throw suspicion off him."

I nod as the words pour out of his mouth. I'm trying to pay attention to each detail, but my brain is shouting, *you are free!*

"Additionally, the police found a dainty necklace under one of Clive's car tires with the initials, SM. They are looking into Clive's contacts with those initials. The money...I searched for that overseas account you said William created. The money is gone, Evie. I'm sorry, but there is no trace left of it. Almost like it never existed. I know William is a successful financial advisor, but I was slightly impressed."

Next, Frank reports that Mitchell turned over Clive's cell phone records which turned out to be very compelling evidence against William. His disclosures aren't completely surprising until the next words come out of his mouth.

"And Evie, there is one more thing. My mom passed away last night. I think she was trying to wait until you were released, but her petite, cancer-ridden body just couldn't fight anymore." After he grabs a tissue and wipes his nose, he shoots me a little smile. "You were literally the last thing on her mind."

Curiosity has my tongue. I don't talk because I want him to continue and finish his story. *What did she say?*

"And some things never change. Even in her last moments on Earth, she was bossing me around. She demanded that I marry you, take the money, and run off into the sunset." He chuckles. "I love my mother, but she is delusional, or *was* delusional. She claimed she had a stash of money that you'd given her. Only my mother can die leaving me more confused than ever."

I'm a bit shell-shocked and speechless. I can't believe that I'm about to bust out of here in less than an hour. My perseverance and overthinking had paid off, but my one confidant is no longer alive. I had said my good-byes to her, but is that really enough? *Thank you, Vera!*

Chapter 32

now

It has been quite a week adjusting to my newly gained freedom. It is all the small things that free citizens don't even devote a second thought to.

Digestion. The food that we cook, marinate, and roast is rich with butter, salt, and fats. After eating bland food in jail, my taste buds came alive as my teeth sunk into a juicy, pink-centered sirloin that Frank grilled to celebrate my homecoming. What that rich steak did to my insides is another matter that I don't want to revisit.

Looking up. When incarcerated, daily yard time is a privilege that all inmates anticipate. As her chin tilts upward, she observes puffy white clouds decorating the light blue afternoon sky. Fresh air tickles the hair on her arms and sends goosebumps up and down her spine. Sometimes, a trapped tornado-like breeze bounces off the buildings and whips across her face. The yard where inmates spend fifteen minutes a day is surrounded on all four sides by tall gray buildings and sharp barbed wire fencing. Looking up is the only option to forget. She misses the horizon, gazing as far as her eyesight would allow. She misses how God paints the skyline when the sun awakens the Earth with its warmth. Long brush strokes of gold, coral, and wine blend together, causing a unique hue that alerts the world to be grateful for a new day. At the end of the day, the blend of lavender, turquoise, and cherry overload the eyesight into pausing in appreciation. Only God is capable of such a masterpiece.

Privacy. After filling my belly with Frank's home cooked meal, I enjoy a warm shower...all alone. I feel the tension leave my shoulders. I haven't been alone in any room for so long that it feels odd. In jail, we could shower every day with supervision but only receive a clean change of clothes on Wednesdays and Sundays. While I towel dry my body, I notice that my keen sense of hearing is still on high alert. In jail, I learned to listen for trouble in the sound of footsteps that came down the corridor. I listened for sarcastic tones in the voices of people that I didn't trust. And now, at home, I hear Hudson, Hazel, and Frank talking in the kitchen. I can't make out the words, but I can tell that Frank is comforting them.

Options. I pull open the top right drawer of my dresser and notice that I have at least fifteen pairs of underwear to choose from. Going to jail isn't like packing for a camp that you signed up and registered for. I didn't bring my overnight bag filled with my nightly skin care regimen. I didn't pack my favorite pairs of undies that didn't give me wedgies. I didn't choose between my six pairs of black heels. After you are fingerprinted, searched, and ripped clean of anything personal, you are handed a pair of underwear, a uniform, socks, and slip on shoes. No options, no choices, no rights.

I slipped on a pair of plain white, no-thrill underwear and my favorite flannel pajamas before returning to the kitchen to be with my family.

***

I have survived, my children are healthy and well, and my family has endured the battle with only one casualty. My marriage.

After the drama of William's arrest and the police department releasing me of any wrongdoings, I decided to entrust Frank with a secret. Only one secret.

Frank and I are enjoying a cocktail at our old stomping grounds, Charley's, to celebrate the end of this nightmarish chapter in our lives. Not long after William was arrested, I filed for divorce because 'my lawyer' suggested it was the right thing to do for my kids and because the shadow of doubt might follow me around for a few years. Even though the law considered me innocent of any wrongdoing, the stench of my arrest lingered.

Charley's still looks like the same bar, with the same pool tables and the same stinky dance floor, but the owner, Mr. Avery, had long since passed away from liver failure, which must be a pretty common disease for bar owners. Because of Mr. Avery's absence, Frank and I didn't receive as warm of a greeting as we had twenty years ago every time we strolled through the creaky back door. But it didn't stop us from choosing Charley's as our primary spot for celebrating any milestone.

"Cheers to Vera." I raise my glass in salute to the woman who neither of us will ever forget.

"Cheers to saving your ass in this very spot a million years ago and a million times." Frank lifts his pint glass.

"And doing it again!"

"Yes, and now I can add plucking your skinny ass out of jail to the list of my heroic saves! That was fun."

"I should have a shirt made for you that reads, 'A good friend calls you in jail. A great friend bails you out of jail. Your best friend sits next to you and says, "Wasn't that fun?"'"

Our glasses clinked with a little too much forcefulness, so the beer foam sloshed over the top of the glass and onto Frank's lap. *Snort.* Whenever something unexpectedly funny happens, I snort. I'm so classy.

"Well, that's the first time you've ever made me wet, Evie." He fires off a sassy comment as he dabs at the wet spot with a napkin.

I slap his arm. "Gross, Buttscab, but now that you brought it up, it's kind of what I wanted to talk to you about."

"Making me wet? Snow White, sorry to break it to you, but I'm still gay. Nothing crazy has happened since you were locked up in the clink." Earlier in the week, Frank met Jilli and agreed to be her lawyer. He quickly adopted her nickname for me, and my only two real friends hit it off. No surprise there.

"Not specifically that, Frank, because it is completely obvious from your outfit today that you still are." I Vanna-White him as I lean back to take a gander at his outfit. His crisp, white buttoned-to-the-top shirt was decorated with a plaid bowtie and a pair of khaki pants rolled at his ankles, exposing his shiny penny loafers.

"Don't knock my outfit. You still wear the same jeans from two decades ago." Teasing each other is a part of our friendship that I've always appreciated. Small slams on each other's fashion sense, or lack thereof, always make me smile. I didn't want the type of friend who agrees with every choice I make. I appreciate honesty and loyalty. My friendship with Frank has filled that requirement for so many years, which is why I wanted to ask him to spend the rest of his life with me.

"Fair observation, but in all honesty, I wondered if you'd marry me."

I pause for dramatic effect. I knew my proposal would grab his attention and be awarded a stunned response. It wasn't often that I could stump Frank into silence.

"You're the most stable person in my life, and in Hazel and Hudson's lives as well. I think every one of us needs that right now. Frank, you need us too. People that we can count on for love and support." During my incarceration, Frank and Benny – who my family fondly nicknamed Beans –

broke up because of Frank's obsession with proving my innocence. Benny had commented on several occasions that Frank's involvement with my case wasn't in his best interest. Even their relationship couldn't withstand digs at me. Frank threw in the towel before I could even talk him out of it. Frank was as alone as my family of three was.

"Oh, Evie, the lead bars have screwed with your brain. You know that's why they recalled a shit-ton of baby cribs back in the nineties. They were coated with paint that had lead in them. Can really mess with fragile brain development." He pretends to be concerned with knocking some sense into me. "And furthermore, being gay clearly means that your taco is of no interest to me." Frank loves to pretend that I'm always trying to make him switch teams. His mother had prayed the same thing every night.

"Thank you for that clarification. I'm asking you to partner with me in parenting your godchildren. Not bedding their mother." I turned my body toward him so that he could witness my serious expression. "Frank, I know where the Blacks' money is. Vera kept it safe." I take a big drink of my beer, letting the information that I supplied settle into his brain. "I'm suggesting that you, me, Hazel and Hudson ditch Miner City and use the money to start fresh somewhere else. My face is rather infamous around here so living on the east coast as husband and wife might help ease us all back into a normal life. The kids could use a fresh start. I could use a fresh start, and I'm asking you to join us. You can retire and live an easy life. You don't have to give up who you are. I'm not offering you a Rockefeller life, but rather a legally binding paper marriage in which we support each other in every aspect *except* physical intimacy."

Frank knows me as well as I know myself. He looks me up and down to verify that my question is serious, to see if my fingers are crossed.

"Wow, Eve. I don't know what to say."

"Just think about it, Frank. I've already talked with the kids about it, and they are one hundred percent on board. And of course, your mother gave us her blessing years ago. It was her dying wish. We are all ready to put this mess behind us." I reach out my hand to hold his, showing the sincerity of the invitation.

Frank takes a large gulp of his beer before responding. "You had me at hello." He put his hand into the palm of mine, and then, in true Frank form, he turned over my hand and looked around it. "Where is the rock, Evie? Don't tell me you proposed without a diamond. Amateur."

***

Getting engaged to your best friend of twenty-some years involved many shots of alcohol. After our celebratory evening of throwing back too many cold ones and realizing that our tolerance level was a lot lower than it was twenty years before, I paused a moment to say a quick prayer to Vera to make sure she was looking down at us and knew I had fulfilled my promise. I was going to marry her son.

Frank told me that before she died, she had urged him to lean close to her face so she could utter one last demand. "Evelyn. Money is Evelyn's."

Her voice was a whisper as if she had used all her strength to vocalize her last words.

During one of her visits to jail, she informed me that she had a plan. She told me she didn't have much time. "In order for you to fulfill your promise, you need to be free of this shit hole."

Vera's cussing was well known at our house. Hazel had bejeweled a mason jar when she was younger and labeled it, "Mimi Vera swears a lot." Whenever Vera visited for dinner or a holiday gathering with our family,

Hazel charged Mimi Vera fifty cents for every swear word. Sometimes, I thought she would drop an enormous amount of profanity just to see how much money Hazel would earn. With her helmet-shaped white hair resting stiffly around her head like a halo, Vera looked like sweet, old Betty White with a dirty sailor's mouth.

Making a pact with a dying woman is more dangerous than any other possible promise. Riskier than a bloody handshake with a member of the mob. More dangerous than a deal with the Mexican cartel. More worrisome than a secret pact with a hitman who was hired to dispose of your own body. Vera had nothing to lose. She was leaving this world and had a sole interest in securing her son's future in a relationship with a woman that she deemed worthy of his love. She'd been on a mission. Furthermore, she never once asked if I was guilty of Clive's murder or not. I don't think it mattered in her mind.

I hinted that I had stored an obscene amount of money and a few other questionable things in the hidden compartment under my gorgeous pool table, and Vera ran with an idea. "I'm a crazy old bat that doesn't trust banks. People will believe that I had that much money stuffed under the mattress in my home."

She probed me for other ideas but pretended we were talking about a daytime soap opera. "I know Victor Newman has screwed every female character on that show, even his own neighbor, who was his wife's best friend. I don't know why the writers don't just write his character off the show."

Vera was anything but subtle. She knew about William's infidelity and believed that there had to be other things shady about him. The afternoon that she claimed to have an upset stomach at our house, she scoured his office and snapped pictures of some work statements that he had hidden in a drawer. Vera wasted no time in leaking damaging information about

William because she didn't believe she had any time to waste. Her late husband's cousin ran the Rapid City newspaper, so she bought a page in the Life section and wrote an article about the shady business practices at William's financial investment company, as well as planting huge clouds of doubt around my arrest. She included copies of the threatening texts that William had sent from his phone to Clive before his murder.

Friends of Vera's populated the streets in our county with a petition to free me. Because of the sheer number of people involved, the local news station became interested in this story. It had all the elements of a hit show – family drama, a wrongful arrest, illegal drugs, financial corruption, and a vengeful murder.

Vera was in her element. She was the center of attention and fulfilling her life's purpose to make sure her son would be happy and taken care of. Not only was she working to free me, but she was also checking things off her personal bucket list.

Chapter 33

now

After getting our affairs in order – which included selling my gorgeous million-dollar home and Frank leaving his partnership at the law firm – we packed up a few treasured items and moved to my all-time favorite vacation destination, the Outer Banks in North Carolina, where William and I had taken Hudson all those years ago before Hazel was born. I bought the little beach house that we had rented twenty years ago and made the owner an offer she couldn't refuse.

Hudson had decided to continue his education, so he enrolled at a local junior college. I worried about how he would handle the pressure that college would put on him, but he shrugged off my concerns. The younger generation always bounces back so quickly compared to the older, damaged generation, which remembers all too clearly the struggles of its own youth. Even though his senior year was filled with tension, disappointment, and pain, Hudson managed to graduate high school on time and with honors. He again exceeded my expectations. I am extremely proud of how far he has come. Furthermore, he has been sober and clean for almost two years. It was all worth it.

Hazel is a freshman in high school and flourishing at her new school. Even though her first love, Phil Loving back in South Dakota, contacts her often, Hazel is making new friends. The kids were fine with Frank and my arrangement, and we all gladly adopted his last name. Hazel didn't feel the need to hyphenate it.

Frank is enjoying his retirement, but itching to get back out there, protecting the innocent. Since he couldn't completely give up his career, he works pro bono for a few clients. Following a lot of encouragement from me and the kids, he finally decided to dabble in acting and joined a local theater company. He scored his first acting gig as Vince Fontaine in 'Grease,' the sleazy, smooth-talking radio announcer.

I decided to leave the editing world and embark on writing my own novel – a love story about marrying my best friend after a very turbulent start to our relationship.

We are starting over, putting the past behind us so we can focus on new goals without having daily reminders of old mistakes and regrets. However, one aspect of life still needs closure so I'm returning to South Dakota the following day to take care of it.

As we relish our current hiatus from the pressures of the working class, our butts are planted on the beach, where we are enjoying the warm sun and cool ocean breeze. The waves crash against the shore, creating the ultimate calming noise. Leaving our past behind and starting fresh across the country was never anything I regretted. Everything we went through to get here seems worth it as I look out at the turquoise-colored water and breathe in the fresh ocean air.

Frank's chin is angled upward toward the sun, soaking up the Vitamin D. He opens one eye and starts a conversation that I'd feared was coming for a while.

"Obviously, I don't want you to expose all your nasty little secrets, Evie, because I don't think I would agree with your immoral decisions. However, there are a few things that have moistened my curiosity."

"Why do you insist on using words that make my mind think you're gonna talk about sex?"

"Honey, that's all on you." Frank knows what will get my attention. "Anyway, because I'm still working on Jillian's appeal, she mailed me back some paperwork today and included a thick envelope in there for you. In big black lettering, she wrote, 'Only for Snow White.' I'm not sure what you two are up to, but leave me out of it."

I pretend that I'm clueless as to what my old cellmate would send me. "Probably love notes from all the friends I made while I was locked up. You know, telling me that they miss me and stuff. Blah, Blah."

Frank's bullshit meter deters my lame excuse. A small, forced chuckle escapes. "Good one. Let's play poker later. Your weak attempt at purity would provide me the opportunity to snatch up your riches." He clears his throat before expressing the real reason for our serious conversation. "Evie, I've got a question for you."

"Is it truth or dare?" I fire back, trying to keep the mood light even though I know that the game is not his intent.

"You and your games. Truth or dare, Evie?" He's sitting up in his beach lounger with his sunglasses resting on the tip of his nose. I know this man like I know myself, and he wants answers – not necessarily the truth, but answers nonetheless. But I want to play a little longer. While he thinks I'm terrible at keeping a straight face, I know that I have many buried secrets.

I mirror him and sit up a bit straighter and slide my sunglasses down so he can see my eyes. "Dare." I always pick dare, and as my best friend, he knows this and plays along.

"I dare you to ditch your itty-bitty string bikini that barely hides your unmentionables and sprint into the chilly November Atlantic Ocean." I'm a beach girl, but not an Ocean swimmer. Besides being terrified of sharks, I hate swimming. He knows these facts and that without a doubt that I'll never follow through with his dare. Frank never makes a bet that the odds aren't in his favor.

"I change my mind. Truth." Game over.

"Okay. I'll allow a change of heart because I know you'll tell me the honest truth."

"Is there another kind of truth?"

"You know what I mean."

I smile at him. This is why he's here with me and my kids. He is my person. He gets me. Sure, we don't have sex, and he sneaks off for 'alone' time about once a month, but our fake marriage is by far the best marriage I've been in. His mother had been right all those years ago – marrying your best friend is so rewarding.

"Back when you were in jail, we were talking about how your fingerprints ended up on the inside of Clive's garage window, you said that you had shut it a few days earlier when you had confronted Clive about the drugs."

"Yeah, I remember. And why are you bringing this up now?"

"You said you shut it because snow was getting in."

"Is there a question coming?"

"On the afternoon that you confronted Clive about stopping his drug dealings, it had snowed earlier that morning, but by the time you said you talked to Clive in his garage – which was after school – all the snow had melted. There would not be any snow accumulating on the windowsill by then. It was a gorgeous afternoon, and the snow was already gone."

He was right. I hadn't shut the garage window on the afternoon that I confronted Clive about his drug dealings. I'd pushed it shut and locked it a few nights later just before I'd turned on the ignition of Clive's car and left it running in his garage.

Suddenly, Hazel burst out of the sliding glass door and ran toward us on the beach. Excitement was oozing from her pores. This conversation would have to wait.

***

Yo Snow White,

Everything is kosher in this black hole of regret and reflection, but it sucks without you. Suzy still screams every night in her sleep, Caramie still thinks she'll get out of here and own her own bison farm. Cassidy still complains about the shouting voices in her head. Now, they are telling her that Cowboy Brandon is Michael Jackson reincarnated. She claims that they are yelling at her in Spanish, which she doesn't know how to speak. I don't understand how she knows what the voices are saying if they are talking in a different language. Same craziness here.

You were right about the lawyer. He's Prince Charming. One of a kind. I'm keeping him busy like you asked, but he'll grow bored soon.

My connection scared your Black friend right out of the country. Ran to Mexico. Don't think she will be back to bother you and your family anytime soon. Before she made like the Roadrunner, he got her to make a statement against Mister. Welcome.

Hope that helps you relax. Now, send me some smokes and more smutty books.

Warmest regards from your princess trapped in a tower,

Rapunzel

Chapter 34

now

Whenever something tragic happens – a sudden death, a surprising arrest, a terrorist attack – people want answers. They demand answers. It is human nature. *Why did it happen? How can we prevent it from happening again?*

When a reckless teenager dies in a fiery car crash, neighbors shake their heads and whisper to each other, "He always drove too fast", as if *that* is the reason something horrible happened. When a woman shouts rape, there are always comments like, "Have you seen how she dresses?" as if her choice of clothing is to blame. When a rich, powerful man is found guilty of stealing money, comments about his greed flourish. Justifications for tragedies. They aren't always factual, but it helps us to sleep better at night.

So, why did I kill Clive? Even though I was secretly punishing him for my own enjoyment for several months – why, when, and how did I decide that that wasn't enough?

No one will like the answer. It isn't easy and simple. It doesn't fit into a box. As a young child, I did not torture animals, nor was I physically or emotionally abused. I wasn't brainwashed by a cult or religion. I'm not made of pure evil, and I never thought I could take someone else's life either. As a mother, I know how fragile life can be, and what a gift it is. But I've also learned to never say never.

Since my answers to why will never satisfy anyone, I will explain how it led to where we are now. I can paint a blurry picture of what went wrong, how my reasoning and logic changed through a course of events. It will not satisfy, but it will have to do.

Chapter 35

For months, I had been secretly punishing Clive for his poisonous choice of becoming a drug dealer. His decision ruined my family. Putting a nail in his tire, stealing their mail, and spreading rumors about him and his family had all been part of my plan to bring the Blacks down. Little jabs to even out the harshness of this life. In my head, I reasoned that these punishable acts would somehow even the score. However, from the outside, where I watched them, nothing I did seemed to create a dent. Their lives were forging ahead, not missing a beat. Clive was attending school and driving too fast down our quiet street, blaring his eardrum-rotting music. Every morning, Mitchell and Becca were heading to work, and during the evenings, entertaining friends around their pool. My pranks weren't causing nearly the amount of pain and anguish I had hoped and planned for. Maybe that was my problem - they were just pranks.

As my disappointment with the ineffectiveness of my sins grew, so did my sinister spiral. My pure heart began to blacken as the darkness invaded my soul. I began to accept that there was no turning back. I decided that it must be my fate. However, I can't completely blame Clive and his drug dealings. William had a huge hand in pushing me over the edge. He had stepped out of our marriage again, and I needed to take control.

We'd been through this infidelity hassle when the kids were toddlers, when he had a very steamy affair with a coworker. As soon as I discovered it and confronted him, he pretended to be over-the-top remorseful. He begged me not to leave him, begged me to forgive him, and begged me to believe that he would never do it again. But the little voice in my brain questioned his sincerity. *Is he remorseful because he was caught? Or is he remorseful for ripping my heart into two bleeding pieces? What is he* actually *sorry for?*

Whatever his reason for his apology, I forgave him and decided to work on our marriage. We attended couple's therapy, went on weekly date nights, and started having sex again three times a week. We were both trying to make our marriage work. I would like to say that I tried harder than he did. He wanted to have sex five times a week. I compromised from none to three.

Then one afternoon, years after William's first affair, I had just laid both kids down for a nap when the home phone rang – this was still back in the day when everyone had both a cell phone and a home phone. It was a Progressive Auto Insurance representative.

"Hi. My name is Vanessa from Progressive Auto Insurance. I need to ask you a few questions about the car accident you were in last week." I blinked rapidly trying to comprehend what she was telling me. I tried to politely interrupt, but she didn't hear me. "The police report says that your white Tahoe was part of a minor traffic accident on a gravel road five miles outside of Deadwood on Ski Valley road. The reports also indicate that no one was behind the wheel of the Tahoe, but two people were in the car when the Toyota hit them. Possibly in the back seat."

"Excuse me." The fast talking insurance agent finally paused long enough that I could get a couple of words in. "I think you have the wrong number."

"Sorry. I should've confirmed who I was speaking to first. Is this the Stanton residence?" I heard papers shuffling in the background.

"Yes, it is. But I don't think our Tahoe was in an accident." However, Vanessa proved me wrong and continued reading the police report, informing me that William and a woman named Carrie were involved in an accident when the Tahoe was hit from behind.

"Are you Carrie?"

"No."

"Sorry, I assumed you were. I shouldn't have done that, assumed, I mean. Is William your son?"

"No. William is my husband."

"Oh..." Vanessa and I, although probably thousands of miles apart and only connected by the phone, both arrived at the same conclusion at the same time: my husband was in the backseat of our car with a floozy named Carrie who was not his wife. Fast-talking Vanessa learned her lesson on assuming anything by trying to speed through the routine questions that her job required.

As Hudson's drug addiction and his attendance in jail increased, I started to notice that William was handling the stress of Hudson's defiance a lot better than I expected him to. He would smile at his phone when he was reading an incoming text. While his work hours increased, he was still finding free time to work out. He had a spring in his step, even though I felt like I was carrying around an extra thousand-pound weight on my shoulders. We were not dealing with the stress the same.

A few months before Hudson's jail time and Clive's death, William announced that he was headed into the office to finish up some paperwork. Honestly, I didn't think anything of it. He'd been busier than usual, putting in long hours. It sounded legit that he would need to catch up on paperwork when no one was there. He strutted out the front door as I finished my second cup of coffee – my limit – and was about to begin my Saturday morning cleaning ritual.

As I was elbow deep into a toilet filled with cleaner and bleach, the little voices in my head started talking.

How could he be so happy right now? How could he not have a care in the world?

I scrubbed harder as if I were scrubbing the poop stains from my life.

How could he go into work on a Saturday morning when Hudson had come home at three in the morning the night before? Did he expect me to discipline him alone? Again?

Suddenly, I knew. That subtle but quiet, honest but kind, blunt but caring voice was back. The Witch. The one that protected my heart announced things that I wasn't always ready to hear but had only my best interests in mind.

Can't you see this obvious pattern, Evelyn? Do you need me to draw you a map? William is having another affair.

I dropped my gloves and cleaning supplies. The voices were right. Before I marched out the front door and raced to his office to catch him, I grabbed my phone and checked his GPS location. The glorious wonders of technology, locating another human with a touch of a button. After the longest ten seconds, the GPS pinned his location at his office building. Well, he hadn't lied about where he was going, just why.

As I strapped on a bra, I vowed to get to the bottom of it. This was the last time William would spit on our wedding vows and screw another woman. I was in no mood to let another one of William's bad choices interrupt our lives and tear our family to shreds. I wanted – I needed – to catch William in the act. This time he wouldn't be able to swindle himself out of the corner, not when I caught him red-handed. I wanted to scream at him, using the pent up anger that was building up. There was no way I was going to sit back and let this happen again. No one messes with Evelyn Sarae Stanton anymore. I deserved so much better.

Hell yeah. The Witch sneered inside of my head.

The first and second time it happened while we were married, she was a floozy from his office. But the last time, it was not.

As I sat slumped in my car outside of William's office, I felt pathetic. I couldn't believe I had to check on the whereabouts of my husband, who I'd been married to for twenty years. *But why should I feel unworthy of him? Why am I crying? I'm not the one who strayed outside of our marriage... again. I'm not the one who broke our wedding vows... again.*

The tender, sweet voice in my head, Angel, reminded me, *You don't have proof that he is cheating.*

My Witch voice shouted, *Yet!*

But I know why I feel this way. The key word is 'again.' I let this happen before, believed him when he was sorry, and believed him when he said he'd never do it again. I let him back into my heart. I forgave him even when I shouldn't have. I saw it in his apology. He wasn't sorry for cheating on me, he wasn't sorry for breaking my heart or ruining my trust in him. He was sorry he had gotten caught. He enjoyed screwing his assistant in the middle of the day, whether it was in his car or at a shady hotel across town. It was exciting, and he thrived on secrecy and sneaking around. He disclosed all of this information and more during our marriage counseling sessions, which he promised to attend with me in an attempt to reconcile our relationship but was late to every week.

I was just as much at fault as he was because I lowered my guard and trusted him with my heart.

I brushed away a fallen tear and checked my reflection in the visor mirror. *Oh my god, I look awful.*

I'd left the house in such a rush that I hadn't even bothered to run a brush through my hair. My sandy brown hair had been thrown up into a bun the night before so not only did I have snarls, but I also had major bedhead. I loosened the ponytail and let my hair fall down to my shoulders. I tried to finger comb it before twisting back into a bun. Then I licked my middle finger to rub the day-old eyeliner from under my eye. *What a mess.* To top off my disheveled appearance, I was wearing my favorite bleach-stained sweatshirt and cut off sweatpants. I hoped I could make it home without anyone seeing me.

Just as I slapped the driver's side visor mirror shut, I saw them. William wasn't in his office building like I thought. He was across the street having brunch with my former best friend.

Becca.

A few months ago, or even a year ago, it wouldn't have been odd. It wouldn't have been a big deal. The four of us were great friends. Sometimes, Mitchell and I would jog together. Becca and William both loved golfing, so they'd take the boys and hit golf balls on a Saturday morning. The four of us simply enjoyed each other's company.

It was different now. William had lied. He'd told me he was going into work, with no mention of seeing Becca. And furthermore, Becca had been giving me the cold shoulder by purposefully not inviting me to coffee dates or happy hours with mutual friends. She brushed it off saying she thought she told me or some other lame excuse. She never responded to any communication. I knew. I felt it. The shift of our friendship. She was pulling away, and I could do nothing to stop it.

But now, it made sense why she was boxing me out. She was sleeping with my husband.

During the shitshow of Hudson's addiction, I felt William pulling away again. We'd been down this path before. I recognized the signs; I smelt the betrayal; there was another woman. But this time around instead of confessing my insecurities to Frank, I leaned on Becca. As any friend would do, she let me cry on her shoulder, she patted my back, and she declared that everything would turn out fine. She consoled me, and I felt relieved to have a friend in my corner.

After I'd revealed all my insecurities about my marriage to Becca, she'd gradually pulled away. It all makes sense when I see them together. It wasn't that my problems were too big for our friendship. It was because *she* was the problem.

Infidelity and betrayal weren't something new to her. Years ago, she had stolen Mitchell away from his wife as well. Furthermore, that wife was also her best friend, Tracie. It was a pattern that she knew all too well. Luckily for me, no freak accident had killed me and made a clear path for her to take over my life. Yet.

With my mouth agape, I watched them walk out of the restaurant. Her arm was looped in his, and her head was resting on his shoulder. They were both smiling and carefree. Suddenly, a gust of wind blew her hair across her face. Because her hands were busy – one was holding a to-go box and the other was locked with William's- she giggled and stopped walking as she tried to brush the wild hair from her face so she could see. William stopped and helped to unblind her, and then he took both of his hands and cupped her face and pulled her in for a deep, passionate kiss.

What the hell?

Everything was making sense. Those Russian dolls were from her. Some inside joke to William. That was why the tattoo looked familiar. Becca had a matching one above her butt crack as well. A tramp stamp. Becca was the woman on the phone who spoke with a fake Russian accent.

It wasn't a floozy from William's office like I thought. It was a floozy from across the street. And this floozy was like an aunt to my children. This floozy used to be my best friend.

Oh, God... I looked around my car for something to throw up in.

***

I hired a local private detective to validate my discovery. I knew what I had witnessed, but I wanted something to hold in my hands, proof that I could use later if I needed to. A small part of me worried that Becca would orchestrate my death in a freak accident so she could take over my life, marry my husband, and parent my children. Just like she did years ago when she stole Mitchell from his wife, her friend, Tracie.

Not only did the detective confirm my suspicions by supplying me with high-quality resolution photographs of William and Becca at hotels, in their cars, at nearby restaurants, and in parks, but he also provided me with even more disturbing photographs. Pictures of my husband buying drugs from a local drug dealer.

Clive Black.

The pictures were taken outside of our local coffee shop in broad daylight. To a stranger or someone passing them on the street, it would appear as if Clive and William were just shaking hands as old friends do when they bump into each other. The typical Saturday morning coffee run. However, the detective was able to zero in on the handshake as a small bag of pills was exchanged for a wad of cash.

William was doing drugs too. How could William be experimenting with the very thing that was ruining our son's life? Talk about a hypocrite!

So, while my heart was building up a tower of hatred for the neighbor-hood drug dealer who used to climb the maple tree in my backyard, my husband was supporting his income. *Are you kidding me?* How could my world crumble any further? That afternoon, when the detective handed me those pictures, it was a pivotal moment for me. I could either sit here and stew and become even more depressed, or I could act. I could make things right. Take control. For too many years, I sat back and let my loved ones wreak havoc on my life and my heart, but I couldn't take it anymore. Every human has their own personal limit on how much abuse they can take. I'd reached mine.

Even though the fact that William bought drugs from Clive was a hard pill to swallow – no pun intended – it did help me later when I used William's phone to order a roofie from Clive. After I returned home from sending the carbon monoxide into Clive's apartment as he slept, I crushed up the pill and deposited it into the rest of my bottle of wine. I assumed that I would be arrested, and the wine would stay untouched in my refrigerator until I could plant the seed in Frank's mind that William might have slipped me something.

The threatening texts to Clive were also my doing. First, it felt good to vent out my frustrations onto Clive, who I knew wouldn't do anything about the threats. What could he possibly do? He's a drug dealer. Plus, he probably received threats all the time. After I sent them from William's phone, I deleted them from his sent file as well as his deleted file. No trace except on Clive's phone. I wasn't concerned if the police traced them back. I only wanted William to be in the dark. It was his turn to feel used.

Chapter 36

It was months later before I formulated any type of plan – a plan to gain control of my life. But during those initial months, I wallowed in self-pity and pretended that everything was okay. While William and I tried to co-parent our son, who was out of control, I stuffed down my feelings of betrayal and bitterness. I learned to be a convincing actress. I didn't want to be the victim again. I was tired of everyone doing what they wanted and how they weren't concerned that it was affecting those around them – mainly me. I remembered something wise and thought-provoking that Vera had said: "The mother is the tree trunk of the family. Roots and branches extend from the life that she gives. You can trim the branches, the root can be severed, but the trunk is still there, standing tall and weathering the storm. Without the trunk, there is no tree."

I was the trunk, and my tree needed to be trimmed.

Recently, I edited a murder mystery, and while I can't and won't blame the fictional story, I will admit that it did help me create major plot twists that would work to my advantage. Who would guess that the friendly, middle-aged neighbor lady killed her son's friend? Of course, after she is arrested, people will come forward with 'I told you so' stories and a few 'I knew it' ones too. But when solid seeds of doubt are planted, their opinions will change, and more people will come forward blaming the angry, cheating husband for wanting everyone out of his way so he could be with his new lover. Public opinion is a finicky bunch. It would make more sense for everyone to question him and blame him for Clive's death. I just needed to be patient. I needed to sit in jail and wait for the mess to be sorted out on its own. If it was too obvious, too easy, no one would believe it. Everyone enjoys a good mystery, especially a whodunit.

When Vera came up with ideas on how to help me earn my freedom, I knew it was only a matter of time. She was my smoking gun.

After our initial phone conversation, Frank's mother came to visit me. Seeing her petite frame of five feet tall, maybe one hundred pounds soaking wet filled my heart with appreciation. This little woman had shown me more love and attention than I ever deserved. After the pleasantries were over, she reached across and clasped my hand in hers. Immediately, I tried to recoil them because that was not allowed. I looked over to Brandon who winked at me as if saying, *'That old lady is harmless.'* I turned my focus back on her.

"I don't have long, dear, so we need to cut to the chase and shake a leg." I wasn't sure if she was referring to the time limit for her visit or the fact that she was terminal, but either way, I nodded in agreement. Vera had a way about her that made me feel like I wanted to please her and agree to whatever she suggested. "I will help." Those three words came out so matter-of-factly that they caught me off guard.

"Help with what, Vera?"

"Eve, dear, you know I'm not a bullshitter." As she widened her eyes and whistled, she rolled her eyes and then put up her hitchhiker's thumb and motioned to the door.

Months prior to her involvement, I had formulated a plan for my arrest and left evidence to show doubt. No nail in the coffin, but I prayed that every little crumb would create enough doubt to warrant my release. But little, stubborn Vera wanted to help by planting even more damning evidence that would secure the overturn of my arrest. It was completely her idea to get involved. No one ever gave Vera enough credit.

The day that Vera refused to leave our house, she had been on a mission. When William didn't answer the front door after ten minutes, she assumed no one was home and decided to retrieve the hidden key when William caught her looking under the mat. She fumbled a little lie, pushed her way through the front door, and then proceeded to lock herself in the bathroom. While she sat patiently on the bathroom floor making noises to indicate that she was in severe abdominal pain, she scared William right out of his own house. Per my instructions, she found the hidden key in my secretary's desk under my embossed stationery to the secret compartment under the pool table where I had hidden the money from the fake charity account. When William was working his money laundering magic, I absorbed every detail while looking over his shoulder. He underestimated me just like everyone did with Vera. I cheered him on, questioned his plans, and then stroked his 'ego' to encourage his participation. It worked like a charm. Sex and money, the root of all evil.

A few weeks after we stole the money, I used the notes that I had collected and transferred the money. Later, I withdrew the money and stored most of it under the pool table. I deleted the fake account as well. Fake accounts are easier to erase than the real thing for obvious reasons: they don't exist Plus, it was not created with the normal procedures and check and balances, so there is less to hide.

That money would help me start a new life after William was safely tucked behind bars.

I lied in my statement to the police. I had already disobeyed the law, stepped out of my comfort zone, and done things I never thought were conceivable for me. So, yes, I lied.

The night of Clive's murder, William couldn't find his phone, and I almost didn't go through with my plan. After the first episode of *Yellowstone*, William jumped off the couch.

"Crap! Have you seen my phone, Eve?" He patted his pant pockets and looked around his immediate surroundings.

"No. When was the last time you had it?"

While his eyes squinted at me, his irritation was laced in his tone of voice. "Are you kidding me right now? If I knew when I last had it, I wouldn't be asking you." The mood in the room had quickly changed. My jaw clenched tight as I choked down a sip of my wine. Not sure if it was because the mood shifted along with my attitude, but my third glass of wine didn't taste as good as the first two. More bitter. Or was that just my resentment? I hated when he talked to me like that, like I was an idiot when I was only trying to help. *Well, he can find his own fucking phone.*

Then he added, "I don't remember even syncing it in the car to listen to music on my drive home." His face lit up, and he flashed a smile in my direction.

A little too late. I wasn't interested in his mood swings. I returned his remorseful smile with a dull, blank look. Three drinks have always been my limit; therefore, my poker face was gone. After three drinks, I either chose to perform circus acts, which I totally regretted the next day, or I retreated to my bed to lay my head down on my pillow before I could embarrass myself any further.

I remember thinking about how quickly everything changed. The balance shifted because William disrespected our relationship, and our friendship *again*. Of course, he wouldn't agree. He'd tell me to get over it like he told me in the past. Those words never worked. I never simply got over his harsh, damaging words or actions. In fact, I secured the memory in my brain vault. The pile of painful memories grew taller and taller until I was ready to burst until I couldn't take anymore, and I'd blow up.

Either way, I didn't give a crap if he found his phone. I was going through with my plan.

When he rushed out of the house to retrieve his phone from the office, I estimated that I had one hour before he returned home and a bit longer if he didn't come right away.

Just days before, when I stormed over to the Blacks' house to hand Clive a piece of my mind, I had already set my plan in motion. In the pocket of my pants, I had crushed pills. After the self-righteous snob dismissed me and climbed the stairs to his little apartment, I pulled open their garage refrigerator where I knew Clive stored his post-workout drinks. From previous conversations while floating in their backyard pool, I learned he pre-ordered them from an uppity juice bar that recently opened. Each drink was labeled by day of the week. I found Friday's drink, popped open the lid, and dropped the four crushed sleeping pills into the mushy contents. Friday night, after he returned from the gym, he would gulp his fancy wheatgrass smoothie before hopping in the shower. His eyes would feel heavy, so he would decide to lie down for a bit before making his Friday night party rounds.

Four pills were sure to knock him out, and I'd have enough time to start up his car to let the magical carbon monoxide bleed through the tiny garage apartment.

I was sure there would not be an autopsy because the gas leak would be a dead ringer for the cause of death. Plus, there was the obvious fact: he was a drug dealer, and his parents wouldn't want to expose the laundry list of drugs that were in his system. That scandal would be unwelcome.

As I was leaving the garage that afternoon, I placed the little SM necklace he had given me years ago under his car tire. I didn't want anything that reminded me of him. When he crushed it with the weight of his car, it would symbolize our broken relationship. I loved a good metaphor. That was when I noticed the small garage window was open. I probably wouldn't have seen it in the dark on Friday night when I planned on returning. I was glad I noticed it. I pushed with my whole weight to shut it and latch it tight. My fingerprints on the windowsill inside their garage would not look good. But I couldn't leave it open because all the carbon monoxide would escape along with my plan. The fact that my nosy neighbor's husband had witnessed me paying Clive a visit a few days before would help with my alibi. It gave me another date and night that put me in that garage. Sure, it didn't look good. It looked more like I was stalking him, but it gave me an out.

In the compartment under the pool table, I locked up pictures from the private detective of William and Becca, notes I had taken on how to transfer the money from the fake charity, the money stolen from the Black's account, a printout of the texts that William sent Clive, the fraud account creation, along with some shady business deals William did through his financial company. Everything I needed to secure my freedom and put an end to William's.

When I received the letter from William while I was in jail, my heart fluttered in my chest because I knew where that stationery was kept. It was in the little secretary's desk where I also stored the key to the pool table cabinet. I truly didn't think William would have any idea that the pool cabinet existed, but I didn't want him to steal the key or hide it somewhere else. Whenever a random key is found, the question of "What is it for?" arises. What do you need to lock up? The key would only lead to more questions. I didn't want to have William questioning the possibility that I had anything to hide.

To cast doubt on my involvement, I planted the idea that someone else made those footprints in the snow. I dropped little bouncy balls in the bottom of my North Face boots and carefully placed boot prints out my front door and to the Blacks' garage. I purposely dropped my cell phone in the snow seconds after I sent that incriminating text to William. I knew the police and the public would want an open-and-shut case, so I wanted to provide an easy solution. The doubt would come later.

Chapter 37

now

"You are sporting quite the tan, Eve." I'm sitting across from my ex-husband and smirking at the irony of the situation. My fair, normally very white skin has responded favorably to the move to the east coast by slowly absorbing the sun's nutrients and coloring my skin a nice shade of tan. When I was married to William and living in the Midwest, sunscreen, sun hats, and shade were a daily requirement. When the sun beat down on our little corner of the world, my skin would react with a bright pink burn. So, while I look healthy and tan, William is dressed in inmate orange and his skin has turned pale white.

"Thank you for noticing. Divorce suits me, don't you think?" I can't help but get snarky with him. The color of skin is not the only physical thing that has changed. My hair is no longer a wavy, wild mess. wishing for something to tame it. When I was in jail, I'd wished to tame it with a baseball cap, a ponytail holder, or even a garbage bag. Frank had suggested that a new look would be perfect for my new life.

"You can't fight the glitter anymore, Evie. You need to embrace it." Frank and his tendency for honesty were a breath of fresh air...sometimes.

After mowing our little patch of lawn, we were enjoying a glass of water on our deck that overlooked the ocean. The view never got old. Turquoise-colored waves crashing on the shore are causing the seagulls to shriek. Once in a while, a fellow retiree would stroll by and leave their temporary footprints in the sand, only to have them erased moments later by a crashing wave. Their existence was quickly erased within a blink of an eye. The clear blue sky steadily grips the bright, golden sun for hours on end until it slowly releases the sun to rest beyond the horizon.

One of the best parts of our arrangement is how well Frank and I get along. There was no awkward first year of marriage period or struggle over household chores. Because we've been friends for over twenty years, our marriage didn't change our relationship. We were just more committed to each other than before.

"Whatever! When a man grays, he's considered distinguished. When a woman goes gray, she's ancient, dried up, and used. It's a bunch of crap."

"If you can't hide it, then flaunt it."

"I'm not interested in flaunting anything, and I don't want to hide it. I simply want my youth back. I want a gigantic life-size remote control that I can press rewind on." I dropped my head into my hands. First crow's feet and now gray hair. Growing old wasn't for the weak. I realized that my pouting wouldn't roll back the last twenty years, but everyone deserves to throw a little tantrum now and then.

Playing into my childish response, Frank pretended to check the front of his cutoff jean shorts. He turned his pockets inside out. "Well, I'm fresh out of miracles today, but I am full of sarcastic comments and witty suggestions. Did you know that frowning causes more wrinkles than smiling?" He yanked on my wavy mane of hair. Reluctantly, I gave him my attention. "Evie, you're overdue for a new hairdo. You've literally had the same untamed style since I met you, and believe me, I'm using the word *style* loosely. Let me make an appointment for you with my guy. Maybe he can perform a miracle."

"Your guy? Is this the one that snatches you away from your wife and kids every other weekend?"

"Hey, my old ball and chain is the one who constructed this nontraditional family." He held the palm side of his hand to his cheek and whispered, "And it just so happens that she was right, but please don't tell her. She has a tendency to get an enormous head when someone compliments her." For dramatic effect, Frank lifts his hands up to the sky and adds, "And now, I have the best of both worlds."

We hardly ever talk about what he did when he packed a bag and left for a weekend. It's his business, and I knew when he was ready, he'd tell me. We have all adjusted to our compromise, and it works extremely well. Hazel and Hudson respond respectively to Frank's parenting and understand that Frank and I are happy.

"I've noticed that when you return home from your escapades that your hair glistens."

"Yes, Arlo practices his skills on my great head of hair." Frank flips his hair like a runaway model.

"Arlo, huh? Can't wait to meet him."

When I settled into Arlo's salon chair a few weeks later, he squinted his eyes, looked me up and down, and whispered to Frank. I could tell he was bursting with ideas and couldn't wait to get his hands dirty. He was a puppet master.

With a thick Russian accent, Arlo explains, "Evelyn, Frankie has told me so much about you that I feel like I already know you. If you trust me, I think I can craft you into the perfect version of yourself." Frank gently elbows him. "Plus, Frankie also wants me to say sheet five times to you." Frank, who was silently observing from the sidelines, busts a gut when Arlo says, "sheet," which actually does sound just like the American word, shit.

As he massaged my scalp, every muscle in my body relaxed, causing me to agree with every suggestion that he made. His fingers were magic. Since I had lost a few unwanted pounds from the stress of my divorce, my jawline was more pronounced, and Arlo suggested an angled hairstyle to frame my face and accentuate my cheekbones. The blonde would automatically hide the gray hair that was sprouting against my will. I looked like a whole new woman. My thick hair is now shaped into a stylish bob, shorter in the back, and dyed blonde.

When Hudson saw the transformed me for the first time, he announced, "You look like Reese Witherspoon with your bangs sweeping to the side like that, Mom." That compliment not only flattered me but also took me by surprise. Even Hudson was taken back by the words that escaped his lips. "Did I just say that? What's happening to me?" We both shared a good, hard laugh.

I feel confident in my new look, and it doesn't bother me that my ex-husband isn't impressed. For a split second, when I witness the hurt register on William's face, I feel guilty for bringing up the divorce that he had fought against. For a man who bedded any female that agreed to his advances, it still surprised me that he didn't want a divorce. But I knew it wasn't the broken marriage vows that bothered him or disregard for our religious pledge, it was the finances and the fact that he felt abandoned. William had lost, and he didn't like losing.

"Yes, we are divorced, Eve, so why are you here?"

That is the million dollar question. The old me feels like I owe him closure, and I know that being locked up behind bars is extremely lonely. But the new me is selfish, and I wanted to show off my look and rub it in his face. He left me. He had abandoned our marriage. He broke my heart, but I crushed his soul, stole his children's love, and managed to get him arrested for a murder that I committed. I didn't let many people in, and I let him in. I married him, but he rejected me and broke his promises. That didn't sit well with the old or new me.

"Honestly, I'm not sure either. Maybe for closure. You've been an important part of my adult life, and now, it's over. I guess I feel I owe it to you and our marriage."

"Our relationship is not over. We will always be connected because we have two children together."

"Not really. Our children are grown now, and although I can't speak for them, I think they've accepted that you will never be the father they deserved." I observe a spark of pain flash across his face. "They each wrote you a letter." I slide them toward him across the table. "I didn't read them, but they are taped shut because the guards were required to read them in order for me to give them to you."

He fidgets in his hard, plastic chair trying to get comfortable. Watching him squirm gives me a warm feeling in my heart. I know it's cruel, but it's the truth.

"Sorry to hear about you and Becca." More fidgeting.

"What do you mean?" He hasn't heard. I get to break the news to him. It feels like my birthday.

"Oh...sorry, I figured you two were still in touch."

"That's none of your business." His tone is sharp, so it's obvious that she hasn't been to visit him while he's been in jail. It doesn't surprise me, but I'm surprised that he actually thought she would.

"She gave a formal statement to the police before she skipped town. And now, they can't seem to find her to ask a few follow-up questions."

"What statement? What are you talking about?" He doesn't want to hear this news from me, but he has no choice. I don't think he can stop himself from asking.

"I don't know what she said word for word, but it was something about how she has evidence that you killed Clive. She also said that you threatened him more than once while you two were sneaking around."

He shakes his head. "Why, Eve?"

I know what he is asking because I know he knows. When things were good between us and he paid attention to me, he could read me like a book. We were in sync; however, even though he had the skills to understand me, he abandoned those rights when he continued to sleep with other women.

"Do you remember our wedding, William?"

"Of course, I remember it." He seems surprised that I'm bringing up a very old memory. Perhaps he thinks I'm going to turn soft as I reminisce about the good ole days.

"You noticed the tears running down my cheeks." As I walked toward him in a long, white, sparkling gown, William looked like the perfect, adoring groom, grinning at his emotional bride. I stared straight at him, my eyes never leaving his face. Everyone in the church thought I was overwhelmed with tears of excitement and anticipation at marrying the love of my life. "You assumed that I couldn't contain my excitement at becoming your wife."

Moments before my grand march, my resentful sister, who had always tried to sabotage my happiness, had decided that that exact moment was the perfect time to confide in me, to unburden herself of guilt. "But in fact, those tears were not tears of an emotional bride who was so excited to pledge her undying love to you. Those wet, cascading tears were created from a sinister, sisterly whisper, where she confessed that she had screwed my soon-to-be husband hours before in the church basement." His face registers shock that I had kept that revelation a secret for our entire marriage. "Some might say that I knew what I was getting into when I married you. Some might say I wanted to change you. Some might say I was too weak to walk out. They are all probably right. It doesn't matter now, because I've decided to change the ending. For twenty years, I was patient and forgiving. For twenty years, I stood by you and suffered through your infidelity, lies and betrayal. But it's finally over now, William. You are getting what you deserve." I nod toward his gray surroundings.

"This is ridiculous. Infidelity isn't punishable by law, Eve. You stood by me all those years because you can't stand being wrong. You can't fail. You always have to win. You loved me, and you looked the other way because you didn't want to lose the life we had. You blame me for the affairs when you're the one who should feel guilty. If you would've been a better, more devoted wife, I wouldn't have had to seek other women for affection. You couldn't leave years ago, because you had no family to run home to. Your crazy mother is locked up, your sister is whoring around somewhere, and your dad's a drunk. You have no one left, Eve. And now, when the only family you have – me – needs you, you walk away. You are a coward, Eve."

"I'm smarter and stronger than you've ever given me credit for."

"You hid. You hid behind the walls that you built because of your insecurities. You hid behind me and the kids. You're too afraid to live, Eve."

"That was the old me, William. I've changed. And you've always underestimated me."

"Underestimated you? I don't think so. You've always been weak."

"Big words from a man sitting in jail wearing an orange jumpsuit."

"This isn't forever, Eve. I didn't kill Clive."

"You are completely right, William, you didn't kill Clive." I point to myself and silently mouth, "But I did." I watch his facial expression change. His head jerked slightly forward as if he choked back a little bile that had risen in his throat, and then he swallowed a big lump. Sweat beads form in little droplets on his forehead. I leaned forward to make sure he heard every whisper. "For months, that was my plan. I didn't care if I rotted in jail as long as I saved Hudson, but then I discovered your affair with Becca and your drug purchases from Clive… and well, this scenario turned out better for everyone." I lift my hand up and count my fingers, "Hudson, clean and sober. Hazel, thriving and safe. Me, free and divorced. Everything is as it should be." As I stand up, I signal to the guard that our conversation is finished. I'm ready to be escorted out. "You should've never taken my love and loyalty for granted. I guess some people have to learn the hard way. Goodbye, William."

"You won't get away with it."

"That is where you are wrong again, William. I already have."

Epilogue

Even five years later, I'm still a major overthinker and big reflector. The past doesn't pain me like it used to. Guilt doesn't consume me. I'm at peace with what happened, and with what I had to do. I never wanted to kill anyone, but my family is my priority, and I would do *anything* to keep them safe. When I reflect on the good times with my family, a smile creeps up on my face. A lot of things had to fall in line in order for me and my family to earn this freedom. I've always been a big believer in Karma. I've always felt that you get what you deserve, eventually. I know Karma is watching me, but I'm sure she is watching me out of interest and wonder. Karma has already dealt me her hand, and I won.

I had no doubt in Frank's ability to defend my honor. It didn't matter to me that he was inexperienced at being a trial lawyer. I just knew he would fight tooth and nail to earn my freedom.

Sure, I feel bad for deceiving everyone. But in the end, it was worth it. Clive is dead. Hudson is clean, and Hazel is thriving. Vera's dying wish was fulfilled because I married her son. And William is behind bars.

Never mess with the mother bear.

"If you quit telling lies about me,
I won't tell the truth about you."
~Mitchell Tenpenny, "Truth About You"

Thank you

Behind every book are countless hours of writing and re-writing, plotting and scheming, tons of self-doubt, and gut-wrenching nerves. I worry that not everyone will like it, that I'm not good enough, and that I'm wasting my time, but I plug away and keep writing. Why? Because I love it! Always have and always will. I know not everyone will like it, and I know I'm not the best. I know it takes a lot of my free time, but it makes me happy. I found a way to release my creativity.

Writers are advised to write what they know. After you knock down the walls of pain, let the words pour out. Unfortunately, I did just that. 2022 was a tough year. I learned that I'm stronger than I think, my immediate family is my main priority, and that drugs and alcohol can throw life major curveballs.

When faced with a make-or-break situation, it's amazing how resilient you can be when your choices are limited. This book would be nothing more than a journal of my frustrations if it hadn't been for the happy ending that my son fought for. When I'm going through turmoil in my heart and soul, I bottle up my feelings and keep them hidden away to not see the light of day. If my son hadn't hit rock bottom and crawled out on his own accord, I don't think this story would've been written. Without a happy ending in my heart, I would never have let it out through my fingertips.

Behind every writer is a group of supportive, amazing people that encourage every step of the way. Those people are my tribe.

To my son, you are back! I couldn't be more proud of how far you've come. When I look in the rearview mirror, I see a whole different person, one I didn't like much. Even though hitting your rock bottom was extremely painful and heartbreaking for our family, you crawled your way out of a dark hole and have blossomed into the young man that I knew was hidden under all the chemicals. I hope you are as proud of yourself as your dad and I are. Thank you for allowing me to write a fictional story based on my feelings as we navigated through our family struggles this past year. You are an inspiration.

As the chief of my tribe, my husband is the person who takes the brunt of my insecurities, frustrations, and my absence when I'm locked away. He quietly shuts my office door and keeps the distractions to a minimum when I've come up with a new twist and need to focus. He is always there listening to me vocalize my ideas and helping uncover new ideas. While I still hold out hope that he'll read one of my books someday, I'm immensely thankful for his continued support and encouragement. He is my rock! I need to thank him for being a stubborn mule and never losing his ground. Every virtue that God blessed him with is for a reason. I guess we found the reason he was blessed with stubbornness and determination.

My editor is the most encouraging, supportive, and thoughtful woman I know. She sends me random messages of optimism and begs me to 'leak' some of my latest chapters to her. I found Caramie Malcolm by pure accident, but what isn't an accident is our genuine friendship. Without her never-ending patience and quality checking, this book would be a jumbled mess with commas in all the wrong places. Not only do I lean on her for her editorial skills but also for her valuable opinion. Sometimes, I sit on the edge of my seat just waiting for her reply. Thank you, Caramie, for being my sounding board and a friend that I rely on.

Beta readers are defined as a group of average readers who are trusted with a copy of an unpublished work to read and make suggestions. These people are key as the first sets of eyes who read a book. For every book, I have selected friends who become essential and important to my process. Thank you, Gena Tarrell, who sails past her bedtime just to read the book in two sittings. Sorry, not sorry, Scott, if you felt neglected for a couple of days. Betsy McIntyre, ole buddy, you have a talent for proofreading like no other. I appreciate you helping me polish my book. Nancy Shade, my ole childhood friend, flew through all of my books in record time. I knew I needed your input and insight into this adventure. Thanks for sharing my love of reading.

Years ago, I started writing my first fictional story to help me deal with some personal issues. It felt good to give an outlet for my pain. Pouring your heart and soul onto paper may be therapeutic, but there are no words for how scary it is to allow someone to read your uncensored, raw feelings. There are no walls. You are vulnerable and wide up for criticism. My good friend, Ashley Hunt, was the first one to read a piece of my work and encouraged me to publish it. Because I valued her opinion and knew her compliments were solid, I took her advice. And here, we are! Book number three. Thanks, Kramer! I will forever credit you for this journey.

Big shout out to my bookstagram buddies who possess a love for everything books as I do. Susan, Jillian, Emily, Nikki, Ashley, Chris, Cindy, Jenny, Bethany, Heidi, Melissa, Liz, Lindsey, Laura, Krissy, Katie, Jen, Farah, Erika, Jenna, Lauren, Denise, Donna, Monica, Michelle, Samantha, and Allison - you are my cheerleading squad, my ARC team. You get as excited as I do about books. I appreciate your endless advice and constant feedback. Thank you so much for being on my team and sharing my book baby with the world.

I have a little posse of friends that I like fondly referred to as my Witches. This group of women has been there for me for different phases of my life, through the good and bad, the highs and the uglies. Even without them knowing, I love to filter their stories into my books, adding a little inside joke to my books. Thank you guys for allowing me to use you as butts of my jokes and use your stories to spice up mine. Scott, sorry that I didn't include you as a character in my book this time, but I'm still praying that I still make it into your Christmas letter.

Readers, you are the group I aim to impress and entertain. Thank you for recommending my books to your friends and supporting my need to tell stories. I love hearing from you and your interpretation of the storylines and characters. Reach out anytime! And be sure to take a minute to post a review or rating on Amazon, Barnes and Noble and/or Good Reads.

If you enjoyed this novel, please check out my others: "He Loves Me, She Loves Me Not" and "Puppet's Shadow."

Thank you!

Emersyn Park

Chicken Parmesan

3-6 boneless thawed chicken breasts

2 Tbsp. melted butter

1/2 C. grated parmesan cheese

1/4 C. bread crumbs or crushed Ritz crackers

1 tsp. oregano

1 tsp. parsley

1/4 tsp. paprika

1/4 tsp. salt

1/4 tsp. pepper

Heat oven to 400 degrees. Spray pan well with cooking spray. Dip chicken into melted butter, coat with the remaining combined ingredients. Bake for 20-25 minutes or until done. Serve on the top of spaghetti noodles and pasta sauce.

Made in the USA
Monee, IL
20 March 2023